MW00614310

NARROWNOOK

Another Maine Mystery

JANE HARVEY MEADE

Designed and produced by:
Maine Authors Publishing
12 High Street, Thomaston, Maine
www.maineauthorspublishing.com

Printed in the United States of America

TO BUCKSPORT, MAINE

My homey hometown, whose caring community and storybook setting have fostered a creative imagination in all of us who are fortunate enough to live here.

ABOUT THE COVER ARTIST

JOHN CHOUINARD GREW UP IN THE SMALL MILL TOWN OF JAY, MAINE. HE inherited his love of the arts from his parents and teachers. After a four-year stint in the United States Army, John married Jill and still refers to her as his true love after twenty-seven years together.

They have a son, Nicholas, and two dogs, Benny and Clyde. They are currently loving life in Bucksport, Maine.

Author's note: John is a very versatile artist. The cover is just a glimpse of his amazing talent. His portrait work is also exceptional.

Thank you, John, for enabling me to present my book with your authentic and beautiful painting of Bucksport Bay on its cover.

ACKNOWLEDGMENTS

My thanks to John L. (Jack) Pooler and Margaret M. Pooler for steering me to their father's research on Bucksport, Maine. For years, their dad, Bernard E. Pooler, was the editor of the Bucksport weekly newspaper, *The Free Press*. During his tenure in that capacity, he produced two very thorough accounts of the town's history.

With Jack's and Margaret's help, I was able to find his first publication, titled *The 150th Anniversary of Bucksport, Maine*, which he published and printed at the Bucksport *Free Press* office in August 1942. Most of the historic references in my narrative are drawn from Bernard's original account, and I thank the Pooler family for their guidance in my research throughout the creation of my otherwise fictional story.

I also wish to thank my readers, Cousin Judith Mountain, my good friend Evora Mattson, and my "like-a-daughter" Tina Simonelli. Their encouragement and advice are always crucial to the successful completion of my manuscripts.

Of course, as always, I extend my gratitude to all of the staff at Maine Authors Publishing:

Jane Karker is not only the president of this remarkable company, but is always someone I can count on for wise direction. I still struggle in this technological age, and during the difficult year of 2020, she went way above expectations to help me get this book published. Her dedication to her authors is one of the valuable trademarks of Maine Authors Publishing.

To Nikki Giglia, managing editor and publicist, thank you for your sense of humor that got us over the hurdles of dealing with my outdated computer—probably at the expense of nearly driving you crazy. Your patience is incredible.

I also thank Michelle Hodgdon, graphic designer, for the beautiful layout of *Narrownook*'s cover and pages.

And to my wonderful editor, Genie Dailey, you already know how much I depend on your expertise. There is no one like you. I am so glad you are there to help me look like a competent wordsmith.

The Atlantic breeze shivers through a tapering funnel of the Penobscot River appropriately named "The Narrows," a natural tunnel created by Orphan Island on its east and Waldo Mountain on its west. Its breath slides under the bridge next to Fort Knox before it exhales completely into the bay of the little town of

Narrownook

Another Maine Mystery

Jane Harvey Meade

1994

THE GRADUATION CEREMONY LASTED UNTIL NINE THIRTY ON THE NIGHT of June 11th. Meghan Murphy wasted no time in discarding her cap and gown as soon as the function ended. There had been no air on the stage where they had been made to stand until every one of the fifty-four graduates had received diplomas. That process had taken twenty minutes during which they actually had to keep their focus on breathing to remain conscious. The effort consumed a large amount of the energy they should have been using to applaud more enthusiastically for their achieving classmates.

By nine thirty-one, Meg was in the front hall meeting up with Stan Russell and a couple of dozen kids that would make the journey that year to Bar Harbor to watch the sun come up on Cadillac Mountain. Greeting the sun on the first day of their new freedom from public school was part of the rite of passage for Narrownook graduates. Every year, carloads of seniors made the thirty-six-mile trip. This year, Lanie Warren and Scott Lanford would go with Meg and Russie in his car and lead the motorcade of vehicles up the long, twisting road to the summit of the mountain.

To Meghan, it was strange being with Russie tonight on this milestone occasion when it should have been Harry helping her usher out the last four years—four years that she and Harry had spent together as a steady couple, sharing classes, cramming for tests at the last minute, and dating exclusively. She had been a cheerleader, rooting him and his football and baseball teams to victory. She had been Harry's girl, soothing her quarterback and ace pitcher through his rare sporting defeats.

In April, Meghan had been accepted to the university in Orono, and since then, she had grappled with the reality that her world was going to change. Gradually, as the vision of her new life developed, she began to realize that the presence of Harry as a steady boyfriend might not be a comfortable fit now that high school was behind her.

Harry had never wanted to go to college. He had opted to remain in Narrownook and had already accepted a job at the paper mill in town like a number of his buddies had done. With Meghan living on campus, they'd be separated by twenty-five miles starting in September. Her parents had begun suggesting that she would have dozens of enriching new life experiences that would no doubt divide the two of them even further.

So Meghan had done the fair thing two nights ago. She had been honest with Harry. She'd confessed to him that she wanted to feel free to participate in and enjoy her college experiences without any encumbrances.

Harry had not taken the news well. First, he'd cried real tears at what he called the sudden hardness of her heart. He pointed out that she was throwing away all the good times they'd shared as if they had meant nothing.

Didn't she remember what they'd talked about since freshman year? he'd asked. They'd been going to build a life together. They had made solid and sensible plans. While she attended college, he would earn money and save for a home and the three children they'd eventually have. After college, she would help build on the existing nest egg until the first baby came along. By that time, they'd be able to afford a house, a four-bedroom home for their growing family.

His reflections had been gentle until he saw that they had not changed her mind. Then he remembered to be offended by the word *encumbrances*. Was that what he was to her now? An encumbrance? Or did she think that now that she was a college girl, she could throw around big words, and poor less-educated Harry wouldn't fuckin' understand what she was saying? Meghan winced as his words became ugly and abusive.

It was nine at night. They had been in their favorite parking spot, a turnout on Wagon Wheel Ridge Road where they had found solitude most weekend nights for four years. Meghan watched Diamond Lake sparkling below them in the moonlight, a sight that had always intensified their romantic urgings. But tonight, its peaceful beauty had lost its appeal.

Silently, she fled the car.

She knew it was a two-mile walk back home along an unlighted and thickly wooded country road, but walking home was better than listening to Harry's foul mouth. He'd always been careful with his offensive language around her, only using foul words when he was with his buddies and didn't think she could hear.

Five minutes later, a car slowed alongside her. She'd expected it to be Harry with an apology, but it was one of her classmates, Stan Russell, returning from Bangor on this back road, a popular short-cut from the city. He gave her a ride back to her house.

She didn't see Harry again until two days later when they lined up with the others for the graduation procession. They didn't speak. Harry wouldn't even make eye contact. More unsettling was his blatant attempt to flirt with Mariah Kennedy, the class tramp. It made Meghan that much more convinced that her decision two nights before had been a good one.

So she was glad that she had accepted Russie's invitation to ride with him and his crowd to Bar Harbor after the graduation ceremony.

And she was comfortable with Stan Russell's company that night. He had been a kind and sympathetic friend. While many of the couples didn't bother to hide their flagrant lovemaking, Russie remained respectful, clearly understanding the turmoil of transition that Meghan was dealing with.

They talked a lot. They talked about his plans. He had dreams of building his own construction company in Narrownook, gradually acquiring a fleet of trucks and equipment that would be the envy of other communities. He would have the most up-and-coming equipment that would eventually expand his business into neighboring towns that needed his broadened capabilities.

She enjoyed hearing about his goals. She'd heard that Stan Russell had a girl in the southern part of the state and wondered if the girl would play a role in his future. But she didn't ask. She did feel a little envious of anyone who would win this nice boy as a life partner.

She shared some of her plans with him and found that talking about them gave them more substance and filled her with renewed enthusiasm about her own future.

By the time the sun had started to rise at four thirty, everyone was too tired to party any longer. When one of the boys suggested they stop for breakfast on the way back, he was shouted down by a chorus of nos.

Russie dropped Meghan off at her house at six a.m. When he started to walk her to the door, she advised against it. She gestured toward the screened window open on the second floor and told him she didn't want their voices to disturb her folks, who would still be sleeping.

So, with a wave, Russie left the driveway and disappeared back up Pleasant Street.

She was aware of Harry before she put the key in her front door. He hadn't rolled himself out of the hammock yet, had just been lying there under the maple tree watching her in silence with his arms up under his head. But somehow, she had sensed he was there.

"How was Bar Harbor?" he asked when he finally spoke. She watched him dangle his left leg over the side of the hammock and secure a footing before he launched himself upright.

"It should have been you who was with me, Harry," Meg said. "What are you doing here?"

"I think we should talk. I don't like the way we left things the other day."

"I don't like it, either," Meghan sighed. "I had hoped you'd understand after you gave it some thought. I didn't mean goodbye. I thought it was wise to have a hiatus now that we're beginning our new lives apart. Maybe, who knows…in four years—"

"*Hiatus.* Another fancy word," he scoffed.

4

"If you came here to continue arguing—"

"I brought breakfast," he said as he retrieved a McDonald's bag from the hammock and let it sway triumphantly in front of her. "Let's go somewhere and talk. My car's just up the street."

When Meghan hesitated, he reached out and caressed her long blond hair, which curved naturally into a silky pageboy below her shoulders. It was a familiar gesture he'd done hundreds of times. "Give me an hour," he said, almost in a whisper, and she nodded and followed him up Pleasant Street to his beat-up Chevy, not bothering to ask why he'd parked so far away from her house instead of in the driveway like he always had done.

They went to Orphan Island, where they usually picnicked at the base of the Waldo–Hancock Bridge. It was a perfect spring morning, summer-warm already with a frisky but soft breeze off the Penobscot.

Harry had coffee and muffins, and she unwrapped her favorite—cinnamon-raisin. As they talked, Harry seemed to relax a bit about their separation.

"We'll be able to see each other Thanksgivings and Christmases," she heard herself suggest. It was an inane effort to help him adjust to their new arrangement.

She deliberately did not mention that she had already taken a job for the whole summer next year on the other side of the state, in Ogunquit. She could have found employment at McKay's Restaurant in Narrownook, but she'd make better tips in York County. She told herself that she needed to help her parents with as much of the cost of college as possible.

"Let's go for a walk," he said when they finished eating, and he took her hand and helped her up from the blanket they'd spread on a patch of lawn in the shadow of the green suspension bridge.

As Meghan rose, the ring on the chain around her neck popped out from beneath her jacket, reminding her that she intended to return it to Harry. Her hand went up to cup the gold nugget as she looked up at him. "You should have this back," she said to his unreadable expression as he gazed at the ring.

Meghan had been wearing it throughout their senior year. It had replaced the sports pins that he'd given her during the first three years of high school.

Harry remained mute as he watched her remove the signet band from its chain and offer it to him.

"I guess so," was all he said when he shoved it into the front pocket of his jeans.

Then they made their way down the sandy embankment toward the base of the massive iron structure.

As they reached the square cement block under the first pylon, Harry put his arm around her and pulled her close.

"We had wonderful moments in there," he whispered, nodding toward the metal door in the cement structure that led to a chamber beneath the bridge. Back in the day, it had housed maintenance equipment, but it had not been used for a number of years.

Meghan smiled in agreement.

"Let's have one more," he murmured. "We need to really celebrate our graduation...unless you and Russell have already—"

"Of course not!" she shot back at him.

"Then we need to reaffirm our hope for a future together one day," he said as he began moving her more deliberately toward the corroded iron door.

He lifted the hefty two-by-six beam that secured the entrance out of its steel brackets and used all his strength to tug the massive iron barrier open. Once there was enough space for entry, he let Meghan squeeze through the small gap ahead of him. As she set her feet on the slick concrete flooring, she suddenly remembered that they had left the blanket back on the lawn. She turned to tell him about it just in time to see the door swing shut and hear the thud of the wooden timber being collapsed back into its brackets.

It would be the last sound she would ever hear except for her own frantic screams in this sealed tomb on the floor of the Penobscot River.

CHAPTER 1

2019

THE DRIVE FROM BOSTON ALWAYS TOOK EXACTLY FOUR HOURS—NOT five minutes less or more. With or without a pit stop, it never varied. It was just one of those curious laws of the road that Lanie had stopped trying to figure out a long time ago. Now, as she glanced at her dashboard clock, she nodded her head. It was noon o'clock, as her brother would say. She'd left Medford at eight thirty this morning, which meant she'd be in the driveway on Pleasant Street at exactly twelve thirty. Perfect timing! Mama would have the television on, and Lanie would slip into the living room and watch the soap with her, just as if she'd never left over a year ago, the last time she had visited. Lanie would unwind from the trip, and during commercials, her mother would catch her up on the latest news in Narrownook.

Just before Belfast, Lanie turned left where Route 3 joined US Route 1 and headed north toward Searsport. She passed over the Belfast bridge and looked down into the picture-perfect harbor to her right. Dozens of sailboats bobbed on crystal waters next to an immaculate shoreline. She always admired what that town had done with its waterfront. She knew that Narrownook had copied them a few years ago and enhanced its own shoreline with new docks and a brick walkway paralleling the main street and the river. Their walk stretched from the Thegan Bridge, which connected Narrownook to Orphan Island, and ended one mile later when one came in sight of the mill through the patch of dogwood trees that had been planted at the west end.

A deep sigh of satisfaction escaped her as she pressed down on the accelerator and urged her white Corolla toward her hometown. Last week, at the last minute, she had resigned from the summer-school supervisory position that she'd held for five years, and citing declining health (not really an exaggeration, what with her allergies lately), had begun packing her bags for a whole summer in Narrownook.

At age forty-two, it was the first full summer she would spend back home since her high school graduation twenty-five years ago. During college summers, she'd waitressed in Ogunquit, then married right out of college and moved even farther away. When her marriage ended in divorce after her daughter was born, she had used her summers to supplement her income in various pursuits including further studies to augment her teaching salary. Her summer-school job had helped pay for the additional courses.

In a way, it had become a vicious cycle, and she was tired. A whole summer off seemed totally opulent, but at this time in her life, totally necessary. She needed to catch her breath. She'd visit with her daughter, who had recently transferred to the Bangor office of the Delta Delivery Company, and of course, she would spend some valuable time with her eighty-year-old mother. "And I will write that great American novel I have always wanted to write," she said out loud to the windshield.

Beware of high expectations, an inner voice scolded. *Remember the other times you've been back.*

She remembered only too well the other times she'd returned home to Narrownook.

Her first time away from home had been when she'd worked in Bar Harbor after graduation. News of Meghan Murphy's disappearance began circulating nationwide that same week. A missing eighteen-year-old who is never found can change a town. Narrownook, which had always been close-knit, became suddenly divided into two factions. One side theorized that Meg had run off with someone unknown to her parents and friends, which would explain her sudden breakup with her longtime boyfriend, Harry Olson, only days before she vanished.

Harry was rumored to have been stunned and devastated not only by her disappearance, but by the stories that there had been someone else in her life, a theory that he bought into quite quickly.

The other side cried foul play. Russie had been the last one to see her alive, and despite his impeccable reputation, many declared Stan Russell the likely suspect. They speculated that Stan might have been silently keeping a thing for Meg during their high school years, and had watched with resentment Meg and Harry's devotion to each other. When he finally secured a date with her (an overnight, for God's sake), that resentment could have escalated if his romantic advances had been rebuffed. His pride being injured and his expectations dashed, he'd resorted to violence.

Authorities had spent many hours questioning Stan Russell, who had stuck to his story of dropping the girl off at her home at six a.m. With no recorded threats and no eye-witnesses, the police were soon left spinning their wheels.

Harold Olson, too, had been interviewed often, but he hadn't been with Meg since their quarrel a few days before graduation, he said, so detectives hit a brick wall each time they looked at him for answers. Besides, he was Narrownook's favored son. No one had wanted to put too much pressure on their high school award-winning quarterback and ace pitcher. Harry Olson was their golden boy.

Throughout that summer, Lanie had been questioned as well. After all, she and her date had been the other couple in Stan Russell's car on graduation night. Her boss, Ann, the owner and operator of the Dunes Diner Restaurant on the outskirts of Bar Harbor where she was waitressing, had gotten annoyed after police detectives descended on her establishment more than a dozen times demanding private conferences with one of her girls. Some of these sessions lasted for an hour, which left Ann strapped for adequate coverage in her dining room, especially if the interruptions were during the breakfast, lunch, or dinner rushes.

And Lanie quickly tired of the same questions. When was the last time she had seen Meghan Murphy? What was she wearing? During the evening on Cadillac Mountain, had there been any arguments or unpleasant confrontations between Meghan and any of the other kids? Had there been any hostility between *anyone* on the mountain that night? What was the relationship between Meghan and Stan Russell? Had they been intimate?

And on and on. Session after session.

All the graduates who had been on Cadillac that night were plagued during the summer by the authorities, too. They had all been transported en masse in police vans to the Ellsworth courthouse for fingerprinting, which took up one entire Friday.

Lanie Warren's parents were besieged with phone calls from worried friends, the annoying press, and local authorities, along with people who didn't identify themselves, but were eager to offer their vulgar suggestions and crude accusations. Lanie could just imagine what Meg's parents were dealing with on top of their gut-wrenching worry.

Lanie didn't want to think what Stan Russell was going through. Such a great kid and good friend during high school didn't deserve the harassment she suspected he was having to endure.

She didn't return home for any period of time before going off to college. She had been in Narrownook just long enough to do laundry and pack for dormitory life. Once at college in New York that year, Lanie was thankfully removed from all the lingering questions and accusations. She had felt guilty about relishing the relief she gained with the distance between her new life and the turmoil she knew was continuing in Narrownook. Her high school classmate was unaccounted for, maybe a victim of foul play, maybe gone forever, and she, Lanie Warren, basked in her new and exciting college life far from the fray.

Her parents kept her updated about everything during her freshman year, but eventually, with no new information, Narrownook's attention to Meghan's disappearance began to dwindle into routine gossip whenever people remembered to discuss the unresolved matter at all.

Every time Lanie came home for short visits over the past twenty-five years, she'd meet up with old friends and be reminded again of that terrible summer when a high school friend had vanished. The memory of it hung often unspoken but palpable at the edges of every conversation among the 1994 graduates.

Lanie had not seen or talked to Russie in all the years she'd been away. She didn't have to spend any time analyzing the gossip about him because from the beginning she knew it was bogus. Some of the newspaper reports she had read years ago hinted strongly that he was the culprit. In today's jargon, he'd have been labeled a person of interest, but never in her mind was he anything but the nice boy she had spent graduation night with in the company of Meghan Murphy and Scott Lanford. Nothing could sway that fact. She would have testified to his good character if court testimony or legally sworn statements had ever been requested, which they were not.

That, in itself, spoke volumes to her. She figured authorities had never asked for statements about his character because no evidence had ever suggested he could have been responsible for her disappearance. It became Lanie's theory that Meghan had been a victim of foul play at the hand of a stranger. Perhaps after Russie had dropped her off at six a.m., she'd been in the wrong place at an early enough hour for no eyewitnesses to have noticed a skulking abductor.

* * *

Lanie shook off the morbid memories and slowed her speed down to twenty-five as she entered Searsport. There were always hidden speed traps through the little village, which maintained its peaceful essence with strictly enforced laws including stringent rules of their roads.

She followed the two-lane roadway along the river into Stockton Springs. The mid-June day was warm, but she snapped off her car's air-conditioner and rolled down her window. She was immediately breathing the sweet and pure scent of east coast Maine and found herself smiling in the delight of it.

She was more alert to her surroundings now because she anticipated, at any minute, a glimpse of the Waldo–Hancock Bridge through the forest of pines on her right. It would be brief, but it would be the first visible sign that she was home, a beacon she always waited for with childlike excitement.

Another memory of all her homecomings in the last twenty-five years suddenly flashed through her thoughts. Somehow, each time she visited Narrownook, Harry Olson spied her car passing through town or parked in the family driveway and showed up at the door. If he tapped the bell, it was always too lightly, because the first time she or her mother had any awareness of his presence was when the front door would fly open, and he'd stride in.

"Harry," Lanie would greet him cheerfully, and he'd hug her, stand her back away from him for a better look, declare her prettier than ever, and without being asked, make himself comfortable in the chair nearest him and stay at least a half hour. It was always nice to see him and hear about all the goings-on in the town, but he had never been a close friend of Lanie's, really. His time in school had been taken up either on the ball field or with Meghan Murphy. Lanie supposed that was a good thing because they'd not had any shared experiences back then to reminisce about and could therefore avoid accidentally slipping into the topic of Meg's disappearance. They concentrated on present-day events in Narrownook which, as mayor, Harry was always anxious to talk about.

* * *

Suddenly, there it was, the high green girders and something else now that dwarfed them. Through the pines were spirals of shiny gray steel. Her mother had warned her about that. Another bridge had been raised to carry, more safely, the multitude of cars and trucks across the Penobscot River. During the past year that Lanie had been away, the Penobscot Narrows Bridge had been erected.

It looked out of place to her. It resembled the one in Boston, which suited Boston, but Lanie immediately labeled it too industrialized to be picturesque. Narrownook was a quaint town, and Lanie felt it needed a more demure entrance.

"It will be christened sometime this summer," her mother had informed her. "I'm so glad you'll be here to enjoy all the festivities that are being planned."

Lanie knew that the beloved Waldo–Hancock Bridge's existence was now in jeopardy, and she felt sickened by the knowledge that it might be demolished.

"Harry is fighting to keep it as a walking bridge," her mother had assured her. "More than half the town wants it to stay as a historical landmark. After all, it was designed by the same man who designed the Golden Gate. The Waldo–Hancock was a practice run for California's bridge, which was built a year after this one. The two are identical except for their size, of course. I believe that Harry and the majority will win the argument and we'll keep the bridge," her mother always concluded optimistically.

Just like that, the bridges had disappeared behind the pine forest, only to reappear again a minute later when the road began curving at the base of Mount Waldo. Now the two bridges loomed up close and commandeering.

Several cars had pulled into a turnout overlooking the picturesque scene, and their passengers were busily snapping pictures with their phones or more deluxe cameras.

Lanie took the next right turn and began soaring over The Narrows. The massive green girders of the old bridge rose magnificently above her, rusted, yes, but still regal.

When she looked to the left, her heart warmed as she gazed down on the little town of Narrownook nestled upon the shore across the bay. Today, it sparkled white in the summer sun and seemed magical.

May it portend a magical summer for us all, she wished silently as her Corolla absorbed the slight bump that signaled she'd left the bridge and entered Orphan Island.

CHAPTER 2

THE TUNNEL NAMED THE NARROWS GIVES THE WIND IMPETUS MOST afternoons. Even late in the summer, gusts can shake the balance of even the fittest adult walking along Main Street on the way to Ben's BookNook or McKay's Restaurant, establishments that sit in the center of town directly in the wind's path.

More folks were seen along the streets in Narrownook proper nowadays. At one time, while the mill was in operation, small businesses in Narrownook operated on the philosophy that one's personal life superseded one's business obligations. It was perfectly acceptable, therefore, to delay a nine o'clock opening for a few minutes, for a few hours, even for a whole day if family needs dictated. Such chaotic scheduling tended to keep customers guessing and businesses closing in short order, so there weren't many folks being drawn to the downtown area back in the day.

As long as the mill kept running, this lackadaisical business practice didn't matter much to the town's economy. Someone in the family could count on employment in the mill and the weekly paycheck and health-care coverage it provided. Likewise, the town kept collecting generous taxes from the industry that had nourished it for decades.

The gnawing fear of losing the paper mill had grown exponentially in recent years. The usual fear mongers had been joined by higher-ups in the paper business predicting, with certainty, the imminent demise of the St. Andrews Company in Narrownook. Then, last year, just before Christmas, the Andrews executives invited a few town officials and the local press to a closed-door meeting where they announced that the mill was shutting down for good. Within the month!

What the town had feared for years had finally happened.

Harry Olson had seen it coming a few years before and had voluntarily left his number two machine to run for town council in the late '90s. He'd been in that position for only a few years when he ran for mayor and won that seat in 2000. He prided the move as the best decision he'd ever made because now he was ensconced as mayor of Narrownook until he chose to retire. That was because he was lucky to have lots of friends in town who looked up to him. They remembered his skills on the sports fields in his high school career. They trusted his judgment now in matters of the town that he'd fought for so brilliantly as a kid on the pitcher's mound and as Narrownook's feisty quarterback on the gridiron. He knew they also remembered his inconsolable grief when he lost his high school sweetheart, Meghan Murphy, to another man. He'd sought their support back then, and they were sympathetic as he lamented his humiliation over Megan's abandonment of him after four years of faithful devotion to her.

He and his friends took up golf together. They coached little league and Pop Warner teams together even now. They never failed to remind him of how important he was to this town. Their backing had been instrumental in winning him the permanent mayoral seat. Harry often chuckled to himself about how secure his position in the town was. He knew if any citizens were fool enough to run against him, they'd lose by a landslide because that was how small towns were—loyal to their friends.

There were times, at night, before he dropped off to sleep, that he thought about Meghan Murphy. It didn't happen often. He'd managed to compartmentalize her into the past as the girl who had done him wrong and paid the price. The way he looked at it, it was a closed door. The pun always made him smile—the few times he bothered to think about it at all.

* * *

He had been at his desk since the town office opened at nine that morning. It was now past noon. Besides a latte and the blueberry muffin his secretary, Gloria, had brought him at ten, he'd had nothing to eat, so it was time to go up the street to McKay's for lunch.

Harry slid his swivel chair back almost with a flourish and stood up, stretched, groaned, and stepped out into the foyer by the service windows. He could see Gloria through the glass partitions just pulling a Saran-wrapped something from a paper bag. Her desk was in front of the center bay window, affording her the best view in town. Today, she'd have a leisurely lunch admiring the sunlit and serene Penobscot Bay with its two signature bridges and the historic Fort Knox.

He signaled her with a sweep of his head toward the main entrance to let her know he was leaving. Once outside, he stretched again and glanced appreciatively over at the handsome stone library across the street, then turned left and started his stroll down Main toward McKay's. Just before he got to the crosswalk that would take him over to the restaurant, he saw the white Corolla with Massachusetts plates turn up Pleasant Street.

He made a mental note that Lanie Warren was in town and wondered for how long this time. He'd get the details later. Right now he was starved.

CHAPTER 3

LANIE HAD MADE THE BRIEF ENTRY ONTO AND QUICK EXIT OFF OF ORPHAN Island, crossing the concrete and low-slung Thegan Bridge, named after a beloved family doctor who had cared for many families in town during the years when a simple phone call, even in the middle of the night, brought the physician immediately to the patient's bedside. The bridge took one from the island onto Narrownook's Main Street.

As she crossed the span, she was pleased to look over a dozen anchored sailboats along an expanded arena of docks that the town had recently developed.

The Veteran's Memorial was on her left as she exited the bridge. It punctuated the beginning of the brick walkway on this side of town. Several flags flew in a light breeze, silently signaling a tribute to the brave citizens who had represented Narrownook in past wars.

The words and melody of the fifties song "Here Comes Summer" began playing in Lanie's mind as she turned left and scooted up Main Street. Between McKay's Restaurant and the historic Jed Prouty Inn, she took a right and gathered a bit of speed to make the long incline to the top of Pleasant Street, then slowed to brake at the fifth house after the hill plateaued. It was twelve thirty on the dashboard clock, Lanie noted, as she pulled into the family's driveway.

Giving the horn three quick jabs, she leaned back to regard the house, her childhood home, totally different in design from the one she'd grown up in. Two years of remodeling inside and out had changed it so significantly that relatives who visited often before its transformation now drove by many times until someone inside spotted them and rushed to signal them in.

For one thing, a high hedge had been added to the front, but even when a car pulled into the driveway, it would immediately begin backing out when the passengers surveyed the home's unfamiliar facade.

The house had doubled in size and morphed from a simple six-room A-frame into a twelve-room expanded Cape onto which a separate two-story dwelling had been added by Lanie's father for an elderly parent. After the death of his mother, the addition had become a guest house.

Lanie's eyes traveled along the lines of the house and came to rest on the new part. My home for the entire summer, she smiled to herself and quieted the engine.

While she gathered her pocketbook and car keys, she looked with appreciation at the well-manicured lawns. On her right, neat green carpets of grass in the front were flanked by carefully trimmed hedges that blocked the view of the Varney home next door and then ran all along the Pleasant Street side, breaking temporarily at the walk and driveway to continue again across the front of their empty lot. Nothing but lilac trees and a large oak came between the Warren property and the Morrisons' home on that empty-lot side.

The flagpole in the flower beds that lined the retaining wall and the new addition was bare, and Lanie made a mental note to keep a flag flying this summer as Dad would have done if he were still alive.

Instantly, she felt the tears that were always just behind any thoughts of her father, and so to break the spell, she glanced over at the long glassed-in front porch. She expected to see her mother, who should have been out there to greet her when she heard the horn. Seeing no one, she left the car and shouted, "Anybody home?" as she covered the short distance to the porch. When she tugged on the screen door, she found it locked so she hit the bell several times.

Immediately, a scuffle from inside and an expectant voice asked, "Lanie, is that you?" just before its owner hurried out to release the lock with an audible snap.

Then Lanie was hugging the tiny woman, and they were hustling back inside the front room, where neither of them spoke again until Victor finished his self-righteous spiel to a teary Victoria.

CHAPTER 4

"SHE JUST ARRIVED, MA." CLARENCE HAYES LET HIS LONG ARMS FLY EXCITedly about his head as he made his announcement even before he'd actually entered the kitchen from the shed at the back of the house on Oak Street, one block over from Pleasant.

Ricky Irving put down the screwdriver he'd been about to use on the second bolt of the new cabinet door he was installing and stood back to regard the six-foot-two seventeen-year-old with undisguised disgust.

"Who's he jawin' about, Sue?" he asked the woman who was absorbed in stripping off wallpaper behind the old woodstove.

"Your girlfriend has arrived, I guess," Sue Hayes answered in a monotone as she concentrated on her task. "If you want to mend any fences, I'd get over there before her daughter comes home and fills her in on your recent termination, if she hasn't already."

"She hasn't," Clarence interjected, swinging his head from side to side with overzealous certainty.

"And Clarence," Sue paused in her work to fix her son with a scornful expression, "you stop sneakin' over there spyin' on Amy and the rest of the family. One of these days you're going to get caught, and you'll feel like a fool."

"If he doesn't feel like a fool by now, nothin' will probably tip him off to it," Ricky mumbled.

"I thought you'd want to know," Clarence whined. His head and shoulders had lowered instantly at his mother's scolding.

"I did. Thank you," Sue said with a rapid change of attitude.

"Now, enough spying. Hand me that scraper there, and grab hold of this last strip while I work it off from here."

"How long she stayin'?" Ricky asked as he ran his grimy hands briefly under the kitchen faucet and wiped smears of dirt off on a nearby kitchen towel.

"All summer," came Clarence's pleased-to-be-of-help-to-you tone.

"How does the idiot kid know that?" Ricky jerked a thumb toward Clarence, who was beaming again with self-worth.

"Why can't you ever address him straight on?" Sue turned on Ricky.

"Because he's an idiot. I don't talk to idiots." Irving unbuckled his tool belt and straightened his paint-streaked T-shirt.

"I talk to you, don't I? Give him the same courtesy. He's smart enough to have figured out he can pick up neighborhood conversations on his scanner when they're talking on portable phones. He's been listening to Amy's calls."

"God a'mighty," Ricky muttered, shaking his head in disbelief. "When I was seventeen, I had better things to do than eavesdrop on the neighbors."

"Yeah," Sue Hayes scoffed, "you were busy *screwing* the neighbors."

"Well, there was this cute little redhead..."

"That was not the kind of screwing I meant, and you know it. I was thinking in terms of your habit of collecting everything that isn't nailed down in Hancock County."

"Benefits you, don't it?" Ricky snorted as he stepped toward the back door.

"Yes, and the fact that Clarence keeps tabs on the neighbors benefits both of us." Sue Hayes stepped around the stove to hug her son and give him a reassuring pat on the back. In response to her gesture and remark, Ricky Irving let the screen door slam as he left the house in a huff.

CHAPTER 5

"What is making my nose tingle?" Lanie asked when the next commercial interrupted their "Young and Restless" drama. Mahitabelle Warren hit the mute button with a vengeance and scowled at her daughter.

"What'd you say, dear?" she asked.

"Do you have your hearing aids on?" Lanie asked with an accusatory squint toward her mother.

"I hate them." Mahitabelle waved off the idea.

Lanie decided to fight the hearing problem another time, and so she repeated more loudly, "The smell. Where are those diesel fumes coming from?"

As if in answer to her question, a low grumble, followed by a lull, followed by a backfire, followed by a still louder roar, deadened any audible reply until a large truck had passed the house and had rattled and growled out of hearing.

"Does that answer your question?" her mother gestured toward the street with a look of impatience.

When the phone rang, Lanie waved her mother back into her recliner.

"I'll get it," she told her.

"It will be Amy," Mahitabelle said as she pushed the mute button to bring back the soap. Instantly, the room was filled with a blast of sound.

"Hello." Lanie fairly yelled the greeting.

"She's called twice before in the past half hour to see if you were here yet," Mrs. Warren prattled despite the intrusive TV and the fact that her daughter had a phone in her ear. "She worries about you like you worry about her."

"Hello?" Lanie tried again.

"Must be in the genes..."

"Ma," Lanie covered the mouthpiece with her left palm and shouted as loudly as she could over the television, "between you and Jack Abbott on the screen there, I can't tell who I'm talking to."

The gray-haired woman across the room leaned forward in her chair and punched a button as if she intended to pulverize it. "I'm sorry, dear," she said, sitting back and staring into her lap with an injured expression.

"You don't have to turn it off, just down," Lanie said, her tone at once impatient and beseeching in an effort to soothe her mother's hurt feelings.

"Hello, McFly," came Amy's caustic response through the phone's receiver. "Argue with Grandmother later. I just wanted to know if you were there in one piece."

"I'm here," Lanie sighed. She was relieved that her daughter sounded like her old self for a change—her old pain-in-the-neck Amy, back to the girl she was before her breakup with Bobby Turner. If she was over him, she was recovering quicker than her mother and grandmother were. They had both been ready to adopt the handsome well-mannered young man into the family. What mother wouldn't love a daughter's suitor who could play a mean game of cribbage and take the time to play it every day with the girl's grandmother during his one-hour lunch break.

"Okay, I'll talk to you when I get home," Amy blurted, and the line went dead.

Lanie had started to ask when that might be, but it didn't matter. Another truck was hiccupping outside in its struggle to crest the rise of Pleasant Street and would be roaring by momentarily. And Grandmother had reinstated the soap on a quieter level albeit still well within the legal definition of deafening.

Ignoring her inner voice beginning somewhere in the distance to remind her of its earlier caution against high expectations, Lanie leaned to smell the dozen red roses in the vase on the breakfast nook counter.

"Who's your admirer?" she asked her mother when the truck had passed and a new commercial had been silenced. She gestured toward the bouquet.

"Not mine," chuckled Mahitabelle, "Amy's. I think Clancy sent them."

"Which one is Clancy?" Lanie tried to remember from past telephone conversations with her daughter.

"Twenty-nine. Married before. Twice."

"Oh, Clancy," Lanie nodded, still trying to fix the boy in her mind. "He's not the one with the ponytail, is he?"

"That's Emerson Hickok," Mrs. Warren waved the thought away with her free hand. The other hand hit the mute button to bring back the audio, just as the doorbell rang.

Lanie walked out onto the porch and unlocked the screen door to a disheveled Ricky Irving, who beamed a toothless grin at her.

"Ricky, hi," she greeted him with a bit more enthusiasm in her voice than she felt at the sight of her mother's handyman.

"Saw your car," he said. "Thought I'd stop in and show you the next project that should have been done yesterday." He began chuckling, as was his custom, at his own perceived joke. As usual, Lanie chuckled with him. He was a funny duck when he wasn't being infuriating.

"Actually, I just got here, Ricky, and you're interrupting our program."

Ricky raised his eyes, looked around, and snorted. "You're kidding, right?" he said. "The house is falling down around you, and you're hung up on fantasy?"

"I earned the right," Lanie said, undaunted by the likes of Ricky Irving.

"By teaching school a few hours a week, a few weeks a year?" Ricky's face lit up like a flashbulb, and Lanie knew he was about to launch into the overpaid, over-appreciated schoolteacher soliloquy if she didn't nip it in the bud.

"Goodbye, Ricky, come back tomorrow when I'm rested and unpacked. The house can take one more night, can't it?"

"Maybe," Ricky extended a hand with splayed fingers and rocked it back and forth in the air. But he turned to go, nevertheless. At that moment, another truck crested the rise of the hill beyond the front hedge and rumbled by. Through the break of greenery at the driveway, Lanie made out the words "Russell Construction" printed on the side of the cab.

"What are all these trucks?" she asked Ricky's back.

Irving stopped in midstride and turned. A smug look told Lanie this could be a long story.

"You went to school with Stan Russell, didn't you?" Ricky asked, stretching back and plunging his hands into the pockets of his splattered dungarees.

"Russie Russell?" Lanie smiled at the memory of the boy who had shared his construction company dreams with all his friends a lifetime ago.

"*Stanley* Russell, now," Ricky corrected, pulling himself up on his tiptoes and lowering his scrawny frame back down in a posture of self-imposed authority as if his information was of great significance.

"What are they doing on outer Pleasant? I haven't been here an hour, and there have been a dozen trucks back and forth already."

"Stanley's building all those development homes. Makin' himself a fortune. He's a big guy around here despite the negative gossip that never ends. He's tough and determined, I'll give him that."

"Good for him," Lanie said, and meant it. "It's nice to know he's etched out a good life for himself."

"More than an etching," Ricky Irving said. "More like a portrait." And he was chuckling at himself again.

Lanie watched, amused, as he leaned over and came back up straight, laughing so uncontrollably that for a second he lost his balance and had to stagger around the lawn a bit to regain it.

"Got to go," Lanie said when Ricky would have plunged on into the saga of "Russie Russell Makes Good." To her relief, Ricky didn't try to keep talking.

"Be sure there's coffee tomorrow morning when I get here," he looked over his shoulder to say flippantly in a tone that went far beyond his place as handyman to the elderly Mahitabelle Warren.

Lanie just shook her head as she watched him swagger to his ugly black van corroding in the driveway. He had to wait until another Russell Construction truck passed by before he could pull out and disappear into the street beyond the hedge.

Lanie was about to turn to go back in to catch what was left of her soap opera, but a florist truck drove into the yard. She waited as a young man alighted, holding a paper-wrapped bouquet.

"Amy Place?" he asked politely as Lanie opened the door.

"I'm her mother," she answered and took possession of the dozen red roses he thrust at her.

"Could this be Clancy again?" Lanie asked as she shared the delivery with Mrs. Warren. "And the name is…Mitch Marlowe?" Lanie gasped as she pulled out the square card that had been tucked inside. "Mitch Marlowe from Massachusetts?" She turned for clarification to her mother.

"He's stayed here a few times this spring," Mahitabelle nodded. "Nice young man. Not Bobby Turner, but no ponytail; no ex-wives."

Lanie was arranging the flowers in a vase when the phone rang again. The television had already been turned off when the soap opera ended, so this time, Lanie didn't have to use a cheerleader voice when she said hello.

"Gloria! How are you?" she greeted when the caller identified herself. Gloria Jordan was a fellow '94 graduate.

"Lanie, is that you?" the voice on the other end of the line exclaimed. "It's good you answered. As you may know, I work for the mayor, and Harry's fit to be tied about your mother's caretaker."

"Ricky Irving? What's he done this time?"

Lanie remembered a couple of years ago when Ricky had brought a gripe to Harry Olson regarding the early arrival of the street-cleaning machine in the residential neighborhoods. He complained it was interrupting the elderly citizens' sleep when it appeared before eight every spring morning. Mahitabelle Warren was one of the complainants, according to Irving. Mrs. Warren, an early riser, had not voiced any objection to it, and Lanie and her brother had had to chastise Irving severely for including their mother in what turned out to be Ricky's attempt to cause controversy where it didn't exist. It was simply the guy's predilection to start trouble for his own aggrandizement.

"He stalked into Harry's office just now, demanding, and I quote, that he 'do something about the construction trucks going up and down Pleasant Street, fouling up the air and overwhelming Mrs. Warren's peaceful home with noise and fumes.'"

"Like the last time," Lanie sputtered.

"There's no love lost between Harry and Stan Russell, but Harry doesn't need Ricky's aggravation, either. On the other hand, if your mother is truly upset by the weekly project Russell is handling for the town, he'll try to use his influence to redirect the truck route or cancel the contract altogether."

Lanie began to seethe. "Oh, Gloria," she said, "this is so aggravating. I just arrived not more than an hour ago. Ricky rang the bell moments after I landed here, and in the course of the conversation, I asked him what all the truck activity was. That part's true, but no one here complained, and we certainly didn't authorize him to speak to the mayor."

"Harry got rid of him fast," Gloria giggled, "but he wants your mother to know that the truck activity is a temporary situation that has nothing to do with Russell's home development. Stan is doing an emergency cleanup of the transfer station for the town. It shouldn't take longer than another week."

"I'm happy to hear that," Lanie told her, "but I'm furious about Ricky. I've wanted Ma to fire him for a long time now, but she's been reluctant to do that. Maybe this will help to change her mind. Please give Harry her apology, will you?"

"I'll do that. Hey, before you hang up, you should know that the day after tomorrow is the first meeting of us old-timers to plan our twenty-fifth high school reunion. Why don't you join us if you're still here in town?"

"Reunion! Oh, my God, it *is* twenty-five years. I'm here for the summer, and I'd love to get in on that."

"I'll pick you up at ten on Thursday morning. Maybe we can grab lunch afterward if Harry will let me take a whole half day off."

"See you Thursday," Lanie told her and hung up feeling elated about getting together with old friends. Then immediately came the stinging realization that any class reunion would surely ignite all the tragic history surrounding theirs. It was sad. Graduations should only be filled with remembrances to treasure instead of memories to shrink from.

"Was that Amy?" Mahitabelle asked when Lanie had rejoined her mother.

"That, Ma, was Gloria Jordan." And Lanie leaned forward to more forcefully explain what Ricky had just done.

"How did he know about the trucks?" Mahitabelle asked.

"I mentioned it, unfortunately."

"When did you see Ricky? You just got here."

"He was the one at the door a few minutes ago."

"What was he doing here?"

"Saw my car, I guess, and thought he'd show me the next project he wanted to tackle. Ma, I think you should get rid of him. He's nothing but trouble. I just don't trust him. Him *and* his girlfriend," Lanie jabbed a thumb in the direction of the next street over.

"Sue's a good friend," Mahitabelle stated firmly with the beginnings of a pout. "She comes and plays Scrabble with me and walks with me and does shopping for me."

"When was the last time?" Lanie squinted at her mother.

"I haven't seen her since Amy moved in at Christmas."

"I rest my case. Some friend."

"She probably feels Amy is able to do some of the things she did for me," Mrs. Warren countered.

"If she were a friend, she'd still come to visit."

The pout took a permanent place on Mahitabelle's mouth as she toyed with the Scrabble tiles on her food tray. "Maybe," she muttered.

"She's too smitten with Ricky, who majors in doing handyman stuff for all the elderly in town. The day he bragged to me that he had keys to half the homes in Narrownook, I started getting nervous. You know he's a thief. He's walked off with half the contents of your garages and Dad's workshop."

"That's why I'm glad Amy fired him," Mahitabelle announced.

Lanie had opened her mouth to keep raving and froze at her mother's self-satisfied declaration, not to mention her smug expression. "When?"

"Weeks ago."

"Why didn't you tell me?"

"Subject didn't come up until now."

"Why was he just here, then?" Lanie wondered out loud.

"What exactly did he say?" her mother asked. "I was so wrapped up in my soap that I didn't notice anyone at the door."

"And you didn't hear the bell," Lanie said, pointing an accusatory finger in her mother's direction but deciding to shelve the hearing problem again.

"It was as if nothing had changed," Lanie mused out loud, instead. "Said he'd be back tomorrow to show me what needed to be done next. Who does the lawns now?"

"Amy."

"Amy does all these lawns herself?" Lanie stared dumbfounded at her mother. "And keeps the hedges trimmed?" she thought to add.

"Insists on it. You know Amy."

Lanie knew her daughter; stubborn and proud and a workaholic at twenty-one. "Well, I'm glad Ricky Irving doesn't work here anymore," she said, setting up the card table in front of Mahitabelle's recliner, "but you need to find someone to do the heavy stuff around here. We'll work on that this summer. I'm glad I'm here for the whole time."

"I'm glad you are, too, dear." Mahitabelle leaned over and squeezed her daughter's hand. When the doorbell rang, Lanie looked at her and waited for a reaction. When there was none, Lanie stood up and shook a finger at her again. "We'll work on that, too," she said.

"What?"

"Someone's at the door. You didn't hear the bell."

"Really?"

"Really."

On her way to the door, Lanie mulled over all of the tasks she had accumulated in just an hour. She would have to visit Harry and apologize for Ricky. She would have to deal with the recently fired Ricky Irving if he had the chutzpah to show up tomorrow. Her mother needed a checkup and her hearing issue resolved. There was a class reunion to help plan. Then there was the business of Amy doing the lawns and a new caretaker needing to be hired before fall.

She stopped in her tracks and hesitated to snap the lock on the screen door when she saw the questionable character on the steps holding a satchel.

"Hello," she said. It sounded more like a question than a greeting.

"Is Amy here?"

Lanie regarded the shoulder-length scraggly hair, the torn jeans, and the battered bag.

"She's working," she answered.

"She said to meet her here at four."

"And you are...?"

"Emerson Hickok," the scraggly hair answered.

Because the name was familiar, she released the lock.

"Ma, look who's here," she announced, aware that she was holding her breath until her mother would officially ID the visitor. It also crossed her mind that she should have asked for a certificate from the health department before she admitted this unkempt character in the first place.

Add to the list of tasks, a long talk with Amy, she mused as she offered the hair a seat on the settee by the door while they all awaited four o'clock.

CHAPTER 6

THE SUN BEGAN STREAMING INTO LANIE'S TALL BEDROOM WINDOWS A little after five a.m., and she was instantly wide awake and full of energy. She slipped out of bed and into a sweatshirt and jeans, a pair of socks and her sneakers. After pouring a quick glass of orange juice from one of two containers in her otherwise empty refrigerator, she went down the back stairs into the garages and out the side basement door into five-thirty sunshine.

It was bracing. Invigorating. She looked up into a cloudless sky the intense Maine-blue color she hadn't seen often enough in recent years. Taking deep breaths, she began a sentimental journey on foot, up the street where she had played as a child, across Pleasant Street, through the St. Jameses' driveway, which had been her shortcut during four years of high school when, already late for class, she'd race in vain to beat the clock. On past the high school, now a middle school, and all the way across town to the west as far as the ravaged mill, its partially gutted-out shells gaping at her grotesquely in their silent pain.

It took her fifteen minutes to wind back along Main Street and climb up Pleasant. By the time she arrived at the house, it was six o'clock, and the trucks were moving busily up and down the street, their brown diesel fumes fouling the early morning air.

She knew Amy would be up getting ready for work by this time. Yesterday afternoon, her daughter had arrived home soon after Emerson's arrival.

"He's a nice guy, Mom," Amy had assured her after he had left on his bicycle.

"Did he lose his license?" Lanie wanted to know as they watched him pedal away.

"Never learned to drive," Amy told her.

"Now that he's a working man, shouldn't he think about learning the skill? And maybe making the acquaintance of a barber, for that matter," she added, knowing full well that her daughter's patience was stretched with her already.

"He's a nice guy, Mom," Amy repeated.

"I think I'm ready to accept a pigtail on a man in the name of neat," Lanie continued, "but the loose, cascading look turns me off. Besides, his hair was filthy."

"He'd just worked all day in the new seafood plant and then worked out before he dropped in to see me. I'm not dating him, Mom, he's just a friend."

"That's a relief, Amy. I had begun to think you were so bent on finding the antithesis of Bobby Turner that you had limited yourself to only his physical counterparts: ugly and unclean."

"Mom!"

"I know, I'm awful," Lanie admitted, giving her daughter a hug, "but I love you, and I worry. It must be hard on you working alongside pretty-boy Bobby Turner every day after finding out he'd been cheating on you the whole time you two were a couple. I probably should shut my mouth and let you alone to ease back into dating in your own way."

"It was hard at first," Amy acknowledged, "but lately it's kind of funny, actually. Bobby hears about long-distance phone calls from Mitch Marlowe, who calls me at work at least once a week. Then Clancy sends me roses, even to the company office, and this one and that one come in to visit me at the station. The pain is still with me, but sometimes the look on Bobby's face across the assembly belt is rewarding, too."

Lanie had hugged her again, and they had talked about Grandmother—about her having a glass of wine with her lunch every day (was it healthy?), about her not using her hearing aids, and, of course, about the visit from Ricky Irving.

Amy filled her mother in on the day she had fired the caretaker. "He'd finished the bathroom cabinets," she told her, "and I found all this crap from the job piled up behind the garage, down back. He said he was going to take it to the dump—stuff like insulation and boards with nails sticking out of them. So the next day, it was gone. He had left a couple of old doors and planks leaning up against the building, which I told him, in no uncertain terms to get rid of, too. A couple of days later, I went into Grandfather's workshop and there was all the stuff! He'd moved it in there to attract mice and rats and pose a safety hazard. When he came to mow the lawns, I told him he was fired, that his days of pilfering from an old lady were over, and that I had found the junk hidden in the workshop. He didn't argue. He knew he was wrong. He just gave me the hairy eyeball and stalked off. Then I called Mr. Snout, and he came and carried away the debris in the workshop."

"Mr. Snout?" Lanie repeated.

"The junk man."

"Mr. *Snout?*" Lanie said again.

"The guy charges Grandmother just one dollar no matter what size load he has to lug off."

"Did he marry Miss Piggy?"

"Oh, Mom," Amy groaned.

But Lanie saw her nose twitch and knew she was trying to stifle her amusement. "I love you, Amy," Lanie said, hugging her daughter again. "You are so cool. So competent. So serious. I hope you'll learn to relax again; learn to ease up on yourself. In the meantime, you do a mother proud."

"Thanks, Mom."

Amy had hugged her back extra tightly for a minute, before Grandmother had come into the kitchen to challenge them both to a game of Scrabble. "I won big today," she had bragged. "I'm on a rollerblade."

"Just a *roll*," they had both laughed in unison.

* * *

Now, Lanie brought a cup of coffee up to Amy in her room in the main house and sat sipping on her own cup while her daughter finished getting dressed. She looked with approval around the remodeled bedroom that had once been hers and her brother's separate bedrooms before the center wall had been removed. Skylights had been added to both sides to make the room appear even larger and brighter. A built-in desk and wall shelves filled one corner, and Lanie saw the picture of her mother and father posing on their wedding day prominently displayed beside a collage of framed family photos on an opposite wall.

Amy was into family memories and keepsakes. There was a polished volunteer police badge that had been her grandfather's pinned to a black-and-white photo of the 1960 volunteer fire department picture showing John Warren with the other members of the department.

Bear, the teddy, none the worse for all his travels through Amy's life so far, perched on the back of a refurbished boudoir chair.

"Your room looks lovely, honey," Lanie told her.

Outside the front window over the sloping porch roof, a large maple rustled against the eaves in the morning breeze. And something else moved outside under the window just before the doorbell rang.

Lanie and Amy turned to look at each other and then at the clock. Seven a.m.

"It can't be Ricky Irving," Lanie gasped.

"Yes, it can," Amy pulled the curling iron away from her hair and reached to pull its cord from the wall socket. "He is one nervy guy. I don't put anything past him. He's going to try to talk you into doing another job around here."

"Don't worry about it!" Lanie declared on her way out of the room.

And there he was on the other side of the door, grinning expectantly.

"Ricky, you've got to be kidding," Lanie greeted him. "Mama's still in her room, and Amy hasn't left for work yet."

"Hey, I'm a busy man," he said self-righteously. "The early bird gets the worm, you know."

"*I* certainly have," Lanie nodded as she unlocked the door. To her surprise, not only did Ricky Irving catch the innuendo, but he found it hilarious and could hardly walk into the house in a straight path, he was laughing so hard.

"Shhh!" Lanie silenced him. "Mama might still be sleeping; we stayed up late last night over a couple of wild games of Scrabble."

"She won't hear us," Ricky said, trying to keep his balance while he tapped his right ear. "Deaf as a boot, you know."

Lanie led him into the kitchen and poured him a cup of coffee, practically shoving it at him, aware that she was abetting his arrogant behavior. She poured a refill for herself and then turned to face him. "You've got five minutes to tell me what's on your mind," she said, "and then I'll tell you what's on mine."

"House is in bad shape in back near the supporting wall around the new construction," Ricky announced in a serious tone.

"Show me what you're talking about," Lanie said, and led him down the back stairs through the family room in the basement and out the Church Street entrance where expansive driveways spread blue-black fingers of pavement to a single garage and then splayed to the left to the three-car garage under the new addition.

"If you'd been here while I was renovating your mother's closet and bath," Ricky said, taking quick strides, "I would've stopped that job until this more serious condition was corrected."

He stopped at the edge of the main driveway and pointed to the stone wall that supported the empty lot above them on Pleasant Street.

"See that?" he asked importantly, jabbing an index finger toward the blue-gray granite.

"Looks okay to me," Lanie shrugged, but she took time to follow the lines of the three cement buttresses reinforcing the wall.

"Oh, nothin' wrong with the wall," Ricky agreed. "Don't you see what's happening to the house's foundation next to it?"

"I really don't, Ricky," she said, feeling her impatience building.

"The cracks," Ricky said with a hint of impatience himself.

"Same ones that have been there for a couple of years," Lanie told him. "The addition is only eight years old. The house is probably still settling."

"The retaining wall is gradually leaning more and more into the house, pressing in on the foundation. Left to do that over a few more years, and the integrity of the house'll be compromised forever."

Lanie studied Ricky's serious face and asked what she thought was the next logical question. "If this were true, what should be done?"

"The house and wall need to be separated immediately to stop further damage," he said. "What I could do—"

Behind them, the familiar clang of the latch on the chain-link fence gate made them both turn at once. A man had left the gate open and was striding briskly up the long driveway toward where they stood. He was a tall man dressed in crisp beige pants and matching shirt. Behind him, parked on Church Street outside the fence, was a truck with Russell Construction emblazoned on its side.

"I thought he might show up," Ricky Irving muttered. "One of the reasons I got here early."

Lanie squinted into the bright easterly sun to catch a better look at the man. Even before he reached them, she recognized the boyhood features, grown fuller yet firmer with age, features made even more handsome with the shedding of naiveté and made leaner with the accumulation of worry and hard work.

"Russie Russell!" Lanie exclaimed, and went the last few yards to greet her high school friend. If her quick but genuine hug startled Stan Russell, he did not let on. In fact, it was difficult for Lanie, afterward, to interpret his reaction. Russie had always been taciturn; that was part of his charm. The sense of humor lurking just behind the unreadable eyes, the hint of amusement almost, but not quite, lifting the firm set of his mouth.

Now, Lanie dropped her arms from their embrace of the man and stepped back to regard him more closely.

For a moment she was young and impish again, carefree, the high school girl before graduation, before that awful day in June had changed so many lives. And so she said in a playful tone, "What have you been doing since I last saw you twenty-five years ago?"

Instantly, the eyes snapped...what?...pain?...certainly not humor as they briefly met hers. "Workin'," came the cryptic Yankee drawl, and then his eyes turned toward Ricky and there could be no question that their expression reflected anger.

"Irving!" Stan Russell stepped around Lanie and confronted the handyman. "My secretary tells me you stormed into my office yesterday afternoon, reduced her to tears, and bullied my sales staff. What's the problem?"

"Your fuckin' diesel trucks are the problem!" Ricky flung at him, and Lanie heard herself gasp.

Ricky heard her, too. "Sorry for my language, Lanie," he said in a condescending tone that made Lanie immediately bristle. "Why don't you go in the house and let me handle this."

His words and tone were suggestive of a personal relationship with her—an ownership, even. Lanie was at once mortified and furious.

"No you don't. Don't patronize me," she growled at him as she raised a flat palm as if to physically halt any further words from him. "Do I understand that you not only took it upon yourself to visit the mayor yesterday in my mother's name, but Russell Construction, also?"

"Something had to be done about the fumes and noise. Big trucks and big money be damned. Elderly lady like your mother can't take that kind of pollution. Her lungs—"

"Ricky, let me worry about my mother's lungs. You had no business making a spectacle of yourself and using my mother's name to do it – again!"

"I just want you to know, Irving," Stan Russell interrupted, "that there is a restraining order out on you as of eight p.m. last night. You'll be served soon enough, but one more appearance anywhere near my office or work areas and I'll let 'em throw the book at you. There are plenty of people who are standing in line for that privilege."

With a defiant glare toward Russell, Ricky Irving pulled himself up as tall as he possibly could and strode off toward the far corner of the house. "Call me when you decide to start the repair," he said to Lanie as he passed her.

"Not that it's any of my business," Russell said when Irving was out of earshot, "but I wouldn't want him anywhere around anything *I* owned." And with that, he, too, strode off, in the opposite direction toward his truck at the gate. Lanie stood dumbfounded as she stared after one and then the other.

"Good-looking guy, Mom," Amy said, suddenly appearing at her side.

They both stood staring after the club cab as it pulled out into Church Street and disappeared around the corner, over the old Sawmill Bridge and up along Sawmill Road, still visible for some seconds as it wound its way across the middle avenues of Narrownook.

CHAPTER 7

AT SEVEN O'CLOCK THE NEXT MORNING, LANIE ONCE AGAIN TOOK AN across-town walk, but she cut it shorter than the day before because Gloria was picking her up at ten for the reunion meeting.

By eight thirty she had showered, dressed, and dabbed on light makeup, filled two cups of coffee for herself and her daughter, and was on her way through the main house to visit with Amy before she left for work. As she arrived at the back stairs, a shortcut to Amy's room, she thought she heard her mother's front door open.

Thinking that Amy must just be coming in from retrieving the morning paper, she detoured into the living room and saw Harry Olson just entering the house.

"Harry!" she exclaimed. "How'd you get in here?"

"I rang the bell, but I guess no one heard me," he answered with a casual shrug. "The door was unlocked, so—"

"The door was unlocked?" Lanie was surprised. They always kept the front door locked at night. Had Amy been out earlier for the newspaper and then neglected to secure the door when she came back in?

"I just wanted a chance to see you before my busy day started," Harry told her. Then, with a wide smile, he stroked both of her shoulders gently so as not to slop the coffees she was holding and, in typical Harry fashion, declared her prettier than ever before backing away.

"You should really get your vision checked," Lanie laughed as she nodded toward the chair by the door that Harry always sat in when he came by. "Have a seat," she said. "You can have my coffee and I'll go deliver this one to Amy and be right back."

Olson scowled down into the plain black liquid she'd handed him.

"You need cream and sugar?" Lanie guessed. "Sugar's on the bar over there. Step into the kitchen and raid the refrigerator for some milk if you need it." With that, she turned and disappeared into the hall.

She was back in a minute finding Harry searching in kitchen drawers for a spoon.

"This one," she said, pulling on a handle next to the stove.

While she filled a coffee pot with water and started a brew for the main house, Harry leaned casually against the counter studying her.

"Our class is getting together to set up a twenty-fifth reunion today," he told her. "You should come. I can pick you up in..." he glanced at his silver-plated watch, "an hour."

"Gloria already beat you to it," Lanie said.

Olson sobered immediately. "She never mentioned it," he said, and Lanie wasn't sure if his tone contained irritation or just surprise.

"Any chance she and I can have lunch together after the meeting, before she returns to work?" she asked. If Gloria hadn't had a chance to make the request, Lanie figured she'd put in a plea in her stead.

Harry pushed himself away from the counter and put his cup down next to the sink before he responded.

"Only if I can join you," he said. "Tell you what I'll do. I'll make a reservation for us at the Jed." And with a light pat to her shoulder as he passed her, he thanked her for the coffee and left.

Lanie heard the front door bang shut followed by the click of the porch screen as it was closed, which reminded her that she had to speak to Amy. She wondered why Amy had been out so early. But mostly, she didn't enjoy the thought that the door might have been carelessly left unlocked, maybe all night.

44

CHAPTER 8

HARRY OLSON HAD RESERVED A TABLE IN THE FORMAL DINING ROOM OF the Jed Prouty Hotel instead of a booth in the breakfast/luncheon section where the locals usually chose to have their midday meals.

The hotel was an old establishment in Narrownook. Originally named the Robinson House, it was renamed the Jed Prouty Tavern after Richard Golden wrote a play called *Old Jed Prouty*. (Prouty was a hotel proprietor in his drama about the hostelry.)

The structure was built as a two-family home in 1783, but not long after that, in the early 1800s, it became an inn and tavern. Daniel Webster visited there often before the Webster–Ashburton Treaty was consummated in 1842. Presidents William Henry Harrison, John Tyler, Martin Van Buren, Andrew Jackson, and Millard Fillmore had all stayed at the Jed Prouty Tavern during the Maine–New Brunswick boundary dispute. That dispute presented a threat of war and resulted in the construction of Fort Knox, today a part of Narrownook's scenic view, on a knoll in Prospect, Maine, overlooking the harbor.

The presidents' names appear on old registers of the Jed Prouty with such notable signatures as John C. Calhoun, Stephen Douglas, Jefferson Davis, and Robert Ingersoll. Admiral Peary made the inn his home while his ship, the *Roosevelt*, was being built on Orphan Island. The USS *Roosevelt* was the first ship ever built in the Western Hemisphere tough enough for successful Arctic exploration, which Peary achieved in 1909.

In the 1940s and '50s, the Jed Prouty was a terminal for Greyhound as the structure blossomed into a more modern hotel.

Buses made a couple of stops a day during their journeys between Bangor and Portland.

* * *

Lanie, Gloria, and Harry took seats at a square table covered by a pristine white tablecloth, and Harry insisted on ordering cocktails for them, joking that Gloria didn't get a lot of work accomplished after lunch, anyway, and he doubted that a gin and tonic or two would make a noticeable reduction in her productivity.

Lanie watched Gloria shoot her boss a dirty look before she evidently decided to laugh along with him.

They gave their drink orders to Crystal Murray, a long-time head waitress there and a '94 graduate who had also attended the reunion meeting that morning. "I worry we won't be able to pull this thing off with such divisions in this town," she said when she'd finished recording their drink orders.

"It's not this town," Gloria answered, "just this class."

"It's too bad," Crystal sighed. "Narrownook is a sweet place to live, and he's a sweet man." She pointed her ballpoint pen toward the opened French doors to their right.

The three of them, in unison, looked down the long hallway of windows beyond the dining room doors. Across the welcoming foyer entrance, they could see into the lunchroom, where a group was gathered at the big round booth at the eastern end of the building. There, Stan Russell seemed to be in deep conversation with a bunch of fellow graduates who had also attended the meeting.

"Stan Russell holding court," Harry sneered.

"He had some good ideas at the meeting this morning," Crystal said, shoving her pen behind her ear and walking away.

"She's had a thing for Russell for a long time," Harry muttered.

To thaw the chill that Lanie suddenly felt come over them, she pointed to her left. "This place has really changed in just a year since I was here last," she said. "The new bright-red carpet lining the L-shaped porch entry is lovely. There must be at least a dozen white wicker chairs and side tables all along that windowed walkway.

It's stunning! What's that room beyond the arched doorway that Crystal just went into? Not a kitchen access, certainly."

"That," Harry smiled, laying a hand lightly on Lanie's arm, "is the new cocktail lounge and dance floor. It's perfect. I'll give you a tour after we eat. I'll even give you a spin around it some night soon if you'd like."

Crystal came with their drinks then, and Lanie was relieved that she'd been spared from making a response to Harry's suggestion. She thought she'd seen a look pass across Gloria's face as Harry was speaking, and it concerned her. She wondered if Gloria was smitten with her boss. Could they be dating?

There was so much she didn't know about her hometown after so many years. It wasn't just the animus around the unsolved disappearance of Meghan Murphy anymore that troubled her. It was the convoluted relationships that had been spawned since that terrible night which also needed to be examined.

The aggravating little voice of warning crawled back into her head as she tried to enjoy her three-decker club sandwich with her old friends.

CHAPTER 9

THERE WAS A CAR IN THE FRONT DRIVEWAY WHEN GLORIA DROPPED LANIE off at the front of the house at two o'clock.

"Do you remember Cousin Penelope?" Mahitabelle asked her the minute her daughter came in.

Lanie regarded the skinny woman perched on the edge of the loveseat and admitted she did not. "I don't even remember *having* a cousin named Penny," Lanie said.

"Penelope," the woman corrected, giving Lanie's extended hand a distracted pump.

"She's not really a relative," Mahitabelle prattled, "but her mother and I were good friends and always referred to each other as cousins. Penelope just drove in from New York for a few days and wonders if you wouldn't take her around and familiarize her with key establishments."

"All three of them?" Lanie joked.

Nobody laughed. Lanie knew her mother probably didn't hear her, but wondered if Penelope hadn't understood the sarcasm or if she just lacked a sense of humor. Why did she suspect the latter?

Lanie had hoped to be able to use the afternoon to line up some doctor visits for her mother, but now, here was Penelope.

"Okay," Lanie nodded, "why don't we start with a quick drive or walk around the center of town. If you don't want to walk, we can take my car; that way you can just concentrate on the scenery."

"I'm perfectly capable of driving. I'll remember where places are if I actually motor to them myself," was Penelope's testy reply, and she stood up, keys in hand, and headed for the door without even a nod of goodbye to Mahitabelle.

"Have a good time, girls," Mahitabelle chirped cheerily despite the disgusted look Lanie tossed her on the way out.

Once in the car, Penelope tapped the button to start the engine, and then activated the radio. She began pressing buttons, pausing just long enough to identify melodies. Apparently finding none to her liking, she kept punching buttons with increasing force until she'd finally run out of options. At the end of her frantic hunt, she turned to Lanie.

"See if you can find a decent classical music station," she directed.

"I'm not sure what station that would be," Lanie shrugged. "I could find some popular or country ones. Stephen King's radio station is the most popular station around here."

"Who?" Penelope asked.

"Stephen King, the author. He lives in Bangor and does a lot for the state, especially this area."

"Never heard of him," Penelope declared as she abruptly shut off the radio and shifted into reverse. "I prefer Faulkner and Hemingway," she sniffed. "Right now, I'm rereading *Wuthering Heights*." Have you read it?"

"I have. It was painful."

Penelope gave her a look that Lanie interpreted to be full of sympathy for a person of questionable literacy, before she began slowly edging the vehicle toward the street. She made a show of straining her neck in a great effort to see around the hedge, which she hadn't reached yet by a yard.

"You'll have to get out and direct me into the street," she finally decided in a tone filled with righteous exasperation. She jammed a heavy foot onto the brake when she spoke and stopped the car with a jerk.

Lanie was glad her seat belt was already on, or she would have been catapulted into the dashboard. She turned an impaling eye toward Penelope. "I don't think so, *Penny*," she said with an emphasis on the nickname, "just ease out slowly. Once you get to the edge of the hedge, I'll be able to see if anything is coming and direct you from where I am. It's done all the time with only a few fatalities so far."

Lanie thought Penelope's face reddened a bit as she took turns tapping first the accelerator and then the brake and inching toward the road again in fits and starts.

Lanie's head began bobbing like a doll on the dash of a 1970s Nash Rambler. By the time they had arrived at a point on the driveway where she could see down Pleasant Street, she was getting carsick and starting to worry about developing a minor case of whiplash.

Eventually, they managed to get onto town roads. They cruised uneventfully for a while through areas where new schools had been built, as well as an impressive performing arts center. The structures sat on the very apex of one of the town's highest hills.

It was when they came down to Main Street that things got weird again. Penelope immediately encountered heavier traffic and lowered her speed. Lanie could see by the speedometer that they were moving fifteen miles per hour in what was a thirty-mile-an-hour zone. With apprehension, she glanced in her side-view mirror and, as expected, saw a solid line of cars forming behind them.

"You probably should accelerate a bit more," Lanie said, trying to make her suggestion in a diplomatic tone. "This is a busy highway with traffic to and from Bar Harbor every day."

"I'm doing the speed limit," Penelope huffed, gesturing toward a sign they were passing that read 15.

"That's the route number," Lanie said, immediately dismayed to feel a surge of giggles bubbling up in her throat and threatening to explode all over the car. "And that's Dunkin' Donuts," she added, pointing through her side window in an effort to divert from an impulse to just give it up and laugh out loud.

"I don't eat doughnuts," Penelope stated, "but that's the motel where I'm staying." She nodded toward a long line of neat-looking units next door to the Golden Arches.

"That's convenient for you. First thing in the morning, you can just walk over to Dunkin' Donuts."

"I don't eat doughnuts," Penelope said again.

"You drink coffee, don't you?"

"I heat up water for tea in the room," Penelope answered, and Lanie, having lost all incentive to laugh, decided to just shut up.

When the two women and twenty or so cars behind them had reached the heart of the town, Lanie leaned forward and tried again to communicate. They were drawing closer to the Jed Prouty Hotel and McKay's Restaurant, and Lanie anticipated the need to quickly identify those key spots if her tour-guiding career was to be successful. Before she could acknowledge the landmarks, however, the car came to a complete stop. They were sitting between the Jed and McKay's on Main Street, blocking access to Pleasant Street. Behind them, horns began blowing.

"Did the car die?" Lanie asked even as she heard the motor still running.

"Crosswalk," Penelope said pointing to the chalky etching on the pavement in front of them.

Lanie looked to her right and left and then at Penelope. "But no one is crossing," she said.

The car horns were getting louder now, honking in unison.

"I always stop at crosswalks regardless," Penelope declared, stepping once more on the accelerator and moving the car forward again at a crawl. There was, after all, another crosswalk already visible ahead, in front of the new art center and the Alamo Theatre. When they reached it and stopped, the beeping behind them began again.

By now, Lanie could see in her side-view mirror an even longer line of traffic had joined their parade. She moved her hands toward her ears to block the ever-increasing sound of horns, but halted when she heard a knock against her side window.

When she looked, she saw Harry Olson gazing in at her.

"Car trouble?" he asked when she had rolled down the window.

Lanie was about to try to explain the ridiculous truth when a Narrownook police cruiser, its lights flashing, pulled up and stopped against Penelope's front bumper.

Penelope had been ready to move again until she found herself nose-to-nose with a black-and-white. A tall uniformed officer sprang out of it and immediately began directing cars around their offending vehicle.

When traffic was flowing smoothly again, the policeman came over to speak to Penelope. His badge said Robinson, and his dark eyes said he was being inconvenienced.

Harry took the opportunity to lean in and chat with Lanie.

"I was on my way back to the office to call you," he said. "I want to invite you to join me at the Jed tonight. I just learned the Tony Boffa Band is here a day early for their weekend gig at the Jed Prouty. The hotel has a band every Friday and Saturday night, and this group is the best so we jumped at the chance to get them an extra night. We'll grab dinner first. How does that sound?"

Penelope, in conversation with Officer Robinson, somehow had been listening to what Harry was saying because she turned the moment Harry extended his invitation and declared that she had already made reservations for Lanie and her mother to join *her* for dinner at her motel restaurant that evening.

Lanie's instinct had been to decline Harry's invitation, but now she reconsidered. If Penelope's plan was her Thursday night alternative… "That sounds wonderful," she said to Olson, and then turned to Penelope. "Mom and I will try to treat *you* to dinner before you leave, but we should only do that at the Jed or McKay's or the new Grotto Winery. They have Narrownook's finest cuisines. I'll talk to my mother and let you know the arrangements."

Silently, Lanie hoped to be done with this woman. Bad enough she was loony, but the arrogance was what was really getting on her nerves.

Harry left then, promising to pick her up at seven o'clock, and Lanie watched Robinson hand Penelope a piece of paper that turned out to be just a warning.

"Next infraction, I'll have to ticket you for impeding traffic," he warned.

The women waited in silence until he had backed his cruiser up enough to do a U-turn up Oak Street.

"Take me home, Penelope," Lanie said. "Follow the cruiser up the hill and turn right at the stop sign. It will take you up to Pleasant.

"I was hoping we could check out the art center and gift shops today," Penelope sighed indignantly, "but I guess you've got to get ready for your big date." Her syrupy voice was tinged with unmistakable resentment. "Who is that handsome fellow, anyway?" she asked.

"His tag said his name was Robinson."

"Not the cop," Penelope hissed, "your date."

"The mayor," Lanie said, figuring this lady who only read Falkner and Hemingway would be impressed by the title. In truth, Lanie knew the position of mayor in this town was a powerless one. A mayor in Narrownook was a figurehead, his power only as strong as the respect the selectmen and town manager had for him. Still, she'd hoped to take a jab at her mother's pseudo cousin after the difficult two hours she'd just had to suffer through. Small of her, she knew, but immeasurably enjoyable.

CHAPTER 10

HARRY PICKED LANIE UP A LITTLE BEFORE SEVEN THAT NIGHT. HE CHARAC-teristically let himself into the house and said a cordial hello to Mrs. Warren when he found her in her recliner in the front room. He was neatly dressed in a white sports coat that complemented his baby-blue dress shirt and navy slacks.

The Tony Boffa Band was already wafting its easy-listening melodies throughout the inn when he and Lanie entered the Jed. At that moment, the soprano vocalist was leaning into the crotch of a baby grand and crooning "Deep Purple" with the haunting accompaniments of trumpets and strings behind her. Crystal seated them at the table closest to the bar's sprawling archway, where they could easily see as well as hear the orchestra.

"I love your dress," she told Lanie, admiring the simple white fitted sheath that slid becomingly over Lanie's slim form. "I wish I could wear those delicious high heels when I come in here," she complained while she took their drink orders, "but I'd fall on my arse if I wore them while I was hefting dinner trays." She laughed as she hurried to the next table.

Lanie and Harry spent the first few minutes quietly enjoying the music as they scanned the menu.

"A toast to a successful reunion," Olson said when the drinks had been served and he'd raised his martini glass toward Lanie's.

"And a salute to you," Lanie replied, clinking her glass against his. "You are brave to put the awful memory of our graduation behind you and help us concentrate on the good parts."

His smile disappeared immediately and his voice fell an octave. "It hasn't been easy," he said in an injured tone.

"I should think not," Lanie sympathized. "You and Meg were so close those four years—"

"Every day," he interrupted, "every day, I go over in my mind how she just ran off with another man after what we'd meant to each other!" Harry shook his head, which had drooped over the drink he was now clutching with both hands. "I thought she loved me like I loved her," he ended, and his voice broke.

Lanie was seized with pity for him. For a long minute, she didn't speak. Then she leaned over to touch his arm for emphasis and stated with as much certainty as she could gather, "I am sure that she did; she did love you. I have no doubt of that."

Harry's head lifted and his face held a stunned expression. "You sound so sure," he said. "How could you know that? You and Meg weren't close. Did she tell you something that last night on the mountain?"

"No. But she was still wearing your ring that night on the mountain. That, to me, was a strong indication of how she was still feeling about you, Harry."

"You remember that," he said. It was not a question. It was a statement, and Lanie heard astonishment in its tone.

She nodded as she studied his face and wondered if her words had helped him to begin to see that Meg could not have betrayed him with someone else. She hoped it would begin to lift the weight of anger and insult he'd obviously been carrying, but she couldn't tell if it had had an impact because his face was suddenly frozen into a blank mask that she found impossible to read. They fell into silence, sipping their cocktails as the music swirled out to them from the dance floor.

They ordered the Jed's famous prime rib dinners and ate with little conversation except to praise, now and then, the preparation and presentation of their meals. Crystal came by several times to inquire about their satisfaction with the food and to deliver a new martini to Harry, who had two more before his steak was consumed. Lanie chalked up his quiet mood to the need to fathom the implications of what she had told him, and she was happy to give him time to reflect.

"Let's dance," Harry suddenly suggested when their main course was finished and Crystal had cleared the plates. The band had swung into a foxtrot when he took Lanie's hand and led her through the arched doorway to the dance floor.

It was easy to follow Harry's lead. After all, they'd gone to school together, and even though they'd never danced with each other, the choreographic techniques they'd learned years before at the same high school sock hops were comfortably familiar.

The band switched into "Stardust," and Harry pulled Lanie closer and twirled her effortlessly across the room. The soloist had just begun vocalizing "The nightingale tells his fairy tale" when Harry leaned into her ear and whispered, "You always reminded me of Meghan. If I hadn't begun dating Meg, it would have been you and me together those four years, and maybe things would have worked out much better for everyone."

Before Lanie could think of a response, they had turned so that she was facing the archway and staring at a familiar figure just entering the room.

Penelope had changed out of the slacks and jersey of the afternoon, which had helped to disguise a thin form. Now Lanie saw a stick figure in a red sleeveless, wide-skirted dress and wondered if the woman could be anorexic. She also wondered what she was doing here. She appeared to be alone—but not for long, because she had spotted them and was moving their way.

For a minute, Lanie was struck by a panicked thought that something had happened to her mother. Perhaps Penelope had stopped in to visit Mahitabelle and, finding her ill, was here to report a crisis. Then Penelope's hand rose to tap Harry's shoulder and her syrupy voice asked if she was permitted to cut in. "I've never danced with a mayor before," she purred.

"Harry," Lanie said, "this is Penelope. I'm sorry; I didn't catch your last name," she murmured as an aside to the woman.

"Penelope's mother and my mother were friends, and she has just arrived in Narrownook for a visit," she went on to explain to a bewildered Harry.

"Oh, yes," Harry said to Penelope, "you were driving the car stopped by Narrownook police this afternoon. Well, any friend of Mahitabelle Warren's is a—"

"Penelope Mageloo?" Officer Robinson was suddenly a fourth in their little group.

Penelope turned from Harry, took in the cop still in uniform, and paled. "You again," she gasped. "What? Are you following me?" She tried a smile to mask the question in humor, but the attempt was stilted.

"You're driving a red 2019 Cadillac, New York license plate DB 7891?"

"Well, I'm driving a Cadillac," she hissed, as she did an eye roll in Harry's direction, "but sorry," she snarled, looking back at Robinson, "I don't memorize my license numbers."

"You're parked illegally in front of the trough. You need to move your car."

Robinson had been writing on a pad while engaged in conversation with Penelope, and now he tore off a slip and handed it to her.

"What's this?" Penelope asked without looking at the paper. "And did you say a *trough?*"

"The horse trough out there where your car is parked," he explained politely, jerking a thumb over his shoulder toward the front of the building. "The No Parking sign is posted clearly."

"Could I wait a bit to move the car? I was about to dance with your mayor, here." Penelope's former sugary and sibilant tone began to return as she flashed a smile in Harry's direction.

"You need to move it now, I'm afraid," Robinson said, still managing to maintain a polite demeanor. "I've given you a parking ticket. You can pay it at the station any time this month or wait for your formal hearing on it next month in Ellsworth."

"I won't be here next month; I'm only staying a week." Penelope's sibilance was an outright hiss at this point. "I had no idea how quaint this little town of Narrownook was," she scoffed. "It is certainly a stimulating experience to be in a village where automobiles must be ticketed for interfering with beasts of burden!"

"I suggest you square this at the station before you leave then, ma'am," he instructed.

Penelope swept the back of her left hand up to her forehead in a dramatic gesture and declared in barely a whisper that she was suddenly feeling unwell. Then her legs began to buckle.

The two men made a grab for her to prevent a fall, and she slumped heavily into Olson.

"I'll call for help," Robinson said, reaching for the radio at his hip.

"No!" Penelope howled in a surprisingly strong voice.

"Let's help her to her car, then," Harry suggested.

"I'm not sure I can possibly drive," she sighed against Harry's shoulder. "This has been so demeaning; such an unpleasant and unkind welcome from my mother's hometown. Mahitabelle Warren will certainly be displeased to hear of my treatment by her town's law enforcement."

Lanie started to follow the three figures, keeping her eye on Penelope, who seemed to struggle to maintain her mobility by clutching onto Harry's arm with such force that he was tilting as he walked. Robinson had a solid grip on her elbow and moved with what looked like sheer intent to get her from the building as fast as possible.

A fairly large group of people had congregated from the main rooms by this time. They were bunched into the archway to get a good look at what had been taking place on the dance floor. With no one still dancing, the orchestra had shifted into elevator instrumentals. Harry had had time to quickly instruct Lanie to order them dessert and coffee before they were separated. "Surprise me," he'd winked back to her as he moved away.

When the crowd had dispersed, Lanie noticed Stan Russell on the fringe of observers. "What's going on, Lanie?" he asked. "Who's the lady that Tyke and Harry are escorting out?"

"Tyke?"

"Tyke Robinson. He's a new cop in town."

"Long story," Lanie answered. "The short version is she was feeling ill—*unwell*, as she phrased it. They're assisting her to her car, which is illegally parked outside which explains the police presence."

Russell looked at his watch. "I was supposed to meet Robinson at eight. What's the long version? Is he going to be tied up now?"

"I don't think so. I personally doubt Penelope is really very unwell at all."

"That sounds like the tip of the long version," he said, and Lanie saw the familiar taciturn expression she remembered from their high school days—the contained amusement threatening to escape from his serious eyes, drawing his mouth into a smile that never quite got released.

"She is a textbook pain in the rump. I don't know where she came from—well, I do—New York, but how I got stuck with her and what she's doing here in the first place is the question. This is her second infraction that the officer has had to deal with in six hours."

"Are you here for dinner?" Russell asked.

"Harry and I ate earlier."

"I saw you two on the dance floor when I came in. How long has this been going on?" That muted expression again, but this time without any hint of amusement.

"He invited me to come to dinner and hear the Tony Boffa Band. Just a case of two classmates catching up," Lanie shrugged. As soon as she had said this, she recalled Harry's surprising comments into her ear a few minutes ago and was swept again with the unsettling feeling that his words had produced at the time.

"You should rethink your choice of classmate," Russell told her, pinning her with an intense look that Lanie thought held genuine concern.

"I know you and Harry are not on good terms. I remember Gloria made a vague reference to your strained relationship."

"Understatement," he murmured, and gave her that pinning look again. "Just be careful," he warned as they watched Tyke Robinson approaching.

The officer was no longer in uniform. He gave Russell a nod when he reached them. "My shift is over, and I'm ready for a drink," he said and turned to Lanie. "Ms. Mageloo said she needed someone to drive her car for her. She insisted it be 'the mayor.'" He raised his hands and made large quotation marks with his fingers. Lanie couldn't help but smile. "Olson wanted me to tell you, Ms. Warren, to hold off ordering dessert until he gets back, which could take a while. It's the change of shifts at the station or one of the patrolmen would have followed him and the woman to bring him back. Now who knows when one of the new guys will pick him up."

"I appreciate your agreeing to meet with me," Tyke said to Russell. "Let's have that drink," he gestured toward a small table in the lounge. "Ms. Warren," he added genially, "while you're waiting, come sit with us. I like getting to know the folks in my new community. I've learned that the sooner I have a sense of my new surroundings, the better job I do for those I serve."

Tyke raised his hand as a signal to Crystal, who hurried over to wait on them. After an hour, when Harry had not returned, Crystal put Harry's and Lanie's dinners on Harry's tab, and Russell drove Lanie home.

* * *

"He was fishing," Stan Russell said as he pulled through the back gate and pulled up to the three-car garage to let Lanie off.

"What do you mean?"

"Didn't you notice how often in the hour we spent together that Robinson kept steering the conversation around to Meghan Murphy's disappearance? I hope they're not reopening the case. It was bad enough the first time. I don't know if I could go through it all again."

"Robinson's just a cop," Lanie countered.

"He sounded more like a detective to me," Russell worried. "Did you notice his reaction when you mentioned that Meghan was still wearing Harry's ring the night before she disappeared? I was actually surprised to hear that, too, because I never noticed any ring that night. And Tyke asked me a couple of times how come *I* hadn't seen it. Many of his questions reminded me of the initial interrogations by law enforcement twenty-five years ago."

"It was pretty chilly that night on the mountain," Lanie recalled. "We all kept jackets on except for those looking to keep warm in other ways," she quipped. "It was only when Meg and I went to the ladies' room in the gas station on the way home that she took her coat off. I'd heard they had broken up, and I remember wondering why she was still wearing it, so I asked her about it. She said she knew she should give the ring back to him, but hadn't seen him to do it since they'd argued, and besides, she confessed to being reluctant to break up with him in the first place. Not the feelings of a girl who would run away with a lover in a matter of hours. I didn't pursue the topic with her at the time. I didn't want to appear nosy."

"Well, Tyke Robinson didn't hide his nosiness tonight," Russell said. "I've got an uncomfortable feeling about that hour we spent with him—about why he asked to have a drink with me in the first place! And why the interest in Meghan Murphy's disappearance?"

"I can think of several reasons he'd ask you and then me to have a drink with him, Russie. He's new in town, and wants to make some friends. As far as the topic of Meghan's disappearance, it's an interesting story. An unfinished story. It's natural for anyone who didn't live through it in '94 to be curious about the details, especially a cop."

"Or a detective," Russell added.

CHAPTER 11

LANIE'S PHONE RANG A FEW MINUTES TO MIDNIGHT. IT WAS HARRY—A furious Harry.

"I didn't get a damn ride until eleven," he told her. "I had to finally get in touch with one of my buddies to come get me. The police detail never showed up, and that woman is a fruit basket. I spent a few minutes with her to be sure she was okay, then couldn't stand it another minute and walked over to DD's to wait for an officer. I owe you coffee and dessert."

"Don't worry about it," Lanie told him, "the dinner was lovely."

"I'll make this up to you," he insisted. "I understand that Russell and the new cop got you home," he added, and Lanie heard an edge in his tone.

"Yes," Lanie answered vaguely.

"That's good," he said. "I didn't like leaving you, and Russell would be the last person I'd want to leave you with. You should keep your distance from him."

There it was again. The friction between Harry and Russie. As Lanie disconnected the call from Harry, Russell's earlier words, *rethink your choice of classmate*, popped into her head. They must both still hold resentments regarding Meghan, she figured, and twenty-five years hadn't been long enough to smooth out hostilities between the two men. Well, the fact that Russie and Harry didn't get along shouldn't mean that she couldn't be friends with them.

The phone call had awakened her from a sound sleep, and now she was wide awake. She got back into bed, but soon realized her racing mind was not going to allow her to drift back for a while, so she eventually went to the kitchen and put a kettle of water on for tea. As she settled over a steaming cup, she let her mind continue to wander.

She kept rehashing the hour with Tyke Robinson and Russie, trying to see the conversation from Russie's suspicious point of view. She reminded herself that she had not been subjected to the depth of inquiry that Russie had been subjected to in 1994. Robinson could be viewed as intimidating, she supposed, and she had noticed a tightening and squaring of his jaw at certain points in their conversation, especially when the ring was discussed. Had that indicated more than casual curiosity on Robinson's part? Did it show a more intense, maybe a professional responsibility toward the case?

Her tea, what was left of it, had grown cold by the time she looked at a clock again. It was almost one a.m., and time to try to get some sleep.

She had no sooner gotten settled into bed than she was suddenly sitting bolt upright. A door had slammed somewhere in the main house. It had been a somewhat muffled bang, but she had heard it distinctly. Who would be up at this time of morning? It reminded her that she hadn't had a chance to ask Amy about the unlocked door the day before yesterday.

The sound she'd just heard hadn't been a heavy door like the Pleasant Street front door. It had been a lighter sound. A closet door?

She would have to ask Amy about two things this morning—that is, if she could just get to sleep now so she'd be up before Amy had to be off to work.

* * *

It had happened again. He'd lost his grip on the damn flimsy trapdoor.

One of these days, Amy would hear and come downstairs to investigate while her sense of direction was still fresh in her mind.

He couldn't keep being clumsy and risk her snooping around the entrance he'd carved out for himself. He had to be more careful.

Silently now, he made his way across the deserted street with no harm done this time and vowed there'd be no next time. He gained speed as he darted over neighboring lawns toward Oak Street.

CHAPTER 12

W‍HEN L‍ANIE WAS SUDDENLY LIFTED OUT OF WHAT HAD FINALLY BEEN A deep slumber, the sun was just casting a warm glow through her east window, and the clock, whose alarm had not sounded yet, read a few minutes before six thirty.

So, what had suddenly roused her?

Hammering answered her question. Hammering that was very close. In fact, the pounding was here, just below her. What would Amy be doing this early on a weekday?

Lanie tore off the covers, stumbled to her robe, and shoved her arms through its sleeves. With the gown still gaping, she went to one of the tall back windows that looked onto the Church Street driveway.

She was focused in the right direction but unable to see any activity below her because it was too *directly* below her.

Savagely, she cinched the ties of her robe as she raced through the apartment. She snapped the bolt lock to open her entrance door and stepped out onto the hall landing above the triple garage.

In her flimsy slippers, she managed to make it down the back stairs two at a time without breaking her neck. At the foot of the stairs, she slammed her finger against the top button on the lighted panel and heard the left garage door begin grinding open. She had crossed the expanse to the driveway before the door had clanged to a stop above her.

It wasn't until she'd stepped out onto the driveway that she saw him, though. He'd been stooped down and tucked into a space under the screened-in porch, his hand raised with the offending hammer when her movement must have distracted him. The hammer came down with force onto his thumb.

The weapon went flying, and Ricky Irving began hopping from one foot to the other as he clutched his left hand and spewed curses into the wind.

Lanie just stood regarding the idiot's flight pattern as he tried to leap out of the way of his pain.

"You startled me," he finally hissed at her when he could speak in sentences again. He still wasn't idle. He'd given up hopping but now was hunched over his injured hand and walking in circles.

She remained mute and staring until Irving finally stopped moving and took his eye off his damaged thumb to look up at her. Then she asked simply, "What are you doing?"

"I just slammed my finger with a hammer."

"I saw that. What are you *doing?*" Lanie gestured angrily at the porch.

"Tryin' to fix an error I spotted last time I was here."

"It wasn't your error. You didn't build this porch. And you don't work here anymore."

"I didn't want to leave something uncorrected."

"Goodbye, Ricky, and don't come back."

Irving shrugged once and turned to head down the driveway toward the street. After only a few steps, he stopped and looked back at Lanie, who was standing with crossed arms, watching his departure.

"To show you what a good guy I am," he crowed, "I don't intend to sue you for injury on the job." And he waved his swollen thumb up in the air before turning again toward his rust-splotched and faded black van, which, interestingly, was parked out on Church Street instead of in their front driveway as had been his habit.

Lanie had to muster a lot of self-control not to show him another finger of hers in response to his arrogance.

When she was sure he had left, she turned to inspect the area of the porch where he had been hammering. One of the front columns had been chipped enough to scatter some nails and a brace on the ground below. There were also pieces of wood hanging in splintered shards off of another support column.

What had Irving been trying to do? It looked like he'd been bent on weakening a well-constructed part of her father's remodeling efforts.

Suddenly, she remembered what had happened *ten* years ago, when Ricky Irving had first been hired by her parents to oversee their property while they vacationed in Florida. Early one morning in mid-January, about a week after they'd left, they received an urgent phone call from him. There had been a major break in a hot water pipe in the furnace room, and all of the basement, which included an efficiency apartment, had been badly flooded. If they agreed, he would oversee the renovation, but it would mean he'd have to live there while the work was being done.

She'd always wondered how responsible Ricky himself had been for the pipe breakage. It seemed as though he had not kept a close eye on the temperature in the basement, which would have been part of his job. Now, she wondered if possibly he had sabotaged the whole thing. It had, after all, given him employment for three months and a place to live rent-free as he worked on the restoration.

Lanie panicked. On a run, she raced up the back stairs and grabbed the phone book from the kitchen cupboard. It was seven thirty, but there was an answer on the second ring.

"Russell Construction."

She recognized his voice. Russie was already on the job, probably answering the phone until his secretary reported for work.

Briefly, she told him what had awakened her and what she had been able to glean from the debris that Ricky had left behind.

"I don't understand why you keep him on," Russell scolded.

"He hasn't been employed here for some time," Lanie sighed. "He just keeps coming back like a bad penny. I hate bothering you with this, Russie, but I need someone I trust to tell me what to do about the damage he just caused."

There was a span of noticeable silence then, and Lanie wondered if he was still on the line. When he finally spoke, his tone had softened. "I'll be there as soon as my secretary arrives," he said and abruptly disconnected.

As she hung up the phone, two quick knocks erupted on the apartment door, and Amy stuck her head in. "You better go talk to Grandmother," she announced cryptically. "She's worried."

"Amy, hold up a second," Lanie responded when her daughter would have closed the door and retreated. "Why did I hear doors slamming around one a.m. this morning? And why were the front doors left unlocked at night during the middle of the week? This is the first time I've been able to catch up with you. Every time I came to see you this weekend, you weren't here."

"We'll talk later, Ma. Right now I'm very late," her daughter huffed, and this time she was successful in getting the door closed before any more questions could be launched.

Lanie reached the landing in time to see Amy's fleeing figure achieve the bottom step. "What were you doing at one a.m. Saturday morning?" she managed to toss down at her.

"Sleeping," came the flippant answer along with the groan of the garage door opening and the sound of Amy's car door closing.

She had to be in Bangor at eight. It was a half-hour drive in the best conditions, and it was now seven thirty-five by the kitchen clock.

"Talk about cutting it close!" Lanie said out loud as she retreated back into her apartment and wrestled with her silent voice that started screaming, *What now?*

She knew the voice was nagging her about Amy's news that Mahitabelle was worried. Where would that problem fit in with the house falling down and unlocked doors being overlooked? Somehow, despite the distractions, she managed to shower and dress and be down in the backyard when Russell drove through the gate twenty minutes later.

He took one look at the porch post and shook his head. "The guy can't even do a credible job destroying things," he said. "I'll send a couple of my men over this morning to do what reconstruction may be necessary, but it's not a big deal; mostly cosmetic at this point."

"Thanks, Russie," Lanie nodded, "that's a relief, and I appreciate your bothering to come over. I know how busy you must be. Can I infringe on a bit more of your time while you're here?"

When Russell nodded, she led him over to the retaining wall on the other side of the property. "Ricky said he was worried that this wall was leaning more and more into the foundation of the original structure and in time would compromise the integrity of the entire home."

Russell turned his normally serious face to stare at Lanie for a second, and then he did an incredible thing. He laughed. He actually lifted his head back and let loose with a deep-throated, genuine, bellyache laugh. It sounded melodious. It was totally infectious, and Lanie found herself laughing with him, though she wasn't sure just what was so amusing.

Russell finally took a deep breath and wiped at his eyes. "You know," he said, "I could have sworn that Irving had the mental capacity of a worm, because that fits his character description, but that story shows a lot of ingenuity on his part. There's a lot of impressive rationale that went into his analysis. But it's bogus!" he ended, chuckling again. "Your home is safe," he assured her as he turned to start down the driveway to his truck.

"Russie," Lanie said, stopping his departure and causing him to turn around. "I want to pay you for your time today, so be sure you add it to the bill when your workmen finish their repair."

"No charge for the consultation," he told her.

"I do so appreciate you coming on short notice like you did," Lanie persisted. "That's worth a whole lot to me, Russie."

"Then do me a favor." Russell took a couple of steps back toward her with what Lanie thought was a chagrined expression.

"Sure," she said.

"Stop with the 'Russie.' I grew out of that moniker a long time ago."

"Okay," Lanie said. "You prefer Stan?"

Now his expression turned back to serious. "My friends call me Russ," he said gently.

CHAPTER 13

Tyke Robinson had arrived early for his shift Friday morning—a good hour and a half early. He was bent on taking a look at the missing person's report on Meghan Murphy. He'd need to ask permission from Captain Brody, of course, to dredge that up after so many years, even though cold cases were all the rage these days. That part shouldn't be a problem, though, because he'd hit it off with Brody almost the minute he'd arrived from Massachusetts. Narrownook needed more cops badly now that the town was growing by leaps and industries, and Ted Brody had been impressed with Tyke's sterling recommendations from Boston.

"I like your interest," the captain nodded when Robinson told him what was on his mind. "We haven't had any people missing from here since Meghan Murphy. Before 1994, the only one unaccounted for in Narrownook was Sarah Ware in September of 1898. She disappeared for two weeks before her body was discovered in Parson's Field. No one ever solved that, either. Talk about a cold case! Hell's freezing over on that one. It won't hurt for a new set of eyes to see the old evidence on this Murphy case," he decided aloud as he picked up the phone and dialed in to Ellsworth.

Whoever he talked to in the records department put a fax through in half an hour. Before Tyke had reported officially for his regular day's work, he was pouring over a stack of papers that contained all the testimonies taken during that 1994 summer.

He'd been looking for one specific factor: the ring. Had that piece of information been missing originally, or just overlooked? Maybe Lanie Warren had neglected to mention it.

But it was there. In several of the many Warren statements, she had talked about it. Someone had been either too dense to acknowledge its importance or had deliberately refused to act on what seemed like a valuable and obvious lead to him.

That girl had not run off with an unknown lover while wearing her high school sweetheart's ring, yet that was one of the popular theories that had been allowed to flourish in the past twenty-five years. He'd dismissed that unknown lover scenario the moment he'd heard about the ring. Now, the only other possibilities were down to two—a stranger had accosted her, or someone she knew was involved.

He read over her sister's statements about hearing Meg talking just outside her home on that morning after graduation. Identify who Meghan was talking to that morning and you had the lead you needed. Why hadn't they done more probing? Had they been reluctant to act on the testimony of a seven-year-old?

If Stan Russell wasn't lying about dropping the girl off at her home and leaving after watching her safely onto her porch, then the police should have been looking for someone else whom she knew.

He'd dismiss the possibility of a stranger abduction if Russell had left her safely at home. If a stranger had grabbed her, Meg's sister would have heard a scuffle, reported screams instead of quiet voices. If Meghan Murphy was calmly conversing with someone the morning she disappeared, he was back to two possibilities, and he knew the names of the top two prime suspects!

* * *

Bubbah Johnson was in Harry's office before the mayor got there Friday morning. Olson deposited his briefcase just inside the door and flicked on the overhead lights to find the town's financial advisor sprawled in a chair in front of his desk. Harry fought the urge to physically pick up the scrawny bastard and throw him out. Instead, he subjected himself to listening to Johnson's same old tune.

"You've got to stop promoting your cockamamie walking-bridge idea," Bubbah declared, leaping like a gazelle from his sitting position and beginning to pace about the room. "We already have a one-mile brick walk along the Penobscot. Give it up, Olson. Let's tear the thing down and move on into the twenty-first century."

Harry had heard Bubbah's rant before. All the mayor wanted right now, first thing on a Friday morning, was some peace and quiet in which to help plan the agenda for next week. He'd already secured his votes and knew his guys were willing to squelch any serious movement toward tearing down the Waldo–Hancock. He wasn't worried.

"I'm afraid, my friend, that this time you're in the minority," Johnson railed as he moved to the door and jerked it open. "Narrownook won't agree to take on the cost of maintaining two bridges once they know the expense that's involved," he said, turning back toward Harry. "Your idea is lofty and enticing until the numbers are exposed. That's why I'm here—to warn you that the hard financial facts will be addressed and voted on next week in committee. No selectman in his right mind will endorse spending a million dollars a year to maintain that bridge. Don't try to say you weren't duly notified," he ended, giving Harry a curt wave before he stalked out of the office without bothering to close the door behind him.

Olson watched him go and decided he didn't have time to indulge in any of that peace and quiet he'd been wishing for, after all. Next week's agenda had just been decided for him. He hit the button on his desk that summoned Gloria. Time to reinforce the orders just to be on the safe side.

* * *

Lanie hurried over to the main house to address her mother's concerns as soon as Russell left. She found Mahitabelle already up, dressed, and in her recliner sipping on a cup of coffee. An empty bowl with the last dregs of cereal grumblies floated in a small puddle of milk on a TV table beside her chair. "What's up?"

Lanie said, surprised to see that Mahitabelle had already applied a hint of eye shadow and rouge, the usual makeup she wore to venture downtown.

"I've got a hair appointment this morning, dear," her mother said. "I was hoping you could drive me down to Callie's Coiffures."

"Of course I can. Were you worried I wouldn't? Amy said you were worried."

"About Penelope," Mahitabelle pouted. "She promised me she would come have breakfast with me this morning and tell me all about the tour you took her on. She didn't come, and she hasn't even called."

"I'll stop by the Buckston Motel and see if I can track her down after I drop you off," Lanie told her. "Remember, she's a big girl and can take care of herself. Please," she emphasized with a bit of fury in her voice, "believe me when I say, she can take care of herself!"

"I hope so, dear," Mahitabelle sighed, pushing her tiny body up from her oversized chair.

"What time do you have to be at Callie's?" Lanie asked as Mahitabelle left the room.

"In fifteen minutes. I just have to brush my teeth and put my lipstick on and I'm ready."

Lanie went back to her side of the house to grab her pocketbook and keys, then returned to check that all the doors were locked in the main house before escorting her mother downtown.

Callie's Coiffures was a tiny beauty shop in the center of town, owned and operated by an attractive local lady who greeted Mahitabelle at the door and carefully helped her into a chair at styling station number one with a mirrored back bar and service counter. Learning that her mother was having the full treatment today—shampoo, perm, and style—Lanie bid them goodbye with a promise to return in three hours.

Her first stop was at the motel by Dunkin' Donuts, where she was told that Ms. Mageloo had checked out early that morning citing an emergency back in New York. Lanie couldn't help but be relieved that the woman was gone, but she felt guilty about her attitude because of her mother's affection for the woman. But her guilt lasted only a fraction of a second.

With more than two hours to herself, she decided to go back to the house and make some phone calls in order to set up some of Mahitabelle's medical appointments. It gave her something constructive to do while she waited for Russ's men to arrive for the porch repairs.

She ducked into the main house to pick up the family's personal phone directory, which she'd need in order to find numbers for all of her mother's doctors. Upon reaching the living room, however, she stopped in her tracks. The front door was ajar! How could that be? She'd bolted that door not a half hour ago!

Crossing to it, she pulled it wider and stepped out onto the porch to inspect the combination storm and screen door that she had also made sure was secure before they left. It, too, was slightly ajar. There was no way this door could have been unlocked from the outside. The lock was a manual switch that could only be turned and released from the inside. No one had *entered* through this front door. It had been an *exit*, which meant that whoever had been here had gained access to the house some other way. But how?

A new worry popped into Lanie's head. The intruder could have heard her come in just now and could have fled in a hurry—or??? She felt the hairs on her neck prickle at the thought of someone still being inside.

Grabbing the phone from the table beside Mahitabelle's recliner, she returned to the front porch, where she felt safer, and dialed 911. A woman's voice answered on the first ring to ask her name and the nature of her emergency.

Lanie quickly explained about her brief absence and how she had returned to find doors that she had just locked either ajar or unlocked.

A police car was dispatched immediately, and Lanie greeted Tyke Robinson less than two minutes later. The swift response was the benefit of living a block away from the station.

"Lanie Warren, right?" Tyke said.

There was a fierceness about him as he moved through the front room, his eyes darting everywhere as he moved to the kitchen. Once there, he jerked open the refrigerator, then the oven door.

Lanie said, "Surely you don't think anyone would—"

"You'd be surprised where we find 'em," he answered soberly, striding purposefully across the dining room toward Mahitabelle's suite on the opposite end of the main level.

With great ease, he did a quick spring down on his hands and knees to gaze briefly under the bed, then with equal buoyancy bounced back up and headed across the room.

Sweeping the hanging clothes from one side and then the other in the bedroom closets, he went on to the adjoining bathroom to pull the shower curtain aside.

Lanie watched him work methodically until he was ready to go into other areas. Then he instructed her to remain where she was.

Tyke was gone for about fifteen minutes. There were, after all, two basements, an attic, and her own two-story apartment to examine. When he was done, Tyke said he had some questions, so Lanie and he pulled out two chairs at the kitchen table in Lanie's quarters where Robinson had ended his search. Lanie poured soda into two glasses full of ice, and Tyke began jotting down notes on a small tablet he'd pulled from his shirt pocket. Temperatures had already reached eighty degrees by this time, and Lanie wished they could have been out on the screened-in porch where it would be cooler, but she was reluctant to go out there until it was repaired.

Tyke first asked her how sure she was that she had locked the house up before she and her mother left. That was followed by asking if they had left in a hurry.

His dark eyes bored into her as he carefully scrutinized her answers, which she delivered with unabashed certainty, saying that she knew with 100% certainty that she had secured both front doors, and, no, they had not been rushed. They'd had a fifteen-minute window to get just two blocks down the hill into town.

Sensing that Robinson was thinking she was a dingbat like Penelope Mageloo, whom he had found her with the first time they'd met, she'd matched his penetrating gaze with her own unwavering glare as she recalled aloud her habit, since she'd arrived, of often checking to be sure doors were locked. Her mother was elderly and her daughter young, busy, and lately, distracted, she explained, and now that she was home, she had taken it upon herself to help in their efforts to keep the big house secure.

She purposely left out the recent recurring history of the unlocked front entrance for fear it would further encourage Robinson's dingbat theory. "How often did you think the door was locked and it wasn't?" she could hear him ask if she ventured there. So she let it go. Besides, during Lanie's explanation, a Russell Construction vehicle beeped its arrival as it backed into the Church Street driveways.

From where they sat at the table near a tall window, the truck's lettering was clear. Tyke immediately launched into a new subject.

"Is Stan Russell doing some work here?" he asked, putting his pencil down suddenly and focusing all of his attention on the backyard.

"A small repair to the screened-in porch," Lanie told him.

"I think you mentioned that you and he graduated together."

It had not been a question, but Lanie responded just the same, "Yes," she said. "He was a great guy. Still is."

"Did you two ever date?"

"He had a girl in the southern part of the state," Lanie answered, feeling herself bristle a bit at such a personal question.

"But that graduation night in 1994, Meg Murphy was his date," Robinson countered.

Now alarm bells joined the bristling. "Not exactly," Lanie shrugged. "I think it was more like seeing someone in need of company on an important day and being a supportive friend. That was Russie."

On a whim, Lanie asked, "Are they opening up the investigation again? Is that why all the questions about Meg and that graduation night?"

"Not exactly." Robinson's cryptic response mimicked Lanie's words of a moment before. Then, standing up abruptly, Tyke turned to leave.

Russie's right! Lanie thought to herself as she walked him to the door and mumbled a thank-you for his time.

She stood at the window and watched Tyke Robinson stop to talk to the two workers who were unloading tools from the truck. Russ was not with them. "Probably a good thing," she decided out loud. She'd be tempted to go out and alert him that his suspicions had been correct. But that would open up a whole new onslaught of worry for him. The longer he could be spared that, the better.

* * *

He was batting a thousand in terms of his B & E, except it was never a B, just an E at the Warrens'. No breaking in there. He had his own doggie door. No need to break anything.

He'd waited until they left. Mahitabelle always had a hair appointment on Fridays. He'd waited to come in until he saw them leave, but Lanie hadn't stayed with her mother. She had come home and surprised him as he searched through the refrigerator for any leftovers that Amy had put on ice. He loved the chicken fingers and Chinese cuisine she often brought home after work.

He'd just begun to explore the meat keeper when he heard one of the garage doors go up and, peering out, saw Lanie's Corolla sprinting up the driveway. He beat it out the front door before Lanie would have a chance to get out of the car. He made it across the lots and over to Oak Street without detection, but without food to enjoy for his lunch, which totally sucked.

CHAPTER 14

On Monday evening, the Narrownook officials held a meeting in the conference room of the town office building. They set a date for the christening of the new bridge for the coming Saturday. It would be an impressive all-day ceremony with activities already in place for the occasion. The council also addressed the future of the Waldo–Hancock Bridge.

Like all council meetings, the proceedings were transmitted into Narrownook on closed-circuit television. Viewers heard the discussions and watched the town officials seated at a long table arguing pros and cons and taking questions from a small gathering of spectators.

"We already have a one-mile brick walk along the Penobscot," Bubbah Johnson said as he kicked off the debate. "There are those who feel, and rightly so, that the bridge should be preserved as a historic landmark. But that's before they know what preserving the Waldo–Hancock Bridge will cost this town. It's estimated that we'll spend a million dollars a year in upkeep, not counting the cost of insurance on the aging expanse. We've just lost our mill, our golden goose that filled our coffers with much-needed tax revenues. Let's not get foolish and blow what we've so carefully preserved. There may come a time in our struggle forward when we'll need the funds for necessities, and we'd rue the day we used them up purely out of nostalgia."

Bubbah yielded the microphone to a confident Harry Olson.

"The town has deep feelings about their old bridge," Harry challenged. "The people want it saved—cherished, in fact." His voice broke on the word cherished. "They are already anguished about the mill sitting there with its guts hanging out. Where's your heart, Mr. Johnson? Folks don't want another treasured landmark demolished in front of them. They deserve a respite from the destruction." He roared that last statement and combined it with a theatrical wave of his fist in the air before relinquishing the mic.

A hush fell over the crowd in attendance. Then Sarah Hamilton, Narrownook's town manager, seated at the center of the table, leaned into her microphone. "We have a brand-new bridge to maintain," she said, choosing her words slowly. "We've been thrifty and wise so far. Our ten million reserve fund is a testament to that fact. It is a credit to us that we have been able to amass a substantial nest egg that would see us through the lean times that we knew would come one day. Let's continue being prudent. Sentiment won't keep this town afloat. Good common sense will," she ended.

The vote to demolish the Waldo–Hancock Bridge was decided minutes later by a 5 to 2 margin.

Harry exploded. He wasted no time in confronting Skip Dyer and Charlie Briggs, former classmates and close friends on the council who he'd successfully gotten elected ten times in a row. Once the meeting was over, he tore after them before they could exit the foyer. "What happened?" he snarled. He was red-faced and almost panting with rage. "You said you could sew up two more votes and save the damn thing!"

"We did the best we could!" Skip was almost whining. "It just couldn't be helped," he shrugged. "No one could justify a town the size of Narrownook, which recently lost its major tax income, spending a million a year for a bridge folks can only walk on."

"And that's only six months out of the year!" Charlie piped up. "We put our council seats in jeopardy just now by voting your way to spend a million a year to keep it for a walking bridge. No one else could be pressured to go for such an extravagant idea."

"You're both pieces of shit, and you can kiss your seats goodbye!" Olson screamed.

"What does that mean?" Charlie almost whimpered.

Harry reached out and grabbed them both by their suit lapels and hauled them up and under his chin. "Your asses won't be in 'em! That's what that means!" he yelled into their stunned faces before viciously shoving them away. He rushed out of the building, slamming the door behind him with such force that the impact thundered through the entire structure.

It was immediately jerked open by Captain Brody, who rushed after him. "Harry, wait," he ordered. "I saw your little tête-à-tête just now. You need to calm down, my friend." Brody gave Harry a gentle slap on the arm and continued studying him with genuine concern.

"Just a mild disagreement," Harry mumbled. "Nothing for you to worry about."

"I can imagine you're upset about the vote," Brody acknowledged. "We all feel sentimental about the bridge. Let me give you some news that will take your mind off it. You'll be happy to know that my office has decided to reopen the Meghan Murphy disappearance based on some new information that has come to my attention."

"Really?" Harry gasped, hoping his reaction didn't reflect the panic that was suddenly tearing through him. "What, ah, what would the new information be, I wonder."

"Actually, it's really old information that was passed over for some reason back in the day when Herman Willett was the captain—a useless human being, Willett," Brody mumbled mostly to himself.

"It has been brought to my attention that there's the matter of your class ring, Harry. Testimony indicates that Meghan was still wearing it when she disappeared, and no one evidently connected the dots or took time to analyze that a girl still wearing her boyfriend's ring would not voluntarily run off with another man. That seems like a logical conclusion to me and one that should have led police, twenty-five years ago, to further investigate the theory of an unknown stalker or even someone she knew. You can thank our new police officer, Tyke Robinson, for stirring up that pot. Great guy—good potential. I'm giving him full authority to run with this, so when you see him, I know you'll want to thank him for caring enough to bring it forward again. This dark and ugly memory is still haunting this town, and the not knowing is still especially difficult for you, I'm sure. Maybe the fact that we are finally once more on the hunt for the culprit will help to lift your spirits."

Harry Olson could only nod as he wondered if this day could get any worse.

Moments later, he tore into his driveway on Center Street, leaped from his car, and shoved the key into his front door lock. He should have gotten rid of the damn ring years ago! He should have at least ditched it that night last week when Lanie let him know that she remembered Meghan still wearing it on their graduation night. Now, after his talk with the police chief, and after the damn vote to tear down the bridge, he'd have to bury the thing. It was probably stupid to have kept it, but it symbolized his young, successful years, and he found it distasteful to throw it away. So he'd bury it for now.

The meeting had dragged on into the evening, so that was a good thing. He had the advantage of darkness to dig a small hole out back in the garden. Later he could take it out of state and hawk it, if he wanted to, after things calmed down again.

He took the stairs two at a time up to his bedroom, reached into the third drawer of his bureau, and retrieved his jewelry case. He had gathered only a few pieces in his forty-three years. A diamond-studded tie clip that had belonged to his father, actually, was the most valuable in his collection. He'd sold his parent's rings after their deaths. He never took off his black onyx ring or his expensive watch, so there wasn't much to rummage through in order to locate what he was looking for.

But it wasn't there!

With the exception of a pair of cheap cufflinks and a worthless tie clip that his aunt had given him for Christmas when he was twelve, nothing else was in the box. The ring and the diamond tie clip were gone!

Harry had never felt real fear before, but a paralyzing dread akin to terror swept him up suddenly. It enveloped him and sent a wave of weakness shuddering through him that made him nauseous.

Again, he rifled through the box, searching with anxious fingers into the corner of the container and along the bottom for a slit, some accidental fault in the construction of the box that could have entrapped the contents.

Of course, he could find none.

Harry stumbled backward against the bed and sat, putting his head in his hands. He remained there for a long time. He was picturing the ring. Just the usual class ring...except it wasn't like the others. He'd gone and had it engraved. At the time, it had meant a lot to Meghan, of course, and that was the point. *At the time.* Now if the ring were in the wrong hands, it could be his swan song. Anyone who found the ring and saw its inscription after hearing about this newly rediscovered evidence, would piece it together in a heartbeat. Either Meghan was still alive, they'd say, or she had met with foul play, and he'd be a prime suspect— especially if that ring should turn up.

What to do? First, get a grip on himself!

CHAPTER 15

THE BLACK BMW CONVERTIBLE CRUISED VERY SLOWLY JUST BEYOND the back gate and stopped. The top was up even though it was a warm June evening, so Lanie and Amy, hanging out on the porch with Mahitabelle after supper, couldn't make out the occupants in the vehicle.

They had been able to use the roomy screened-in porch as soon as Russ's workmen had repaired the damaged post. They wasted no time in setting up, once again, the comfortable chairs and large table that could easily accommodate twelve people at a time.

"Friend of yours?" Lanie teased her daughter when they heard the motor and looked up from a game of Scrabble that Mahitabelle was winning hands down.

Amy looked again and shook her head. "I wish," she said, "but I don't know anyone with a Beamer. Then a stunned expression appeared fleetingly on her face.

"What?" Lanie asked.

"What?" Amy echoed.

"What was that strange look that just crossed your face?"

Amy looked back at the car, which was still idling by the back fence. "I think it's the same car that was out there yesterday when I was mulching around the flower beds," she mused aloud.

"Let's see—Clancy, Mitch, even Bobby Turner could be a possibility," said Lanie. "It's not a bicycle, so we can eliminate Emerson Hickok."

"That reminds me," Amy said after she'd thrown her mother a disgusted look for the bicycle comment, "I want to have a yard sale next week. I'll set it up. You won't have to worry about it."

"I'll be glad to help," Lanie told her.

"I'm a champion yard-seller," Amy bragged.

They watched the black car finally move away and disappear down the street.

"When is your sale, dear?" Mahitabelle asked Amy as she made an eight-letter word on Lanie's four-letter one. "It better not interfere with the new bridge dedication," she cautioned. "That will be a whole day plus evening affair."

"I'm thinking about next Sunday."

"Sounds lovely, dear," her grandmother said, a bit distracted as she calculated her score before sitting back with a self-satisfied sigh. "I've been invited to the evening celebration for the new bridge's opening, you know," Mahitabelle boasted. "The mayor knew how disappointed I was with the Waldo–Hancock vote. He said he knew just how I felt and asked if I would do the honor of sitting with him at his reserved table at the Jed Prouty Saturday night—with Lanie, of course. What a charming man, and so funny. He said misery loves company, so he was gathering all the disappointed citizenry around him for a high-class pity party."

Amy looked suspiciously over at her mother. "Another date with the mayor?" she challenged.

"The mayor is your grandmother's date," Lanie told her. "I'll just chaperone."

Amy nodded with a sarcastic expression and a comment that her mother didn't quite hear. Lanie wasn't happy about this turn of events at all. Harry had gone completely around her by inviting Mahitabelle first, knowing full well that the elderly lady would love a night out at the Jed on the arm of the mayor. What could Lanie do? She couldn't send her mother off alone. She'd have to be there, which she knew had been the idea. She couldn't think of anything she hated more than manipulation, and Olson had just crossed that line big-time by using her mother as a ploy.

She'd have to nip that kind of nerve in the bud, and that meant she'd have to have a confrontation with Harry soon, something she did not look forward to. Somehow, she sensed he was used to getting his own way, and she worried about how to approach the conversation without alienating a friend and fellow classmate. There was enough dissension in this town as it was. She really didn't want to create any more tension.

CHAPTER 16

THE BANGOR DAILY NEWS GOT WIND OF THE FACT THAT NARROWNOOK had begun again to explore the disappearance of Meghan Murphy. On Monday morning, large headlines on the front page reported that authorities were focusing on a vital piece of evidence that had been overlooked in the original investigation. A story surrounding the fact that seventeen-year-old Meghan had been seen wearing Harry Olson's class ring on the eve of her disappearance speculated about whether that oversight had been accidental or intentional. "How had the original investigation missed such an important clue?" the article asked.

They named Lanie Warren as the credible witness who had reported seeing the keepsake on a chain around the missing girl's neck the night she accompanied many of the high school graduating class of '94 to Bar Harbor's Cadillac Mountain.

In subsequent paragraphs, speculation continued about the meaning of this long-overlooked detail. The article mentioned Stan Russell, prominent businessman and builder, and Mayor Harry Olson as important persons in Meghan's life. The paper was careful not to accuse either of foul play but left no doubt in the reader's mind that one of them might know more than they had ever proffered up to now.

* * *

Ricky Irving poured a cup of coffee when he arrived home on Monday morning after briefly visiting a couple of homes he had been hired to look after. He knew he should have mowed both of their lawns and started trimming some of the shrubs around the properties, but it was a hot day, and he told himself that once four o'clock came around, he'd do a better job of landscaping in the cooler late afternoon. So he'd grabbed a newspaper he saw sticking out of a mailbox on Center Street and sprinted home.

He got himself settled at the kitchen table with the intention of making a leisurely hour for himself, just like a true professional— sipping on his coffee as he caught up on the latest current events.

Except today's current event struck him cold:

MISSING GIRL WAS WEARING
OLSON'S CLASS RING
ONLY HOURS BEFORE
SHE DISAPPEARED

The headline seemed to scream at him, and he momentarily froze in shock. Then Ricky shoved the paper with such force that it ended up scaling across the slippery steel table and onto the floor. He was halfway through the kitchen on his way to his little room under the hallway stairs when Sue stopped his exodus.

"You don't board here without rent so you can litter the place," she yelled as she swept an accusatory finger at the newsprint scattered across the linoleum.

"I'll be right back," he muttered, and Sue heard an uncharacteristic quivering in his voice. That was when she saw the front-page headline and understood.

When Ricky returned, he was clutching the ring in his fist. With a shaky hand, he released it onto the table.

"I've got to get rid of this," he gasped at her.

Sue picked up the heavy gold nugget and bounced its weight lightly around in her palm.

"Why?" she asked calmly.

"He must've killed her," he mumbled, a little to Sue but mostly to himself. "How else could it have ended up in his jewelry case if Meghan was wearing it when she disappeared?"

Sue turned the ring over in her hand, still admiring its heft.

"Why are you so nervous, Ricky?" she wanted to know. "Why feel you have to get rid of what must be just one of dozens of similar '94 class rings?"

"This one is marked as belonging to Olson," Ricky said, lowering his voice to almost a whisper. "In two ways," he added.

Sue turned the ring more slowly and then thought to gaze into the inner surface of the band. "He had it inscribed," she nodded. "MM and HO."

Ricky took the ring from her and jabbed his index finger onto a small stone at the base of the school's insignia. "Olson was a real superstar athlete for Narrownook, and they added this diamond chip in honor of his four-year contributions. If I'm caught with this ring, I could be implicated in Meghan Murphy's disappearance, don't you see?"

Sue gave him an exaggerated eye roll that he was meant to see. "How old were you in 1994?" she sneered.

"Ten," he said.

"So you think they're looking for a fifth grader as a possible suspect? Use whatever scanty brain cells God gave you and figure out how you can make use of this piece of information to your advantage."

"What're you getting at?" Ricky asked. He'd stopped shaking and had started scowling at Sue in obedient concentration.

"What do you think Olson would give to keep the existence of this ring a secret?"

"Huh? You talkin' blackmail?"

"What? Does blackmail insult your moral integrity?"

"'Course not, but it might get me killed."

"Not if you insure yourself against any violence before you approach Olson. What you need to do is get yourself a safety deposit box at the bank and leave the rest to me."

"How much does one of those cost?" Ricky whined.

"About two cents next to what you stand to make when you talk to Olson. You've been sitting on this gold mine for how long?"

"I've had the ring since 2010, when I did some renovation work on his bathroom. How was I supposed to know it was a piece of evidence?"

"Now you do," Sue declared, going to a kitchen drawer and taking out a pad of paper.

"What're you doing?" Ricky wanted to know.

"Leaving a note detailing where the ring came from with instructions on the envelope for the authorities to open it in the event of your death."

"Hey! I don't like the sound of this!" Ricky yelped.

"You're not going to die, idiot. You're going to put the note and the ring and whatever else you took from Olson into a safety deposit box at the bank, and make sure you tell Mr. Mayor about it so he won't even *think* about retaliation."

Ricky thought about it for a good minute. "It's a risk," he finally decided.

"So's your favorite pastime—breaking into houses. Ricky, you've just hit the trifecta, and you're too dense to know it. Just do what I tell you, and soon enough you'll be glad you listened to me—and grateful to me, too, I hope."

Sue chuckled to herself as she thought about what she would do with the cash that Ricky would cut her in on in just a matter of days.

CHAPTER 17

Narrownook filled the front pages of the papers that week. Stories continued about the Meghan Murphy case, of course, and then there were the headlines about the upcoming Penobscot Narrows Bridge dedication and the proposed demolition of the Waldo–Hancock span. Maine papers ran two- and three-page stories about the upcoming Saturday celebration and featured large colorful pictures of both spans that presently arched the peaceful flowing Penobscot River.

At nine thirty on Saturday morning, Lanie dropped Mahitabelle and Amy off at the entrance to the new Penobscot Narrows Bridge and left to park the car. Folding chairs and benches had been set up all along the sides of the new 2,120-foot span for folks to quietly observe the festivities, and that's where Lanie found them waiting when she returned.

On the way back to the entrance, Lanie had met her cousin, Lawrence, whom she hadn't seen in years. Growing up, he had been a year ahead of her in school and busy with his own group of friends, but their families had managed to get together for important occasions a couple of times a year. Now, it was good to see him and catch up with developments in each other's lives.

They made sure that Mahitabelle was comfortable on a bench before the two girls and Lawrence joined the growing crowds of people who were on a ceremonial walk along the expanse. There would be hundreds strolling back and forth across the length of the new bridge that day—when they weren't taking advantage of the concession stands that had been set up on adjacent plots of land on Orphan Island.

Lawrence had been raised on the island. The shore by the Waldo–Hancock Bridge had been his playground as a kid. They hadn't gone far in their walk before he began pointing out areas where he and his brother and his friends had spent memorable moments.

"See that door in the footing of the first pylon down there under the bridge?" he asked them.

The two women looked and at first didn't understand what he was indicating, but with closer scrutiny, they could make out what appeared to be a steel door in the base of the huge concrete block.

"We used to play in there as kids," Lawrence boasted.

"*In* there?" Lanie asked. They had stopped to look and were leaning against the rails of the Penobscot Narrow Bridge, peering down at the other bridge's structure.

"Back in the day, when we were kids and exploring and conquering, it was pirate headquarters or whatever we were imagining on a particular day. It was really a room where equipment was stored. There was an opening in the floor of that room that intrigued us, too. It had a rope ladder down to another level. We never dared to descend into that part. The closest we got was to lie on our stomachs and take turns shining flashlights down into the hole."

"What was down there?" Lanie wanted to know.

"Just some rope and more tools," Lawrence shrugged.

"I'd have been hesitant about even going into that equipment room," Lanie told him as they started walking once more toward the Waldo County line at the western end of the bridge.

"Oh, look." Amy pointed upward. "That's the observation tower that will be opening soon. It's the tallest bridge observatory in the world and the tallest occupied structure in Maine. It also can brag that it's the only observatory bridge in the Western Hemisphere. The only others are in Thailand, Slovakia, and I forget the other one."

"I'm impressed you know so much about it already," Lanie said.

"I'll never set foot in it," she laughed. "Heights aren't my strong suit, so I learned all I could about it without leaving terra firma."

The sun was angled into their faces as they looked straight up. By shielding their eyes, they managed to glimpse, only briefly, the windowed top of the high deck glistening above them before the light completely blinded them.

They kept walking but paused once in a while to look over at Narrownook across the water, singling out specific streets and buildings nestled on the shore. They commented on portions of the mill still in its obscene state of collapse and sadly noted the mounds of stones strewn over areas where whole industrial complexes had once stood.

It took more than a half hour for them to walk the span up and back. When they arrived at the Hancock County side again, Mahitabelle was not where they'd left her.

"Where's Mama?" Lanie asked, beginning to panic. "We shouldn't have left her alone for so long."

"She wasn't alone," Amy said, seemingly calm as she looked up and down the crowd in either direction. "How many people kept saying hello to her in the few minutes it took her to be seated here? She knows more than half of these people. What'd I tell you?" she said pointing then toward a crowd by one of the food stands.

There was Mahitabelle, ice cream cone balanced in one hand and the other hand on the arm of Willard Varney, her next-door neighbor. Willard had lost his wife in the same year that John Warren had died.

"How long has this been going on, Mama?" Lanie teased Mahitabelle after Willard had returned her to her family and bid them hello and goodbye.

"It's just our neighbor being neighborly," her mother smiled demurely as she waved off any further speculation.

"And I thought I just had to keep my eye on *you!*" Lanie laughed, turning toward Amy.

"What?" Amy asked, looking back from her focus on the hill, where cars cruised for parking spaces on the island's main road.

"What were you staring at?" Lanie wanted to know when she saw her daughter's distracted look.

"Nothing," she shrugged. "What did you say?"

"Nothing," Lanie echoed, "just teasing your cavorting grandmother."

"My what?" Amy asked just as a loudspeaker sent a blaring greeting out to the hundreds of people gathered on or near the new bridge. It was Mayor Olson welcoming the crowd of spectators to this auspicious occasion.

Suddenly, the people ceased their chatter and halted their movements to focus their attention on the makeshift staging that had been set up on the grassy mound beside the bridge.

Harry was beaming. He had had a few days to reconcile himself to the fact that his ring was missing and had decided that he must have been the victim of thieves. Further, he had speculated that if the ring ever turned up, the robbers would have a lot of explaining to do and might surely be the prime suspects in Meghan Murphy's disappearance.

He'd convinced himself that it was actually to his benefit that some poor fool had been stupid enough to swipe such an incriminating item. Yes, he was one lucky bastard.

"Good afternoon," he declared. "What a beautiful day for a celebration! Clear a path for the marching bands from Belfast, Stockton Springs, Ellsworth, and Narrownook as they officially open the Penobscot Narrows Bridge."

And the crowd cheered.

CHAPTER 18

THE JED PROUTY HOTEL WAS JUMPING THAT NIGHT. THE LIQUOR WAS flowing into crystal glasses, and the smells of sizzling beef entrées and seasonal seafood dishes wafted enticingly through the dining rooms and out onto the dance floor of the crowded cocktail lounge.

There was no band for the occasion, but a popular local pianist played a constant medley of soft, slow music that many couples couldn't resist waltzing to. The melodies were mellow enough to inspire plenty of uninterrupted conversations around the fifty or so tables in the inn's two restaurants.

Harry Olson had gathered fifteen people at a rectangular table in the main dining room near the archway to the lounge, where he presided over his invited guests, making sure everyone was properly attended to. He insisted that their drinks be kept replenished and their dinners served right out of the kitchen piping hot.

Stan Russell was at a large table in the main dining room, as well, with his entire staff and their families. Lanie had stopped on her way by him to thank him for the wonderful job his men had done repairing the porch. She remembered to address him as Russ several times as they talked, bringing a flicker of amusement into his eyes each time.

Lanie was surprised to see Ricky Irving at a table for two over in a corner on the other side of the room. Sue was with him. Each time Lanie happened to look over, they were laughing and seemed to be enjoying the evening.

When the main course had been consumed, someone activated a microphone in the bandstand section of the lounge, and a male voice began requesting the appearance of the town manager to the microphone.

Sarah Hamilton rose from a table of six where she had been seated with her family and spoke with emotion about the enormous blessing the new Penobscot Narrows Bridge afforded not just Narrownook, but the whole State of Maine.

"Don't forget," she reminded them, "we are the gateway to Downeast for the rest of the country, and never doubt that folks will want to visit here very soon because this town is going places!"

Thunderous applause filled the inn. Even those who were still lingering over their dinners stood to endorse the manager's words with more applause and whistles.

"We begin anew, but not from scratch this time," Sarah continued when the room quieted again. "Now we have a solid educational system already established. We have our beautiful churches, our historic library and movie theater, a lovely new art center and brand-new performing arts center, a thriving golf course, and a deep harbor that is railroad accessible. We're the envy of coastal communities up and down the New England coast because of our enormous resources, and let's not forget," she gestured toward the front porch that overlooked the Penobscot, "no place can claim a more splendid harbor view. Soon we will welcome a brand-new seafood industry and a pleasure craft manufacturing plant that promises to bring with it a bustling yacht club whose members will need good food and lodgings and will encourage further establishments to be built like our beloved Jed Prouty Tavern where we dine in style tonight."

Sarah Hamilton paused and took a breath before concluding her address. There had been a hint of tears beginning to form in her eyes and her voice had cracked when she mentioned the Jed Prouty.

"In April of 1909," she said in a stronger voice, "Admiral Peary launched his famous schooner *Roosevelt* from the mouth of the Narrows after building it on Orphan Island. Its destination was the North Pole. Because its first-of-a-kind heavy wooden construction was reinforced with steel, the ship was able to penetrate through the icy North Pole and conquer a new frontier."

"It is only fitting that we now will construct beautifully crafted yachts on these same waters. So do not despair about what we have lost. Tonight, we celebrate what we are about to gain as we rise from the cement ashes of our beloved St. Andrews paper mill and mourn the passing of our beautiful Waldo–Hancock Bridge. They are and always will be an integral part of our heritage and will remind us of what we have already accomplished. Remembering them will give us courage to push on to even greater goals."

Harry had sat stone-faced throughout the entire address and did not join the robust applause that erupted when Sarah stepped away from the mic.

He was seated at the head of the long table. Lanie was on his right facing her mother, who was at his left. Out of the increased bedlam of applause and renewed cheers and chatter, Ricky Irving suddenly appeared beside him. Harry had just turned to speak to Lanie when Ricky tapped him vigorously on his shoulder. "Mr. Mayor," he said, and his greeting had an undisguised mocking tone. "I need to talk to you." Irving looked up and down the table at the people who had paused in their conversation to stare at the rather shabbily dressed intruder. "Somewhere more private," he amended, smiling a toothless and vacuous smile at each one seated at the table before resting his gaze back on Olson.

"Not tonight, Irving. Ms. Warren and I were about to dance. Call my office on Monday." And with that, Harry stood and held out his hand in Lanie's direction.

Ricky unfolded a piece of paper he'd been holding in his hand and snapped it open with a degree of ceremony before he dangled it in front of Olson's face.

"What's this?" Harry growled.

"What *you* need to talk to *me* about. In private," Irving added again as he arched his eyebrows in exaggerated fashion and came up a bit on his toes to look down on Harry Olson. All the time, he kept grinning that snide, empty grin.

Harry took the paper and held it closer.

"*M.M. & H.O.—Does that ring a bell?*" was printed on the small white sheet. A double circle had been drawn around the word *ring* and shaded in yellow to roughly resemble a gold band. Those at the table watched every bit of color leave Harry Olson's face.

"Let's go out on the porch," he said, grabbing the paper and crumbling it up in his fist. He was almost shoving Irving forward in his haste to get outside.

"What was that about, I wonder?" Skip Dyer remarked to everyone ingeneral. "Who was that guy, anyway? Anyone know him?"

"A handyman in town," Lanie said without further commentary.

"Harry turned as white as a ghost," Charlie Briggs said. "Maybe we should go out and make sure he's okay."

But everyone stayed seated, just staring at the far-off center door through which the men had disappeared.

Lanie caught a glimpse of Sue at the table for two. Crystal had just laid the bill down next to her elbow, and Sue immediately handed it back to the waitress with a nod toward Lanie's side of the restaurant. As she puzzled over what she had just witnessed, Mr. Varney, their next-door neighbor, approached their table and asked Mahitabelle if she would like to dance. When she said yes, it evidently prompted all the others to move to the dance floor, too. In the confusion, Lanie never had a chance to see what Crystal ended up doing with the bill.

"Was it something you said?" Russ asked as he moved someone's empty dishes back to make room for the drink that he'd carried over with him when he slid into the seat next to her.

Lanie scanned the dozen empty seats at the table and laughed, then sat back and stared at him. "Did you just see Harry and Ricky leave together?" she asked him.

"I did. What happened? They don't even pretend to tolerate each other."

"Ricky said he needed to talk to him, and when Harry refused, Ricky showed him something on a piece of paper. It must have been important, because Harry almost beat Ricky out the door, he was suddenly in such a hurry to have that conversation."

"Irving is always playing an angle; maybe he thinks he's got one up on Olson this time."

"Maybe this time he does," Lanie shrugged. "Whatever was on that paper caused Harry to lose every ounce of color in his face."

"I should think by this time you're beginning to figure out what a loser Olson is as a date." Russell said, sitting back a bit to study Lanie. He had tried to plant a serious expression on his face, but it seemed contrived when you detected a smile playing at the edges of his mouth. "Didn't he desert you the last time he took you to dinner here? If I remember correctly, he skipped out before paying *that* bill, too."

"This was not a date," Lanie snapped. "He asked my mother, not me. I was here just looking out for her."

"Right," Russell nodded, the smile finally breaking into an uncharacteristic grin. "Well, I'm available again to get you home," he offered, switching his tone and facial expression to one that held a more genuine look of concern.

"Thanks, but we can hitch a ride with Mr. Varney," Lanie said and gestured toward the dance floor, where Mahitabelle and Willard had just swung into the easy cadence of "Deep Purple."

"Let's find out," Russell said, taking Lanie's hand and giving it a tug.

When Lanie looked at him questioningly, he tugged again. "We'll dance over to them and make sure about that ride home," he explained.

"Oh," was all she said as she was pulled the short distance into the lounge.

As soon as they were on the other side of the arch, Russ's arm encircled her waist and he swung her quickly into the rhythm of the melody as the pianist entered into the second verse of the age-old tune. *In the still of the night, Once again I hold you tight...*

He was surprisingly adept at swirling her effortlessly, and she found herself folding into him, confident immediately that he was capable of controlling their united movements.

"We haven't reached Mr. Varney yet," she said.

"We'll get there eventually," he replied as he swirled her in another direction.

"I think they're to our left," she suggested.

"We'll find them, eventually," he answered against her ear.

The piano whisperer segued into "If Ever I Should Leave You" and after that into a long medley of Sinatra favorites. It was Mahitabelle who spotted them about fifteen minutes later from several couples away and shouted a "Yoohoo."

"I haven't seen you since John's funeral, Stanley, dear," Mahitabelle greeted him when they reached them. Then, to Lanie, "It's time we headed home, I'm afraid. My feet have had enough dancing for one night. Willard is tired, too. He'll drive us. Evidently, Harry isn't in any hurry to return to his party," and she pouted her famil-iar *I'm annoyed* pout.

Russ wished Lanie a good night as they followed Mahitabelle and Willard toward the archway. "I can't tell you the last time I enjoyed dancing as much as I did just now," he told her graciously, and squeezed her hand briefly when he said it.

Lanie had a chance to tell him what a wonderful dancer he was before he turned toward his table of friends, then she hurried to catch up with the elderly couple now several paces ahead despite their professed exhaustion.

CHAPTER 19

THE FOURTH OF JULY WAS ON A THURSDAY, AND THE BRIDGE WALK WAS on a Saturday, so Amy scheduled her yard sale for all day Sunday, after all the celebrations were over.

She had advertised ahead of time in the Bangor and local papers and plastered fluorescent cardboard signs all over town on trees and telephone poles.

Clearly, the time of the sale was stated as eight to four, but on that Sunday morning, at six thirty, while Amy was starting to set up tables and sawhorses for makeshift tables, she was surprised to see two women sweep through the opened garage doors where she was working as if they were storming a Walmart going-out-of-business sale.

"Excuse me!" she said firmly as the ladies began rummaging through the fishing gear hanging on the outer wall in the first bay of the garage.

The women paid no attention to her but began removing and studying some of the colorful tackle in a basket on the lower shelf. They conversed loudly with each other as they giggled and oohed and aahed about each item before strewing bobbers and lures over the shelves and allowing some to fall and scatter on the cement floor.

"Excuse me." Amy tried again with a bit more volume while she set down the piece of plywood that was to be a tabletop and rushed over to her enthusiastic early-bird customers. "This is not a garage sale," she said in what she tried to make a polite tone. "This is a *yard* sale that doesn't start outside in the yard until eight o'clock."

"How much for the lawn mower?" one of the women asked, gesturing toward a Craftsman in the far corner and completely ignoring what Amy had just told them.

"You'll have to come back at eight when I have things ready. In. The. *Yard*," Amy said, emphasizing each word and pointing toward the lawns on the other side of the opened garage doors.

One of the women spotted a pair of Amy's hiking boots on the back wall next to the stairs that led up to the living areas. Feeling panicked by this time as both ladies suddenly moved in that direction, which was well into the interior of the garages, she made a decision to call for her mother's help.

She hated to do that. She remembered how she had declared herself a yard sale veteran capable of handling things on her own, and just last night, when Lanie and Mahitabelle had returned from the bridge celebration and found her knee-deep in boxes and newspaper wrappings, Lanie had offered to help her set up again. But Amy had still insisted there was no need, and made it sound, even to her own ears, like she was some kind of yard-sale guru.

Now she took the stairs two at a time and pounded on the apartment door. "I need some help down here," she confessed to her mother when Lanie answered her frantic knocking.

Amy took in her mother's baby-doll pajamas and floppy blue slippers and felt terribly guilty for bothering her, but her panic had plastered a look of abject terror on her face that Lanie could not ignore. "I'll go grab a wrap," she said, and returned less than a minute later, still in the floppy slippers, but covered adequately in an ugly chenille robe. "What's the problem?" she asked Amy as they exited the apartment.

Amy gestured below, where, by this time, one of the women had both feet in Amy's boots and was clomping and stomping back and forth at the bottom of the stairs.

"Aren't those your boots?" Lanie asked her.

"Therein lies the problem," Amy mumbled as they finished making their way down the stairs.

"Excuse me," Lanie said to the booted woman, "why are you wearing my daughter's boots?"

"I like them. I want to buy them, but I don't know how much they are. They are not marked."

"That's because they are not for sale," Amy said. "Nothing is for sale until eight, and only outside sales are being conducted here today—that is, if you would please leave and let us set things up."

"Well," the Walmart shopper huffed, "with that kind of tone and attitude, I doubt you'll have a very successful enterprise at all," and she began yanking the boots off of her feet and tossing them indiscriminately in two different directions. "Mildred," she yelled to her friend as she shoved her feet into her own shoes, "we're outta here."

Amy and Lanie watched in relief the departure of the two characters down the driveway and kept their eyes on them all the way down Church Street until they were out of sight.

"Thanks, Mom," Amy said. "I'm sorry I had to bother you, but my coworker Lewis and his crew haven't shown up yet. They were supposed to be here by this time."

"I'll go change and be back down to give you a hand," Lanie told her.

"After Lewis gets here, I'll be fine," Amy said. "He's bringing Dexter, Veazie, and Verona to help."

"You've got whole towns pitching in?" Lanie exclaimed.

"Dexter is Lewis's brother, and his two sisters are Veazie and Verona. The girls will do the jewelry and clothing area, and Dexter and Lewis will do a tool table."

"They're all named after Maine towns?" Lanie asked.

Amy nodded as she ripped open a sealed box and exposed dozens of long-playing record albums from the mid-twentieth century if the one on top, Sinatra's *Only the Lonely*, was an example of the rest.

"I'm just curious," Lanie said, "how did Lewis end up with a normal name?"

"His name is Lewiston."

107

"Ah," Lanie nodded. "Are there any more siblings? Any Ogunquits or Berwicks or, God forbid, a Vassalboro?"

"Funny!" Amy scoffed, refusing to even smile at her mother's sarcasm. Then she paused in her work, stood to face Lanie, took a breath, and finally admitted that there were two younger brothers, Charles and Rick.

"Let me guess," Lanie mused, "Charleston and Limerick?"

Amy did break down and crack a smile then. "That's correct," she nodded tearing into another box to expose dozens of 45's. "And there's one more on the way, but they haven't decided on a name yet. We're raffling off tickets to bet on what name they decide. We'll use the money to throw them a baby shower."

"That's considerate," Lanie said dryly, and gestured toward the records. "You should get a good price for some of those. Collectors would be here early if they knew about them."

Amy went to retrieve a boot by the right wall and then another one in the middle of the center bay. Her mother watched her tag and then place them in a box of shoes.

"What are you doing?" Lanie asked.

"Putting them up for sale," Amy frowned.

"Your hiking boots? You love those boots!"

"I'll never put my feet into them again!" Amy declared, and they both laughed as they grabbed the sides of a piece of plywood and carried it to a waiting pair of sawhorses in the shade of a pine tree.

With her mother's help, Amy managed to have everything organized within an hour. Early birds began arriving around seven thirty, but by that time, Lewis and his family were in place arranging the tables they were in charge of and managing to negotiate some sales while they put last-minute touches on their displays.

By eight, over a dozen people were meandering around the yard. Amy and her mother went upstairs then to pour cups of coffee for themselves and their helpers. Ten minutes later, when they brought two trays of refreshments downstairs, cars lined both sides of Church Street and roughly two dozen people were browsing and buying.

Lewis, at the tool table, signaled Amy and her mother with a wave. "I didn't know what to tell that couple over there about the cost of the record collections," he told them, gesturing toward two people at the jewelry display in conversation with Veazie.

"Oh, brother!" Lanie sighed, recognizing Ricky Irving and Sue Hayes. "Each record is marked. The price depends on the artist and the year it was produced."

"They want the entire collections, the albums and the 45's," Lewis told her.

"They can't *afford* that," Amy said. "I'll go talk to them."

"Money's no object!" Ricky crowed when Amy had warned them of the cost. "Name your price."

So Amy borrowed the calculator from Veazie's table and started adding up the price of fifty-three albums. The tally came to over $1500. She relayed the cost to Irving and waited for the inevitable decision that he'd changed his mind about getting the whole collection.

"Okay, now figure the forty-fives," he said without batting an eye.

"There are seventy-five of those," Amy told him. "Each one is fifteen dollars. That comes to $1,125. So now, if you'll excuse me, I'll go help wait on some real customers, but thanks for helping me itemize the stock for the serious patrons."

"I'll take 'em both," Ricky said.

"Sure you will," Amy nodded beginning to walk away.

"Hey," Irving yelled after her, "does this look like I'm joking?"

Amy turned to see her former caretaker waving what looked like a wad of bills.

"Where'd you get the play money?" she laughed as she watched Ricky stoop and pick up the heavy box of albums and start heading for his car. "Not so fast!" Amy hollered as she raced after him.

Ricky laughed and set the box down carefully so he could pull the currency back out of his pocket. Then he handed her the whole wad. "Take out the two thousand and change for the two boxes," he ordered arrogantly, "and give what's left to Sue. I'll come back for the other box and then head home. Tell Susie I'll meet her back at the house."

Amy thumbed through the rough lump of paper he'd shoved into her hands and stared blankly after Ricky's scrawny frame as he juggled his burden of records up the street to his decrepit vehicle.

* * *

The BMW cruised for the fourth time down past the line of parked cars on Church Street and finally pulled into the furthest available spot seven houses down from the Warrens'. The driver exited his vehicle and stretched his tall frame once before he walked back up the block to the property bursting with so much activity that he could mingle unnoticed around the tables like just another yard sale enthusiast.

He was able to identify Amy quickly enough. He'd pulled her up online enough times and had been following her for several weeks. He strolled through the crowd until he became sure that her mother was the attractive woman Amy kept conferring with, a woman who certainly resembled an older version of pretty Amy.

Before he strolled back to his car half an hour later, he made sure to purchase a keepsake from the "memorial table"—a framed copy of an original photograph of Narrownook's fire department circa 1950. A young John Warren, in the first row of the group of men, smiled at him as if he knew.

* * *

Harry steered his Mercedes up Pleasant and made the sharp right down into Church, slowing as he threaded his way through the cars lined up on both sides of the street. The yard sale was obviously doing a robust business.

He'd just wanted to see how it was going. He wouldn't stop in. Not today. He needed more time to collect himself, figure out what he'd say to Lanie about last night. He could say he had suddenly felt ill, which wouldn't even be a lie—not even an exaggeration.

He still felt nauseous. He'd feel sick to his stomach until he could decide how to deal with that weasel Ricky Irving.

He could say he'd been called away by a pressing issue that had to be resolved that evening. He could say he had hoped to be able to take care of it quickly, but it had taken most of the rest of the night. A lie, since it wouldn't be resolved until the threat Irving posed had been eliminated.

And what would he say today? Tomorrow? The day after that?

He was suddenly walking on eggshells and worrying constantly about Irving, with his big braggy mouth, spilling the beans in a moment of careless bravado.

Fleetingly, he caught a glimpse of Lanie as he inched by, and it stirred up the anger that would motivate him to fix this momentary problem that had put a glitch in his plans for the two of them.

CHAPTER 20

GLORIA REPORTED FOR WORK ON MONDAY AND WAS IMMEDIATELY AWARE that Harry was not his usual self. He could often be curt in his dealings with the office staff, especially with those who took orders from him, but on this day, he'd hurried into the building and into his office, passing several coworker friends without even so much as a nod in greeting.

Gloria waited forty-five minutes for him to buzz her to come into his office for their daily discussions of pending matters, but her desk monitor remained silent. Finally, she picked up her notepad and took it upon herself to cross the foyer and tap lightly on his door.

"I'm busy," Harry's voice thundered from his inner sanctum, and Gloria backed off. Without a directive from Harry about the morning's agenda, she went to the staff room and poured herself a cup of coffee much earlier than she would normally have taken a break.

The room was unusually quiet. Folks were getting their drinks without much repartee; just heading right back to their stations. Had they, too, noticed Harry's demeanor? Were they saving their discussions of it for when they were in a more private setting?

Gloria took a seat at an empty table in the staff room and absently moved the swizzle stick around in her coffee laced with cream as her thoughts flashed back to the strange scene Saturday night between Harry and Ricky Irving.

She knew Irving. He had done a few odd jobs at her house in the past. He was a ne'er-do-well, picking up jobs here and there to keep spending money in his pocket; at least that was her perception of the man. What he could have had to discuss with her boss that would keep Harry away from his table of guests for the rest of that special night was beyond her. She had stayed until closing and knew he had not returned.

Probably, one of the reasons she had lingered as long as she did on Saturday night was to see if Harry would leave with Lanie Warren. Not that she really cared. She and Harry hadn't been an item for ten years now, but she remained interested in his activities just the same. She no longer even loved the man. Her feelings for him had wavered and died during the five years they were together. The night she began having second thoughts about him was still clear in her mind.

They had been asleep when his voice jarred her awake. He was obviously dreaming. He seemed to be in an angry conversation with someone. Gloria bristled now as she recalled his exact words: *You'll never hurt me again, you little bitch.*

He had begun thrashing at that point, and his arms raised up for a split second before they slowly lowered as if they were carrying a heavy weight. Then, the final utterance before he drifted back into quiet repose was a gruff *Goodbye, Meghan, and good riddance.*

Gloria had not been able to go back to sleep that night, and what she had heard haunted her in the weeks that immediately followed. Gradually, she and Harry ceased being intimate, but they remained friends, good enough friends so that when Harry became mayor, he asked Gloria to be his personal secretary.

She never told him that she had heard him talking in his sleep, and she had buried the memory entirely until something triggered the recollection—like a change in his behavior.

Over the years, she had managed to rationalize his dream as a subconscious reaction to his enormous hurt at being rejected by Meghan, who he believed had run off with another man. Yet something else more sinister crawled around in the back of her mind now and then that she was unwilling to address. She sensed it was something dark; something too frightening to bring into the light.

Besides, to dwell on it would be a betrayal of a man held in high regard by his community, a man who remained her good friend.

When Gloria got back to her desk, she found Harry had left a note saying that he would be out of the building for the rest of the day. With a shrug, Gloria caught up on some last-minute shopping online until it was lunchtime, then decided to take a longer lunch than usual at McKay's.

* * *

There was no way Harry could concentrate on town business that Monday morning. Over the weekend, he had been devising a new plan, and after reaching the office, he had called Ricky Irving to demand that he meet with him for another discussion. He could think of nothing else until he presented his new idea. He just hoped Irving would respond well to it and not force him into a plan C. He didn't have a plan C yet, but he knew if he had to make one, it would not be pretty.

Now he drove the mile and a quarter out on Pleasant Street and was relieved that Ricky was already there in the lot waiting for him.

"I thought we came to a clear understanding Saturday night," Irving hissed before Harry had even reached the creep, who was spread-legged in a defiant stance.

"We did," Harry nodded, keeping his voice as upbeat as he could make it with his insides churning. "I've had a chance to mull things over since we talked," he ventured slowly, "and I just don't like the idea of the drip-drip payouts once a month with no end in sight. I'm prepared to make you a one-time gigantic offer."

"It would have to be pretty damn huge," Ricky scoffed, shuffling his feet into a position that allowed him to rise up on his toes as a signal to Olson that he was the one in charge.

Harry gave a sharp nod and then swept his left arm around to encompass the flat, treeless area where they stood. "I own all this," he announced. "Ten acres. It would be part of a one-time package of assets I'm prepared to offer you."

"I don't need no barren piece of land," Irving sputtered.

"How about I put a house of your design on it? Landscape the acreage." Harry stopped to point toward Ricky's dilapidated black vehicle parked out on the street. "I'll throw in a brand-new SUV and a quarter million dollars in one lump sum. It would take forever for you to save enough to acquire what I can give you right now."

Ricky paced a bit as he thought about it.

"I'd want a house like the one on the corner of Church and Main," he declared, stopping as he turned to regard Harry and catch his reaction to his choice for a luxurious estate like the one that had been built almost a century ago by a mill executive.

"Okay, your choice," Harry said without flinching.

"A Cadillac SUV," Ricky stipulated next.

"Sure, go pick one out this afternoon if you want to. I'll write you a check including enough for insurance and registration costs."

Irving seemed overly stimulated now as he began walking around again at a brisker pace. Then he stopped abruptly. "Sue would need a car, too," he said.

"Pick it out and let me know," Harry sighed and then pinned a direct gaze on his blackmailer. "That will be it, you understand," he was punctuating this decree with a finger fiercely jabbed in Ricky's direction. "Ten acres, a large home, two cars, and two hundred fifty thousand fuckin' dollars, and we're done! That will just about wipe me out of most of my assets, so the well will be pretty much dried up, anyway. And, oh, I want the ring and tie clip back."

Ricky nodded and all but leaped into his black van, so enthusiastic was he to get home and tell Sue about his sudden windfall.

Harry watched as Irving rattled away back down Pleasant Street. He began to review his losses for the umpteenth time. He had two other smaller pieces of property in town, but the quarter of a million and the cost of building the estate-sized home that Ricky was requesting would leave him roughly only another quarter of a million of the inheritance his parents had left him. He'd finance the two new cars and try to pay them off gradually from his own monthly earnings.

Still, if it meant he'd be free of any further shakedowns and worry that his secret was going to be discovered, it would be worth it in the long run.

Harry got into his car unwilling to congratulate himself just yet, but at least feeling a lighter load on his shoulders until, on his way back to the center of town, he suddenly braked at the corner of Pleasant and Forest Streets. Had his eyes deceived him, or had he just seen someone going into the old Murphy house, which had been vacant since the death of both of Meghan's parents? They had died within a few months of each other in 2017.

Then he noticed the black-and-white parked in the driveway. A chill crawled up his back as he stepped on the accelerator and sped away.

Must be part of the reopened investigation, he mused and decided to contact a buddy on the force to ask how the inquiry was progressing. He knew folks would view his interest as a normal reaction by one of the two people still alive who had suffered the trauma of Meghan's disappearance.

He thought of Meg's sister, who had come to town for both funerals and stayed only long enough after the second one to close up the house and put the property up for sale. It still hadn't sold two years later. Maybe no one wanted a house with such a tragic history.

As for the sister, Katherine Murphy, the gossip was that she lived in the western part of Massachusetts and held down a lucrative position as private secretary in a prestigious law firm there. Whether that rumor was credible was anyone's guess. Katherine had not touched base with any old friends since her graduation, not even during the two times she'd made an appearance in Narrownook for the funerals. She had tended to her immediate family obligations and left town as quickly as she could.

Harry went home and dialed Dale Robershaw. His son, Bill, answered the phone and told him that his father was on the eight-to-four shift and still on duty down at the station. When Harry asked him to tell his dad to call him later, that he was interested in how the Murphy case was developing, Bill, who was an EMT at the same facility, was happy to impart what information he had on the subject and show the mayor what a trusted witness of local affairs he could be.

"They're keeping everything pretty close to the vest," he told him, "but Tyke Robinson seems to be heading up the operation."

"Oh, the new guy," Harry said. "I saw a cruiser at the Murphy place just now so I guess he's on the job."

"That would be Tyke, all right. He's staying there."

"Living in the Murphy house? How did that happen?"

"You'd have to ask Brody. Maybe because he's heading up the inquiry, he got an okay to live on the scene for a while."

The turmoil in the pit of Harry's stomach that he'd gone to bed with the night before had suddenly returned in spades.

"That's about all I know right now," Bill was saying. "How're you doing, Mr. Olson?" he added in an effort to be cordial.

"Tell your dad I called," Harry said as he disconnected.

"Who the hell is Tyke Robinson?" Harry asked the carafe of Johnny Walker that he poured neat and generously into a cocktail glass before settling down in his den for some serious reflection.

CHAPTER 21

TYKE HAD MADE A LIST OF THE NAMES OF THE MAIN CHARACTERS IN Meghan Murphy's final hours.

Lanie Warren stood out as the number-one witness. Scott Lanford, who had also been in the car with Meghan on Cadillac Mountain that night, had died in an accident at Brown University during his sophomore year there, or he would have been on that short list, too. It had occurred to Tyke that Scott might have shared some details with his family back in the day, so he had added the parents' names with a question mark.

Having personally determined that the girl's disappearance was not at the hands of a stranger made Tyke's job easier. The enigma lay in how to proceed without offending the townspeople. They could help put the pieces together for him, but he had to be careful in the way he approached them. He knew he had both alarmed and angered Lanie Warren that day in her apartment when he began asking questions about Stan Russell.

On this Monday morning, Tyke stepped out of the shower, wrapped a thick blue towel around his lean and muscular frame, and gazed with a critical eye at his reflection in the mirror over the sink. He wondered briefly if it was the same mirror Meghan had used the morning of her graduation, when her reflection would have been one of hope and enormous possibilities.

He was using the small suite that had been hers while she was growing up in this cozy Maine home. He hoped that somehow the karma here would help him find his way to a successful answer to what had happened to her.

He was aware that small towns had the propensity to be protective of their own, especially if they thought an outsider was suspicious of one of them. In this case, he had his laser on two of their own—Russell and Olson, and he knew each one had a healthy following of devoted friends.

It didn't take him long to shave, comb through his thick mane of dark hair, and get into some chinos and a blue shirt that he'd laid out the night before. Technically, it was his day off, but he'd be using it to scout around town, and if all went well, he'd be interviewing at least one of the people on his list.

At first, he'd hoped that Lanie Warren, who had not been a resident of Narrownook all these years, would have a weak tie to his suspects, Russell and Olson, which would make her more easily forthcoming than his other key witness, Gloria Jordan. Gloria had been a resident of Narrownook her whole life and still worked for one of his persons of interest.

However, when he'd had the Jed Prouty details, he'd interrupted Lanie and Harry dancing when he issued a ticket to Penelope Mageloo. And more recently, he'd noticed Lanie and her mother flanking the mayor at Olson's table of guests the night the new bridge was celebrated. It was possible that there was a close connection brewing between Lanie and Olson.

On the other hand, he couldn't forget Lanie's strong defense of Stan Russell each time his name came up in a conversation. She had contracted with him for repairs on the family home recently, and the first time he'd met her, she had been with Russell at the Jed Prouty bar.

He still had a clear image of a beautiful woman in a fitted white dress, her long brown hair flying as she swirled effortlessly around the dance floor in Russell's arms this past weekend. He began to enjoy the heat that memory had produced until he caught himself wasting time, swept up his keys off the table in the hall, and left the Murphy house to get down to business.

CHAPTER 22

AMY WAS DRESSED AND READY FOR WORK WHEN LANIE MADE HER COFFEE run on that Monday morning. Her daughter had actually asked her to come over early, before Lanie's exercise walk. "So we can have a chance to talk," she had told her mother.

Unprecedented! With more than a small degree of worry about what Amy could be so anxious to tell her, Lanie got to her daughter's room by six thirty.

Unlike the normal cannonball girl that she was, always in a hurry to get going once her lipstick was blotted and her pocketbook snapped shut, Lanie was surprised to find Amy fully ready but lounging in a chair as if she wasn't in a rush to be anywhere else.

"I need to ask a favor of you, Mom," was her daughter's opening statement as Lanie sat down in the boudoir chair with Bear and fought back a surge of foreboding.

"I may have opened up a Pandora's box," Amy ventured, which only increased Lanie's apprehension. "Would you be willing to send a sample of your DNA to AAAA? I've already sent mine, and the result was a match of either a first cousin..." there was a slight pause as Amy turned to retrieve a small vial from the bookshelf... "or a sibling."

"What in the world are you talking about? What is AAAA?"

"The Double A Ancestry Agency," Amy said in a tone that could have been interpreted as a chastisement for not knowing such a popular twenty-first-century facility.

Lanie stood up, taking the time to adjust Bear back into his original spot before she turned to respond. "Your grandmother's family is a large one. It is certainly possible to have many first cousins whom we've never met," she said.

"That's true, but if I have a brother or sister out there, I want to know it. I never told you, but I always wished I hadn't been an only child. I'm thinking Dad could have had a child we don't know about, couldn't he? I mean, we never saw him after he walked out on us. I need to see if the match of cousin or sibling is from your side or his."

"What, exactly, do you want me to do?" Lanie asked.

"Spit in this vial," Amy said, thrusting the transparent plastic tube at her mother.

"Do *what?*"

"I already did it; now I need you to give your sample so I'll know if the match is the Warren family side or the Place family side. You have to fill it up to here," she ended, indicating a faint line partway up the tube.

"How soon do you want me to do this?" Lanie asked, eyeing the vial she was now holding with a look of trepidation.

"Let's do it now," Amy shrugged, taking her mother's hand and leading her across the hall and into her bathroom, where she left Lanie with instructions to keep spitting.

"There's one more thing," Amy said when Lanie returned with a sample that her daughter approved of. Amy pushed the vial into an envelope already addressed and stamped for shipping, then blurted, "I'm being followed!"

"Let me guess—the BMW."

Amy nodded. "It showed up after I had gone online and made contact with the match," Amy confessed. "It could be him."

"Him? Couldn't it be her?"

Amy shook her head no. "He was at the yard sale Saturday. He bought a picture. He's very tall and quite handsome."

Lanie backed up and sat down heavily in the boudoir chair, nearly squishing Bear.

"You saw him drive up?"

"He parked the car way down the street out of sight, but I was curious who the stranger was who had purchased a picture taken of our fire department back in the fifties, so I kept watch and at a safe distance followed him all the way down the street to the BMW."

Amy glanced at her watch. "I better get going," she declared abruptly. Lanie watched her seal the envelope and grab her pocketbook. "We'll talk more when I get home," she threw back over her shoulder, and left her mother and Bear gaping silently after her.

* * *

It was ten thirty that Monday morning before Lanie finally arrived on the shore of the Penobscot. She had been too stunned by her daughter's revelation during their six-thirty talk to work up enough energy to even think about exercise after such startling news. Three cups of coffee and two hours later, she had finally reconciled herself to the distinct possibility that her daughter had found her brother! Ultimately, she decided that exercise would help clear her mind so she could begin to decide how she would handle this going forward.

Since the decision to demolish the old bridge had been made, she had begun a new route for her exercise regimen. She now did the one-mile waterfront walkway up and back several times each day. It achieved two ends at the same time. She got her walk in and positioned herself to be witness to the removal of the bridge once the process started.

Last week, after word got out that the council had voted to destroy Narrownook's historic bridge, Lanie remembered reading an anguished headline in a local paper. Screaming in capital letters were the simple words IT'S OUR GOLDEN GATE BRIDGE!

Lanie felt the same way. The suspension bridge pioneer, David B. Steinman, went on to design the Golden Gate Bridge in San Francisco the year after the Waldo–Hancock Bridge was built. The magnificent and stately structure, the gateway to Downeast, Maine, had become her personal gateway to her home, and would soon be razed. There was something sacrilegious in the very thought of it. It would be a sad thing to watch it fall, but sad or not, it was part of Narrownook's history, and Lanie wanted to say she had been witness to it.

She spent over an hour completing her walk along the Penobscot that Monday, slowing to study more thoroughly some of the facades of the Main Street stores on the river side of their establishments. She loved the lighthouse edifice that had been constructed on the back of the new art center. It had been cleverly designed with a flickering lantern atop a tower that overlooked the bay. Along the way, there were plaques containing bits of town history, and stone benches contained the names of their donors, one of which was her own class of 1994. She often paused for reflection at a few of them during her walks.

There was, of course, no visible activity as yet on the old bridge, but there was plenty of action on the new one, whose observatory would be ready right after the bridge opened for traffic this coming Saturday.

Only when Lanie had climbed up the short incline back to the main thoroughfare of town did she have a second to refocus back on her early-morning meeting with her daughter and examine again the options available to her.

She knew there was only one option, really, and that was honesty. She would handle the situation straight on, probably within a day or two.

So absorbed was she in her thoughts, she hardly heard the rapping against McKay's large window until she was nearly past the restaurant. When she finally looked up, she saw Gloria frantically signaling and waving when she wasn't attacking the glass with her knuckles.

"Come join me," Gloria mouthed when Lanie had finally backed up a couple of steps and waved hello.

Lanie went around and entered through the front door, planning to just chat a few minutes before getting home to shower and change.

Gloria had returned to her chair at a table for four in the second dining room by the time Lanie had walked through the restaurant. She looked lonely with three empty places stripped of place settings around her, not to mention the lack of any other people seated with her.

"Are you waiting for someone?" Lanie asked.

"You," she answered. "Please join me. I forgot what it's like dining alone. I feel like a turd in a punch bowl," she laughed.

Lanie spread her arms out. "Look at me. Do I look like someone dressed for lunch at McKay's?"

Gloria took in Lanie's blue sweats and clean white Nike sneakers and pronounced her gorgeous. "Where have you come from?" she asked her.

"My daily exercise jaunt around town," Lanie told her. "Now I need a shower."

"Please don't make me eat alone. At least have a cup of coffee while I nibble my way through this chicken Caesar salad," she gestured with her fork at an untouched plate in front of her, which was teeming with veggies and greens and delicately sliced pieces of roasted chicken.

"For just a few minutes," Lanie conceded and pulled out a chair across from her.

Their table was up against one of the massive front windows overlooking the fort and bridges that were the backdrop to the Narrownook Motel and the town park across the street. "This is my favorite seat in the house," Lanie said. "I always love sitting here and admiring the prettiest tree in town over there at the park entrance," she gestured toward a perfectly shaped maple across the street.

"Always wondered who Googins was," Gloria said, studying the sign under the tree that announced "Googins Park."

"Rufus," Lanie nodded. "He ran the Jed Prouty Hotel way back when it was the Robinson House. In fact, he was the one who actually renamed it the Jed Prouty Tavern after Golden's play became famous. Rufus was a businessman in town, operated a thriving livery stable."

Gloria had signaled the waitress, Kristen, when Lanie arrived, and now she was beside them poised with a pen and notepad. Lanie ordered iced coffee. "I'll sip on this while you eat," she told her friend. "Where's your boss today? Why are you all by yourself?"

"He left for the day around ten this morning," she shrugged. "Didn't leave me any instructions, so decided to give myself some time off, too."

"How often does he do that?" Lanie asked.

"Never," Gloria said, sobering noticeably.

"He's upset about the old bridge," Lanie suggested by way of an excuse for his truancy.

Gloria shrugged again and leaned forward over her plate to look straight at Lanie. "I'd like to know what went down between that Irving fellow and Harry on Friday night."

"That was weird, wasn't it!" Lanie agreed. "Did he say anything about it to you?"

"From what I've observed, at least this first day back to work, he's hardly said a word to anyone about anything."

Gloria sat back then, and something caught her eye out on the street. Lanie turned and watched a man in a blue shirt just exiting a police cruiser that had pulled up in front of the restaurant. As he came around to step up onto the sidewalk, he looked up and made eye contact with Gloria, who immediately gave him a wave. "What a hunk our new Officer Robinson is," she said to Lanie as her cheeks took on a crimson blush.

"I guess," Lanie said with a scowl.

"You know him?"

"We've met. He's already asking a lot of questions about Meghan's disappearance."

"Yes, I heard they're opening that up again. Maybe that's what's bothering Harry."

Lanie turned her head when movement appeared in the periphery of her vision. "Speaking of bothering," she mumbled under her breath as Tyke Robinson started heading directly for their table.

He *was* a handsome man. She'd give Gloria that one. The free strand of dark wavy hair falling over his forehead, the piercing dark eyes above the firm jaw—classic Adonis, but Lanie didn't feel romantic stirrings when she looked at him, just a sweep of discomfort roiling around in her gut.

"Wow," he said when he'd reached them, "this must be my lucky day. Here are the two people I'd hoped to see soon, and both of you are here in one place just when I happened by. May I join you?"

"Absolutely," Gloria smiled and couldn't get up fast enough to move her salad, her lemon water, and herself over to the next chair by the window to allow Tyke a seat without the hassle of working his six-foot frame over and around one or the other of them.

Lanie sat silent, her discomfort growing by the second. Kristen came over all smiles, called Tyke by name, and took his order.

"Aren't you eating?" Tyke asked Lanie when the waitress had left.

Lanie told him simply that she had been on her way home after her exercise routine and had just come in to keep Gloria company. "But now that she has someone to chat with," she said, standing up, "I'll be on my way."

She drew three dollar bills from her pants pocket and placed them next to her iced coffee, and would have turned to leave except she heard Tyke say, "I'd appreciate it if you'd reconsider and stay for a few minutes." Both his serious tone and the dark eyes he had pinned on her were riveting. Afterwards, Lanie wasn't sure if it was a sense of urgency in his request or her own sense of civic duty to law enforcement that compelled her back into her chair… or maybe something else entirely. Anyway, she sat back down.

"Thank you," he said simply, his eye contact never wavering until she was seated again, when once more he addressed them both.

"You've no doubt heard I'm reopening the Murphy case," he said.

Both women nodded.

"Eventually, I'll need to go over some of the details with you that you remember from that night, but right now, I would like you to be candid about anything you've noticed in the twenty-five years since graduation; anything that may have triggered special notice and could be relevant to Meghan's disappearance."

When no one spoke, Tyke leaned back with a sigh. "Let me start off, then, and I'll try to be as candid as I can be. Meghan did not come in contact with a stranger that spring morning back in 1994. Someone she knew was involved."

"That's certainly candid, but how in the world did you come to that conclusion?" Lanie challenged him.

"Because Meghan's little sister heard two calm voices at six a.m. Had Meghan been threatened or kidnapped, there would not have been quiet conversation. There would have been either silence or screams."

"That's a guess, isn't it?" Lanie argued.

"After you're in this kind of work for a while, your instincts get sharpened to a common-sense point." Tyke's dark eyes grew blacker as his smoldering passion to solve this crime flared. "For twenty-five years, most of Narrownook believed in only two possibilities—either Meghan ran off with a lover, or Meghan was abducted by a stranger. They were easier answers to live with than the obvious two intelligent possibilities. Meghan was still wearing Harry's ring, right?" Tyke raised his brows in Lanie's direction.

Lanie nodded.

"Then common sense dictates that we have to disregard the unknown-lover scenario. No one runs off with another man while she's still wearing her boyfriend's class ring. I'm also scrapping the kidnapping theory because Katherine heard no screams, and records show no signs of a struggle."

"Katherine was only seven years old," Lanie argued. "She could have been half asleep. How serious should we take her statements?"

"Did you know the girl?" Tyke asked.

Both women nodded.

"Was she an intelligent child?"

Both nodded again.

"She's the only witness that we know of. We owe it to Meghan to believe her sister and approach this with a new perspective."

"Were you ever a lawyer?" Lanie asked. "Because you sound like one."

"I'm just a cop with a job to do," Tyke said. "I've been candid about where I stand on this. I'm hoping you'll give me the same courtesy."

"I'm concerned about what this whole reopened investigation business will do to this town," Lanie said, "specifically to innocent people who have carried the burden of suspicion placed on them by a biased section of the community to this day."

"You're talking about your friend Stan Russell," Tyke said.

"Stan and, to a lesser degree, Harry, I suppose," Lanie told him. "You're being candid. Are they suspects?"

"Persons of interest, yes," Tyke conceded.

Lanie looked over at Gloria, who had remained uncharacteristically silent. Now, Lanie saw that she had lost every bit of color in her face and seemed suddenly restless, as if her chair was becoming uncomfortable.

"I'm sorry," Gloria murmured, bracing her palms squarely against the tabletop to boost herself onto her feet. "I'm suddenly not feeling good. If you'll excuse me..." And she somehow propelled herself out into the aisle and weaved her way toward the restrooms.

That left Lanie and Tyke momentarily speechless and staring after her and then at each other.

"Did you always have this effect on people?" Lanie asked Tyke, managing an ironic smile.

"Only since my arrival in Narrownook," he told her, and his expression seemed to reflect a bit of regret mixed with a dash of chagrin.

"I have nothing to contribute, Officer Robinson, except my deeply held belief that Stan Russell is and has always been a fine person."

"I understand that you haven't been in this town for twenty-five years except for the occasional visit. I assume you're basing your opinion mostly on your early association with Russell."

Lanie agreed with a quick nod and a shrug.

"But you haven't mentioned Harry Olson," he said.

"I really didn't know him very well growing up."

"And now?"

"I'm not sure how to answer that. He seems to me like an unhappy man sometimes, still dealing with what he sees as a betrayal by a girl he thought he would spend the rest of his life with."

"Is that what he told you?"

"In so many words," Lanie nodded.

"And you found him credible?"

"Of course. I told you, he seemed—I guess *haunted* would be a good adjective to describe his demeanor the only time we talked about what happened to Meghan."

"When was that?"

"The night at the Jed. The night you interrupted us to tell Penelope to move her car. Before that, we had had dinner, and he had opened up to me briefly about how devastated he'd been at losing Meghan to another man."

"Is that what he said?"

"It was. And I saw the torment in his face, in his eyes."

"I appreciate your candor, Ms. Warren," Tyke said and sat back to allow Kristen to serve him the McKay's whopper burger deluxe plate that he had ordered.

Lanie watched him lift the top bun and smear a generous helping of catsup all over the patty, which was already flanked by a thick slice of onion.

"I'll go find Gloria and make sure she's okay," she said, pushing back her chair. "I truly hope you do find out what happened to Meghan, Officer Robinson, but I hope it will be without causing my friends any more unpleasantness."

"I will try to do it as painlessly as possible," Tyke said. He had been placing the top of the roll back on his garnished burger, and he took a moment to look up at Lanie. "I do have one more question before you go, though." He dusted his hands off on a white napkin, and Lanie held her breath and stayed seated.

"Your friend, Penelope Mageloo, can you tell me how to contact her?"

"She is not my friend," Lanie said defensively. "I'll try to find out from my mother. She's a daughter to one of my mother's close friends. I met her for the first time the same day you did."

With that, Lanie finally got to her feet and escaped to the other side of the restaurant in search of Gloria.

Tyke saw them leave a short time later as he enjoyed large bites of his deluxe burger. He saw Gloria shake off Lanie's attempt to help her down the stone steps to the sidewalk and saw her stumble a couple of times without the assistance.

His instincts told him that Gloria Jordan had a tale to tell, and he'd have to follow through on that even though it might be a bit painful to a woman who had been visibly shaken by the brief discussion they'd just had.

Maybe it meant that Olson would turn out to be the number-one suspect after all, so he could ease up on Russell.

He liked Lanie Warren, admired her dedication to her friends, wondered briefly if she was in love with Russell. Wondered if Russell would come out clean and get the girl in the bargain.

Wondered why the last part of that made him uncomfortable.

He didn't finish his lunch. He left a sizeable tip for Kristen and got back into his cruiser feeling uncharacteristically weary, and it wasn't even two in the afternoon yet.

CHAPTER 23

For the fifth night in a row, Lanie awoke startled from a dream. It was, as usual, in the hour of three a.m. In the dream tonight, she had been struggling with a bag of groceries as she wound her way up a steep set of familiar back stairs to a screen door that opened into a sparsely furnished living room. Somehow, she knew it was her third trip up those stairs that day. She also knew that her struggle was caused not only by the weight of the groceries she carried, but also by the baby she carried. She was seven months pregnant.

The other four nights of dreams had been similar reviews in sharp pictorial images of the six months of her life she had spent hiding her pregnancy in an obscure town in a state far away from her family, whom she had chosen to protect from the scorn of a daughter pregnant out of wedlock. Her self-deprecating scorn was painful enough; she didn't have to share it, to see it reflected in the eyes of the people she loved.

The dreams always left her weak and shaken. The very first dream had been the worst. It had occurred the night Amy divulged finding an ancestry match. In that dream, Lanie was in the bedroom off the kitchen of that three-room, second-floor apartment over a bar in the middle of a city, and someone was knocking on the bedroom door, which was also a fire exit into a common hallway at the front of the building.

When the knocking stopped, she got up from where she'd been lying on her bed and went to the window. Lifting a couple of slats of the yellowed venetian blind, she saw a figure dressed in a floor-length black winter coat walking away with a slow, gliding gait. It gave her the willies. It was late October, and the person could have been dressed for Halloween, but she knew it was her neighbor lady in the next apartment, whom Lanie often saw leaving the building. The woman had tried numerous times to make contact with her by slipping notes under the door when she wasn't rapping on it.

Lanie knew the dream had mirrored her feelings of loneliness and abandonment. She had dealt with a lot of that back then, and now she wanted desperately to shake off the haunting uneasiness tonight's dream had left her with, and so she threw on a bathrobe and went into the kitchen, turning on every light along the way. The bright Italian tiled floor and modern cabinetry leapt up and embraced her, helping to dispel her unease. A little.

As she made a cup of chamomile tea, she couldn't help but think about how she had waited all alone in a strange city for the baby to be born. She had friends who became contacts with her parents, and they had been willing to cover her story that she was teaching in a poverty-stricken area devoid of even phone service. Her friends were too far away to visit her, but they were immeasurably helpful in keeping her parents calm during her unprecedented lengthy absence, which unfortunately included the family holidays of Thanksgiving and Christmas that year.

By the time Lanie had finished two cups of tea, she was ready to try to get back to sleep. It was now four thirty, and a hint of light had begun to tease the eastern horizon.

It was the day the new Penobscot Narrows Bridge was opening and the Waldo–Hancock Bridge would close. Lanie hoped to take her mother down to the walkway to watch the ceremonies, but first she needed some more sleep.

* * *

It turned out to be a miserable day. Sheets of rain started coming down sideways, pushed by a violent wind about seven o'clock when Lanie woke to the sound of the heavy downpour lashing her high windows.

Her first thought was that her mother couldn't be out in this kind of deluge. Lanie showered and dressed quickly and went in search of her.

Mahitabelle was not happy to hear Lanie tell her that she couldn't be out in the rain. "I don't melt," she scoffed, waving away her daughter's misgivings.

When Lanie couldn't persuade her mother to give up the idea of seeing the opening, she went to the phone and dialed her friend Sarah.

She had reconnected with several of her high school chums in the last few weeks, and one of them was Sarah, who lived in the top-floor apartment of a building on Main Street that overlooked the harbor. She had often urged Lanie to visit and enjoy her view of the bridges and fort. Today would be a perfect opportunity to take advantage of the offer if Sarah didn't already have guests coming.

As it turned out, her friend had not been looking forward to watching the event by herself and was delighted at the thought of some company. "I'll put on a pot of coffee and defrost some homemade breakfast cakes," she told Lanie.

When they walked into Sarah's apartment an hour later, they were face-to-face with the fort and the bridges over the Penobscot through a series of high windows that lined the south wall of Sarah's home.

Lanie actually gasped.

"Isn't it wonderful?" Sarah grinned. "I love it here. I'm very fortunate to have found this place. And," she added, "I have binoculars for everyone."

Wet coats were hung to dry in the bathroom, coffee and coffee cake were placed on stands next to the easy chairs that were lined up in front of the living room windows, and the three women made themselves comfortable.

They had about a half hour to chat and were on their second cups of coffee when they noticed, through their binoculars, that a small crowd of people who had been standing in the middle of the Penobscot Narrows Bridge had raised their arms in unison as if cheering en masse.

"I'm going to open my windows," Sarah declared. "The rain seems to have diminished a bit, and maybe we can hear some of the goings-on."

When the windows were cranked open, the raspy sound of motors was carried to them across the water. They saw a line of what must have been about three dozen ancient cars creeping in very slow motion, bumper to bumper, along the Waldo–Hancock Bridge in the direction of Orphan Island. Their headlights made watery halos as they cruised like decrepit phantoms from a bygone era through the present midday mist.

It was a powerful symbolic exhibition. Seventy-five years ago, the same vehicles, with rumble seats rattling, had once crossed the span for the first time, and now they became the last cars to exit the once mighty bridge.

At this point, there were no dry eyes in the apartment, but the women were suddenly distracted by a line of fire trucks and emergency apparatus they later learned belonged to a dozen neighboring towns, moving single file toward Orphan Island, the first vehicles to cross the new Penobscot Narrows Bridge. Their lights flashed in syncopation and their sirens blasted and wailed through the downpour that had resumed even more torrentially.

"I could not have missed this," Mahitabelle Warren told Sarah as the visitors shrugged into their rain gear to take their leave about two o'clock. They were having trouble finding words enough to thank Sarah for allowing them to share her cozy home with a perfect view of the historic moment.

Lanie instructed her mother to wait in the vestibule while she brought the car over from a parking space across the street. She shoved the hood of her raincoat up over her head, peering out from under the soaked drapery as she looked both ways before entering the crosswalk. Just as she lifted her right foot to step out, a big SUV was suddenly upon her doing a rate of speed far above the limit.

Lanie jumped back, but not in time to avoid being further soaked with a cascade of dirty road water. She glared after the offending vehicle, then gave a wave of thanks to both lanes of traffic that had stopped to allow her to cross.

Five minutes later, she had retrieved her car and was getting out at the entrance of Sarah's building to escort her mother, when she spotted the same SUV coming back down the street. As it went by, the driver waved. For a minute, Lanie thought he was being flip, that he knew he had almost hit her and was mocking her. Then she recognized him. Ricky Irving!

This time she stared after him again, but only because she was having a difficult time equating him with a bright-red, brand-new 2019 SUV.

"That's Ricky's new car," a voice said beside her, and Lanie looked down at her mother, who had walked out on her own and now stood in the pouring rain with a flimsy transparent plastic cap tied under her chin, staring after Ricky's flickering taillights as they disappeared down Main Street.

"You're going to get soaking wet," Lanie scolded as she grabbed her mother's arm and scooted her into her car.

As she settled into the passenger seat with a sigh, Mahitabelle reminded her daughter again that she didn't melt.

Once Lanie had gotten behind the wheel, she didn't start the car. She leaned back and sat motionless, staring vacantly at the rain streaming down the windshield. Finally, she looked over at her mother. "How can Ricky afford a new car, and a Cadillac SUV, no less?"

"I like Sue's better," Mahitabelle declared. "It's pink. Custom-made pink. Like Elvis's cars."

"What's pink?" Lanie asked, gaping at her mother.

"Sue's new SUV. Looks like it could have come out of Graceland."

"How do you know that?"

"Sue took me for a ride day before yesterday."

"You never told me you'd been out for a ride with Sue."

"I have my life. I don't necessarily have to tell you everything," Mahitabelle said, giving her daughter a smug grin. And she emphasized the word *everything*. "I wasn't deliberately keeping it from you, dear. I just haven't had a chance to mention it," she shrugged.

Lanie nodded numbly and started the car. "Did Sue tell you how they happened to be able to possess not one but two new SUVs?"

"I think she said something about a rich uncle who's dead."

"Well, that's as good a story as any, I guess. Certainly better than trying to convince everyone that he got a good trade-in on his corroded black van, circa 1950."

On the way back to the house, Lanie remembered the yard sale items Sue and Ricky had bought last weekend. She had thought that was strange. Now, add two brand-new Cadillacs, and it got even stranger.

"Sue's really excited about the new home they're building up on the corner of Pleasant and Surry," Mahitabelle said as Lanie reached the house and steered the car into the second bay.

"*What?*" Lanie asked, staring at her mother with a dumbfounded expression.

"Sue says it will be modeled after the Johnson house."

"The mansion?" Lanie was incredulous.

"That's what she said."

"Handyman jobs must be getting very lucrative," Lanie sneered as she wondered how to find out more about Ricky Irving's "dead uncle."

CHAPTER 24

THE FOLLOWING MONDAY, CREWS DESCENDED ON THE DOOMED WALDO–Hancock Bridge to begin the demolition. A little-known fact is that federal rules make it necessary to photograph, in detail, historic structures before any destruction begins, so the Maine DOT teams stood in wait as cameras began filming every nook and cranny of the bridge.

At ten o'clock, one unlucky cameraman entered the base of the pylon on the Orphan Island side.

At ten oh five, a call came into the Narrownook Police Department. Tyke Robinson took the call and summoned Chief Brody, who was still at home after a late shift the night before. The two men met at the bridge at ten fifteen and helped string the crime tape around the area near pylon number one.

Photographing continued elsewhere, but the demolition company was told to leave until further notice. No explanation was offered at that time, but newspapers and television crews miraculously began arriving by noon. They'd been tipped off by passersby, curious to know the reason for the appearance of the crime tape.

On the six o'clock news, all Maine TV stations were broadcasting that a brief announcement would be coming from Captain Ted Brody of Narrownook and Sheriff Tommy Tate of Hancock County by seven p.m.

Just before eight o'clock that evening, as the sun began setting over the scene, dozens of eager journalists, their cameras flashing, and over a hundred spectators were gathered in front of two microphones where Captain Brody and Sheriff Tate had finally made an appearance.

The two men gave short statements that capsulized four simple facts. Bones had been found in the equipment room of pylon number one on Orphan Island, and they were already en route to an out-of-state facility for analysis. No further information would be known until that process was completed, which would take in the neighborhood of ten days. In the meantime, the removal of the bridge would be on hold.

Immediately, the reporters began shouting questions. When was the last time anyone was in the equipment room? Were there any other pieces of evidence found with the bones, like clothing or jewelry? Any identification? Were the bones scattered or were they, in fact, skeletal? If a skeleton, could the sex and/or the age be determined?

To all of these questions, the responses were the same: either "We do not know," or "We cannot say at this time," or "We must wait for the forensic report."

Lanie and her mother, like most of the folks in Narrownook, watched the broadcast live on a Bangor station that had interrupted regular programming to bring this momentous piece of local news to the concerned public.

When it was over at eight thirty, Lanie felt shivers radiating throughout her body. "No one has gone missing in this area except Meghan," she commented weakly.

"Maybe some homeless person we wouldn't know about," Mahitabelle suggested.

"When was the last time you saw a homeless person in or around Narrownook?" she said pointedly.

Mahitabelle thought for only a moment before she just shrugged.

For the rest of the evening, the two women turned off the TV and tried to enjoy a game of Scrabble. But even Mahitabelle's mind and heart were not into her favorite contest.

* * *

Meanwhile, Harry Olson had consumed two scotches during the thirty-minute broadcast. Once his television was silenced, his phone started ringing nonstop. He made no attempt to answer any of the calls but continued to drink until he was snoring on the couch, still fully clothed but peacefully oblivious.

CHAPTER 25

THAT NIGHT, LANIE DIDN'T HAVE ANY DREAMS ABOUT THE TIME SHE'D GONE into hiding when she was pregnant, but she did not have a restful sleep. She found herself awake several times, but if her arousals were triggered by dreams, she had no memory of them at two a.m., four a.m., and seven a.m., when she finally got out of bed with a nagging headache and a weariness that hinted she hadn't slept at all.

She drank three cups of coffee during the time she showered, dressed, and applied makeup to camouflage the dark circles under her eyes.

She had gotten a call yesterday from Gloria Jordan begging her for an enormous favor. Tyke was meeting with her at one o'clock the next day, she said, and she wanted Lanie to sit in on the meeting.

Remembering how unnerved Gloria had become the last time she'd spoken with Tyke, and knowing now that the discovery of bones was one more thing to make any discussion of Meghan Murphy even more difficult, Lanie had agreed to join her. "But on one condition," she had qualified, "be straight with him. If there is anything that you know that might be relevant to his investigation, tell him. I think he's probably one of the good guys."

Lanie spent the bulk of the morning figuring costs per person for the reunion dinner scheduled in August at McKay's Restaurant and licking envelopes containing information about the event that were being sent to each '94 graduate.

After a quick lunch, she checked on her mother one last time before she left for the one o'clock meeting. She found Gloria still in her car outside the police station, waiting for her to arrive. "I didn't want to go in alone," she confessed.

When they reached the glass door, they found it locked. "I haven't been in a police station for years," Lanie said. "I guess even police have to keep their doors locked nowadays when fewer people are showing them the respect they deserve," she said as she rang the bell.

It was Tyke who responded. He had posted himself near the entrance anticipating Gloria's arrival, and exhibited momentary surprise by raised eyebrows when he saw Lanie. Then an impish grin curved his mouth and spread an amused glimmer into his dark eyes. "Didn't dare to face me alone," he joked to Gloria as he stepped back to admit them.

That made Lanie smile, but Gloria quite clearly tensed as they followed Tyke into a small room at the rear of the facility.

The women took seats side by side at the nearest end of a long conference table. Tyke pulled a chair out on the opposite side but did not sit down.

"Can I get you a cup of coffee or a soda before we get started?" he asked.

When they both declined, he sat down, too, and began by addressing Lanie. "I'm going to direct my questions to Gloria, but any time you want to jump in with anything, please feel free to do that," he told her, his expression now a serious one again.

Lanie nodded, feeling the sudden shift into professional mode.

"How long have you known Harry Olson?" was Tyke's first question.

"Since before kindergarten," came the stilted reply.

"Did you date at all in high school?"

"He was Meghan's boyfriend exclusively."

"When did you start seeing him socially?"

"About a year and a half after Meghan disappeared."

"Can you pinpoint what it was that later ended your romantic involvement?"

"It was a gradual drifting apart, I guess," Gloria answered hesitantly.

"But you ended up being his secretary when he became mayor."

"We remained friends."

"Did he date others after you?"

"Of course. We both dated afterward."

"How did his dating others make you feel?"

"At that point, he was just a friend again—like back in grade school."

"Give me your impression of how he dealt with what happened to Meghan."

"He was devastated. I don't think he ever really got over it, even to this day."

"Tell me what you have observed that makes you think he never got over it."

There was a long pause. Gloria sat back and sighed. Lanie reached out and briefly put her hand on her shoulder. When Gloria looked over at her, Lanie gave her an encouraging smile and a quick nod.

"He had low moods," Gloria murmured.

"Describe what you mean."

"He was quick to anger—over little things; often over nothing, really."

"Would you say it was a change in his personality after Meghan disappeared?"

"I didn't know him well enough in high school to say," Gloria shrugged.

When Tyke sat back in his chair, Lanie wondered if they'd reached a dead end. But no; he took a breath and leaned forward again.

"Remember how I talked about being candid at McKay's last week?" he asked.

Gloria nodded.

"I want you to give this next question a lot of thought, and try to be as candid as you can be when you answer. Did you ever consider, for even a minute, in the last twenty-five years, that Harry might know more about Meghan Murphy's disappearance than he has let on?"

"Of course not!" came the defensive response. Too quickly.

Tyke sat back again and waited for what seemed like a long time before he spoke again.

"Why do I sense there is something…something that may really be nothing…but something that has bothered you over the years that you're not saying?" Tyke remained sitting back with his arms folded in a relaxed pose, but with a look of deep concentration—or was it concern?—on his face.

Gloria shrugged again and squirmed a bit in her chair, beginning to appear the way she had at McKay's before rushing from the dining room.

Tyke turned to Lanie. "Has she ever confided in you about any misgivings she had about Harry Olson?" he asked.

Lanie shook her head and opened her mouth to say something, but Gloria spoke up. "It was just a dream once," she said.

"You had a dream?" Tyke asked, sitting forward again.

"Harry did. When we were a couple." And she told them about the night she woke up while he was having a conversation with Meghan. She included the arm gestures she had witnessed.

"Is that what finally ended your affair with Olson?" Tyke asked kindly.

"That and his anger issues, I suppose," Gloria acknowledged. "He's not an easy man to live with."

"If you think of anything else…" Tyke ventured, standing to signal the end of the meeting. "Sometimes things get tamped down and hidden for years. If anything else surfaces, you need to let me know, Ms. Jordan, but you've been a big help today. I appreciate your cooperation."

Gloria nodded and didn't try to disguise her desire to flee the place. She was at the front door before Lanie had gotten out of the room.

At the conference-room doorway, Tyke reached out and placed a hand on Lanie's arm, managing to delay her exit a bit longer. "I appreciate your help today, too," he said. "I know your support was key in helping Gloria open up to me. Thank you."

146

For a moment, the dark eyes that could be hard and riveting were warm and genuine, and Lanie felt her cheeks begin to burn.

She never blushed!

She was too old to blush!

Now it was her turn to escape the building. Later, she remembered muttering a stupid, "You're welcome," before she, too, fled.

She found Gloria sobbing into a tissue outside. "I've never told anyone that story before," she said to Lanie as she swiped at her tears. "It felt good, actually," she said, and she was suddenly laughing as she wiped her wet cheeks.

CHAPTER 26

THE OPENING OF THE PENOBSCOT NARROWS OBSERVATORY, SCHEDULED to be held that Saturday, was put on hold. Since the discovery of the bones, there had been an influx of people swarming the bridge areas, and authorities could not deal with an extra attraction that would increase crowds to unmanageable sizes.

Historic preservationists from several states had descended on the area overnight to challenge the building or destruction of anything until an analysis of the bones was concluded. "The pylons may be sitting on old farmsteads that have family cemeteries in their yards," the historians worried.

Then there were the groups afraid that the bones might signal Indian burial grounds, which under no circumstances could be disturbed. Both groups were in the area to make sure sacred ground was preserved regardless of any cost that might be exacted by the halting of the work.

Lanie had put off a talk with her daughter regarding the results from AAAA for too long. With the postponement of the observatory opening, the day had been freed up, and she had no reason to wait any further. So, early that Saturday morning, over coffee and omelettes on the porch of a popular restaurant overlooking the harbor, they had a chance to talk.

There was a lot of movement on the bridges even at the early hour of seven a.m. when they arrived. The weather was already July warm, with a small breeze affording a bit of comfort as they sipped coffee and watched the activity across a river that lay still as glass.

Being aware of other patrons at nearby tables, Lanie spoke in an uncharacteristically low voice as she prefaced her confession with a firm qualifier. "What I tell you," she began, "I ask that you not share with your grandmother—not yet, anyway," she instructed. And then she told her that she had had a child, a son, out of wedlock when she was too young and too poor to raise a family.

"Oh, Mom," Amy responded, her eyes filling with tears as she heard about her mother's isolation far away from home or friends and how she was virtually forced to deal with the pregnancy by herself.

"Did you ever consider abortion?" Amy asked.

"Briefly. I was scared and wanted my situation to suddenly be over, but not that way. I could find no justification for killing a child."

As they kept talking, Amy got a little peeved. "You weren't going to ever tell me I had a brother, were you!" she accused. "I always wished I wasn't an only child. Why couldn't you tell me?"

"I'm sorry," Lanie nodded. "I should have told you when you reached adulthood. I guess I was still trying to protect Grandmother from any embarrassment."

"Like you were doing back then," Amy nodded.

"I thought I'd wait..."

"Until Grandmother..."

"Yes," Lanie acknowledged. "Tell me what you would like to do with this information now that you have it. Where would you like to go with it?"

"I'm not sure. That fellow must be your son, and my brother. I guess we should wait to see where he wants to take this. The fact that he's here, that he's tracked us down, shows that he's interested, but so far, he's kept his distance."

"I think we should respect that," Lanie said, and Amy agreed.

They finished their breakfast and went back to the house. As they got out of the car in the first bay, Lanie admonished her daughter one last time: "Remember, not a word to Grandmother," she said.

They found that Mahitabelle was already dressed and had applied her usual touch of going-to-town eye makeup. She was sitting in her recliner with what little was left of her cereal and coffee on the TV tray beside her.

"You're up and dressed early," Amy said.

"I have great news," Grandmother announced, all smiles. "Guess who's in town!"

"Who?" they chorused, looking at each other in alarm as they immediately equated their conversation, just concluded, with Mahitabelle's remark.

"Penelope Mageloo called me first thing this morning from the Buckston Motel. She's back," she said.

Lanie's look of alarm intensified. "What's she doing back?"

"She said something about being a member of a historical group interested in doing what's right about the discovery of the bones on the island. I'm going with her this morning to the library, introduce her to Pauline, our librarian, and help her, if I can, sort through some maps and old chronicles that may provide assistance to their mission."

"Is she picking you up?" Lanie asked, trying to keep her voice positive for her mother's sake.

As she asked the question, they all heard the sound of a car door slamming, and seconds later, the front doorbell chimed.

Amy answered it and ushered Penelope in. The woman didn't stop gushing over Mahitabelle, exclaiming how wonderful it was to see her and hugging her numerous times. She kept thanking her for agreeing to escort her to the Narrownook Public Library and introducing her to the right people.

Lanie wondered who Penelope envisioned to be the "right people," since the librarian would be the only person there with the wherewithal to guide them to appropriate materials.

Their visitor hadn't acknowledged either Lanie or her daughter until Lanie spoke up, interrupting Penelope's fourth embrace of her mother, which allowed Mahitabelle to sit back down for a rest.

"Nice to see you again," Lanie lied.

Penelope turned and looked startled to find anyone else in the room. "Oh, yes, Elaine," she said, "and...uh..."

"Amy," Amy prompted.

Lanie didn't even bother to correct Penelope's misnomer. She was, at the moment, trying to keep her distracting hidden voice of warning on a lower frequency as it screamed that chaos was about to begin again.

Again? Lanie mentally replied after taking a quick tally of all the chaotic things that had already descended on them since she'd arrived for the summer. The list seemed endless already. So what was one more dilemma? Except that this one would be orchestrated by a dingbat. What in the world was Penelope doing on a historical committee, anyway? She'd be better suited for a *hysterical* committee.

"How did you become part of a historic organization?" Lanie asked in a voice she hoped bordered on polite.

"I'm studying archaeology and naturally belong to many such groups, Janie," Penelope huffed. "This one is the New York chapter of the United National Historic Preservationists League. U.N.H.P.L."

"That's quite a mouthful," Lanie said. "I think you do well to remember such a lengthy title. By the way, my name is pretty easy. Not Elaine. Not Janie." Lanie caught a glimpse of Amy looking aghast at her mother's rude behavior. "Lanie," she said, poking herself with her thumb.

"Let's go," Penelope said to Mahitabelle without further comment.

Mahitabelle pushed herself up and out of her chair with a sweet smile and declared she'd go get her purse.

"I'll get it for you, Grandmother," Amy said, moving toward the hallway.

"That's all right, dear," Mahitabelle said. "I've got to put lipstick on. I'll be right back," she added in Penelope's direction before she left the room.

Penelope turned to face Lanie. "Where is your handsome friend lately?" she asked.

"Which one?" Lanie asked.

Penelope paused to give her a look of disbelief that implied that even one handsome friend of Lanie's defied logic. After an exasperated sigh, she hissed out, "The mayor. I tried to speak to him several times yesterday after I arrived and again this morning. I was told each time that he wasn't in his office."

"I'm sure he's extra busy with this business over on the island. He'll probably have little else to deal with until that matter is resolved."

"That's one of the issues my committee and I need to see him about, of course. Then there's another matter that has just come to our attention."

"Your parking ticket?"

"Hmph!" Penelope snorted, waving the idea away with a skinny hand. "I'm talking about that disgusting monument you people have erected just as you come into the heart of Narrownook."

Lanie scowled and shook her head to indicate she had no idea what Penelope was talking about.

"You know—the graveyard with the black wrought-iron fence around it just before the Buckston Motel where I'm staying."

"Oh, yes, the famous grave of our founder."

"It's hideous, is what it is. Such a spectacle to be out there for all to see."

"I don't think I understand."

"A woman's leg is on that tombstone. It's immoral, degrading to womankind, embarrassing for a town to maintain such a sexually offensive display on such sacred ground."

Lanie almost laughed. "It's just some kind of flaw in the stone."

"It's indecent, is what it is. It should be removed."

"I think they've tried that, but it keeps coming back."

"Well, I intend to bring the matter up to the mayor when the committee and I meet with him," Penelope declared. "Where in the world is your mother?" she suddenly railed.

"Right here," Mahitabelle said as she strolled into the room looking quite stylish for her age, in a two-piece suit, her pocketbook on her arm and a sweet smile still on her face.

"Have a good time," Lanie told her. "Call me if you get tired, and I'll come rescue you," she said quietly into her ear when she hugged her mother goodbye.

"I see what you mean about Cousin Penelope," Amy commented when the door had closed behind them. "She *is* a little out there."

"Not far enough out there to suit me," Lanie complained as the two of them watched the car weave in slow motion out of the driveway. "At least she didn't make Grandmother get out and direct traffic while she did that."

"She wouldn't do that," Amy said, turning to stare at her mother. "Would she?" she had to ask when she saw the serious expression on Lanie's face.

CHAPTER 27

MAHITABELLE ACCOMPANIED PENELOPE A COUPLE OF TIMES DURING THAT next week whenever she visited the library. By Friday, when Penelope still had not been able to see Harry Olson, Mahitabelle went with her to the town office to use her influence with her friend, the mayor, to persuade him to meet with her. Surprisingly, Gloria informed them that Olson had not been in all week. He had been at home nursing a head cold. "You know how difficult summer colds can be to shake off," she had told them.

* * *

That night, Lanie moved a few of her clothes and personal items over to the main house because Amy had left directly from work that afternoon to spend the weekend with friends in Boston. Lanie would camp out in her daughter's room to be closer to and within earshot of Mahitabelle until Amy returned on Sunday.

The night was humid, and in the upstairs bedroom, even with two fans going and all the windows, including both skylights, wide open, Lanie still could not keep cool enough to sleep well. She kept waking up about every hour. Around two a.m., she padded downstairs to the kitchen for a glass of water.

When she got to the main floor, she peeked in on her mother, found her sleeping comfortably, and was about to turn toward the kitchen when she heard what sounded like something falling in the living room to her right.

She flipped the light switch on the wall beside the front-room archway and went in. Her breath caught in her throat and her hands flew up to cover her gaping mouth at the sight of a man standing in the middle of the living room!

"What are you doing here?" she screamed.

"Looking for my hammer," Ricky answered calmly with a casual shrug, as if it was only natural for him to be standing there in the dark at two a.m.

"Looking for a hammer? Looking for a *hammer*? Looking for a hammer in our living room?" Lanie said, still screaming.

"Yeah, you remember. I lost it here the day you spooked me and made me hit my thumb. I need it back. I'm building a new house, you know."

"And you thought you'd find the hammer in our living room?" Lanie heard herself caterwauling, but she couldn't help it. "How did you get in here? Tell me that!" she bellowed.

Ricky gestured toward the front door. "Through there," he said. "It was unlocked."

Lanie looked at the door and saw that the dead bolt was in its upright position, indicating that the door was locked.

Of course it was locked! She knew it was locked! She had locked every friggin' door in the house before they went to bed!

"The dead bolt is on! That door is locked!" she shrieked.

"Well, it's locked *now*," Ricky said with an exasperating nod of his head, still speaking in that infuriatingly arrogant voice. "I made sure I locked it once I got in here."

"You broke into a house in the dead of night and locked the door after you got inside?" Lanie screamed. "That's insane. Do you hear yourself? You're crazy!"

Ricky rose up on his toes to peer down at her with a condescending look. "This time of night," he said professorially, "it's not safe being in a house with unlocked doors."

"You are Narrownook's village idiot," Lanie yelled. She had been rooted in one spot since the moment she'd entered the room and found him standing there, but now she began to move toward the other side of the room; to a phone sitting on the counter of the breakfast nook.

"I wish you'd stop shouting at me," Ricky griped. "It's really making me nervous. I can't see what all the fuss is about, anyway."

"You can't see what all the fuss is about? Are you *kidding* me? You're standing in the dark, at two a.m., in my freaking living room, and you can't see what all the fuss is about?"

Lanie hit 911.

"Kinda late to be calling anybody at this hour, don't you think?" Ricky said, keeping his eye on her and beginning to back slowly toward the door.

"Lanie Warren. Seventy-four Pleasant Street. There's been a break-in," she said in a modulated voice that surprised even her.

Ricky Irving turned around and took several long strides toward the exit. "I don't know what you're gettin' so almighty excited about," he growled back at her as he released the dead bolt.

"Go ahead, leave, you idiot. I know where you live, and I'll send them right over."

Ricky had a bit of trouble unsnapping the screen door lock and lost a couple of seconds there, but finally he was able to get out onto the front walk. Just as he made a beeline into the street, a cruiser, with its lights flashing, had to swerve to miss hitting him.

Ricky took off running in earnest. Tyke Robinson leaped out of the squad car and tackled him in the Morrisons' front yard.

"Is this the culprit?" Tyke asked Lanie after he had cuffed him and dragged him back to the Warrens', where Lanie was standing on the porch.

"That's Ricky Irving. I found him in my living room when I came downstairs to check on my mother and get a glass of water about fifteen minutes ago."

Suddenly, Lanie didn't feel so good. She had started to shake. Then, she looked down at herself and realized, for the first time, that she had on only her skimpy baby-doll pajamas. She had been so warm fifteen minutes ago. Now she was freezing, not to mention indecent.

"Go get a robe on," Tyke instructed, trying to make himself appear completely disinterested in her summer-sheer nightwear.

"I'll make this clown comfortable in the cruiser and be right back in."

"You think you got yourself a criminal, don't you, Hot-Shot," Ricky snarled as Robinson grabbed his arm and began jerking him toward the car. "I'll have you know I'm a personal friend of the mayor," Lanie heard him say as she rushed upstairs.

When she returned, Tyke was seated in a chair with the familiar notepad on his knee, scribbling something.

"Can I get you something cold to drink?" Lanie asked him. "I've got Pepsi and ice water. I need some ice water."

"Ice water sounds wonderful," he said, looking up at her. She had donned a light-blue, floor-length smock. He thought she looked beautiful. His next thought was that he had to get over his obsession with this woman. He hadn't been attracted to anyone for going on three years. Even before she'd appeared tonight in the see-through shorts and halter set, he'd felt the stirrings. The reality was that he was only here temporarily for this one case. The way things were going, he'd be back in Boston before the summer was over.

That made him think of Brody. The captain would miss him and be pissed when he learned that, from the very beginning, he'd never intended to make Narrownook his home for very long. He could only hope that once the case was wrapped up, Brody would understand, and his appreciation about the cold case being solved would soften his anger at being hoodwinked.

However, if he didn't curb his feelings for Lanie Warren, Ted Brody wouldn't be the only one regretting he was leaving. He was already beginning to be sorry he had to leave Lanie, who had begun making him feel alive again. He'd gone through the last three years thinking for sure he'd died himself that day his wife passed away.

Lanie brought tall glasses of water full of ice that clinked enticingly when she set them on a stand between two chairs and sat down.

"What time did you find him here?" Tyke asked when they had both taken copious gulps of the liquid. "Did he say anything that might give you a hint about what he was up to?"

"He was looking for his hammer."

Tyke stopped writing to regard Lanie with skepticism.

"That's what he said," she shrugged. "I should tell you that I've heard him brag about having keys to half the houses in Narrownook. That has always bothered me, but I can assure you he never had a key to this place. That makes me worry about how he did get in. As you remember, this isn't the first time I've had suspicions that someone had been getting into the house."

And Lanie finally told Tyke about hearing a door slam in the middle of the night, and about the morning Harry Olson had been able to walk right in through the screen door and the front entrance that she knew she had locked.

Tyke listened and jotted down more notes.

"I'll have a lot more worries after this until I find out how he got in tonight. There isn't a key to the screen door, so that should disprove a stolen key theory."

Tyke paused again, his pen in midair. "Those are the exits, then," he mused. He closed the pad with a snap and stood up. "You needn't worry tonight," he told her. "He'll be with me tonight. I'll be interrogating him, or he'll be locked in a cell. Tomorrow… that would be later today, I guess, we'll come over and do a more thorough job looking around here. He did some work in the house a while ago, didn't he?"

Lanie nodded.

"I'll see you, say, around ten a.m.," he said. "You get some sleep now," he added, and for a second, the expression in his eyes shifted from serious cop to a look full of tenderness. Lanie was surprised to feel a rush of warmth sweep through her in response. Like the last time.

CHAPTER 28

HARRY WAS RUDELY AWAKENED BY THE RINGING OF THE PHONE AT NINE o'clock Saturday morning. For a minute, he just lay there letting it ring. When the caller began leaving a message on his answering machine, he decided he'd better pick up.

"Yeah," he growled. His head was throbbing and the voice, sharp in his ear, made it worse.

"I'm sorry, Harry," the female police dispatcher said, "I know you've been sick with a cold, but we have Richard Irving here, who insists, for some reason, that you'd want to know that he is being held for breaking and entering."

"What the hell!"

"I'm sorry, sir."

"Put him on the phone," Harry mumbled.

"What?"

"Let me talk to him."

"Yes, sir, just a moment."

This was followed by quite a lengthy period of time during which Harry heard low voices and some shuffling sounds. Finally, a too-familiar voice said hello.

"What the hell did you do?" Harry railed.

"Something stupid," Ricky acknowledged in an adolescent tone.

"I'll say. What are you bothering me for?"

"I need your influence to get me outta here. Today. This morning."

"Don't bother me again, but I'll see what I can do," Harry groaned, and hung up.

This was the way it was going to be from now on, Harry thought as he collapsed back on his pillow. If he didn't help that menace to society, there was no telling what he'd do in retaliation. He might spill the beans, or at least throw out enough innuendos to raise suspicions.

He had grappled with what his next move should be all week as he drank himself into one oblivion after another. When he finally came out of every coma, he couldn't make heads or tails of anything he'd been trying to decide.

Any day now, the bones would be identified. Unless, by some miracle, they turned out to be ancient settlers or Native Americans, he'd have to go to Plan B.

Or was it Plan C?

Whatever, he needed a clear head when the time came, so starting today, there'd be no more drinking. He'd get busy putting together a step-by-step method of getting out of Dodge, if it should come to that. In the meantime, he had to get back to normal activity so *he* didn't arouse suspicion.

* * *

When the doorbell rang Saturday morning at ten fifteen, Lanie opened the door to Tyke just as a Russell Construction truck pulled in behind his cruiser in the driveway.

"I've asked Stan Russell to go over your house with a fine-tooth comb," Tyke explained when he saw Lanie's surprised look. "If there's an unknown access, he should be able to find it."

Lanie introduced Tyke to her mother as the two men entered the living room, where Mahitabelle was in her recliner reading the morning's *Bangor Daily*.

Then the two men disappeared for quite a while. When they returned, both Lanie and her mother looked up expectantly from the Scrabble game they'd been playing.

"Did Ricky Irving do any work in the bedroom on the main floor?" Tyke asked, gesturing toward Mahitabelle's area.

"He built that wonderful new walk-in closet for me," Mahitabelle told him.

"He built more than that, by the looks," Tyke told them. "He built his own version of a doggie door."

"Where?" the women chimed in unison.

"Stan will go outside, and you both come with me," Tyke said, leaning to assist Lanie's mother as she began pushing herself out of her chair.

Lanie and Mahitabelle followed Tyke into Mahitabelle's bedroom, where he slid open the walk-in closet door to a long and deep mini-room with clothes racks on either side. Along the back wall, which was an outside wall, a higher rack had been installed to accommodate longer hanging garments like formal dresses and winter coats. These items were mostly stored in bulky garment bags for extra protection.

Tyke swept apart a section of those clothes to expose the wall. "Unless you look carefully," he told them, "you'd never notice this fine line that can be traced about two and a half feet up and two feet across. You miss it because Ricky was clever enough to put fancy paneling on the walls in here to distract the eye."

As he was speaking, Robinson had been tracing the rectangle he was indicating with his index finger. "It's a door," he said.

No sooner had he uttered those words than the wall fell open, exposing a patch of green lawn, and there was Stan Russell leaning over to look in at them.

"Russ just hit the 'open' button outside," Tyke explained to their horrified expressions. "There are two open and close buttons. One set is in here," he pointed at two silver spots to the right of what had been the horizontal line, "and two are against the foundation outside. The hinges are outside, too. They're placed low up against the foundation and camouflaged with paint that matches the color of the siding. This one," Tyke raised his finger to the silver spot under its matching mate above him, "closes the door." Tyke signaled Russ and gave him a few seconds to stand out of the way before he poked the lower metallic dot.

The door lifted on command, and the women heard only a muted snap as Tyke guided the section into place.

A minute later, Russ let himself in the front door and returned to the bedroom.

"Do me a favor," Lanie said to them. "Go through that one more time, but this time, after you have it opened, let it close on its own."

Russ touched the top silver button, and they watched the wall fall open again. When he hit the second button, Lanie closed her eyes and waited for the sound. When it came, she looked at Tyke. "That's what I heard that night I told you about. The sound was muffled over in my apartment, but I know that was the thud I heard. I could tell that it wasn't a heavy door that had closed. At the time, I thought it might have been a cabinet door somewhere over here in the main house."

"We've got Irving dead to rights," Tyke said, and Lanie saw his jaw tighten.

"I guess he'll have to stay where he is a little longer," Mahitabelle commented with a smile. Lanie had filled her mother in on last night's two a.m. drama. Amy, in fact, was now on her way home early after hearing about the break-in.

Tyke spoke into his portable radio and the women were surprised to hear him give the order to pick up Richard Irving.

"Isn't he still in jail?" Lanie wanted to know.

"From what I understand," Tyke said, "the mayor pulled some strings and got him released just before I got here."

Russ and Lanie exchanged puzzled looks. "Harry and Ricky hardly know each other," Russ said.

"And they certainly don't like each other," Lanie added.

Both were suddenly remembering the strange scene in the Jed Prouty a few weeks ago between Ricky and Harry. Surely Tyke would remember it, too...

Tyke asked Stan Russell how soon he could secure the closet entry. When Russell said he could do it before the end of the day, Tyke asked that he give him an hour to let the department photograph the site as a crime scene.

Lanie, initially dismayed to hear that Ricky had been released, now breathed a sigh of relief to know that she wouldn't find anyone standing in the middle of the living room in the middle of the night ever again.

CHAPTER 29

TED BRODY GOT THE RESULTS ON WEDNESDAY, JULY 31ST. IT WAS TYKE Robinson's day off, but Brody immediately called him in. Fifteen minutes later, when Tyke stepped into his boss's office, one look at the official document in his captain's hand and a second look up at his tense jaw, and he knew.

"It's Meghan, isn't it," he said.

"It's Meghan," Brody nodded soberly. "I've called Katherine Murphy already. She'll be here as soon as she can throw a few things into a suitcase and make the four-hour trip. I've arranged for the remains to be brought back to Narrownook for burial. The Murray Funeral Home has been notified, and they're making preparations. Based on what you've learned in your investigation and at the crime scene, how do you read this now?"

"Unless she went in there by herself, and someone walked by, saw the bar out of its brackets and put it back on, I'd say it's a deliberate case of murder. Why would she even go to the island that early in the morning? I wager that someone deliberately lured her there, got her inside that tool room, and then barred her exit. I've been in communication with the DOT. They tell me that no one's been authorized to go into that space for over thirty years, which is too bad. If there'd been someone regularly going in and out in 1994, they might have found her in time."

"You still concentrating on just two suspects?"

"Russell or Olson," Tyke nodded.

"And the motive?"

"Vindictiveness," Tyke said. "The dictionary describes vindictiveness as unforgiving. That would match the mindset of someone who would do such a heinous act. Vengeance is a better description, in my opinion. Vengeance is described as violent retribution. This crime was heinous *and* violent when you allow yourself to visualize what that poor girl endured for what was surely an excruciatingly long period of time."

"Your two suspects are two of our finest citizens," Brody reminded him, shaking his head back and forth in slow motion. "Do you think either one of them could have orchestrated this? Could either of them have been cold-blooded enough to live with themselves while allowing this unspeakable act to play out? Could either have spent the days that followed in normal routines, knowing what that poor girl was suffering and not lift a finger to rescue her?"

"Sometimes love makes people do terrible things," Tyke said, "and sometimes love gone bad can make a certain type of person snap. Teenage love can be a particularly destabilizing emotion for immature minds. The fact that he didn't go back for her shows extreme vindictiveness, so yes, cold-blooded describes our villain to a T."

"Some think Russell was getting even for being rebuffed," Brody mused out loud, "but this would be a pretty extreme reaction to rejection, especially for someone as level-headed as Stan Russell."

"I agree," Tyke nodded.

"So you're leaning more toward Olson?"

"He and Meghan had been dating exclusively through four years of high school, and suddenly she breaks up with him because she wants to go to college and enjoy a freer lifestyle while there. To me, that would be more likely to enrage a guy to this extent."

"He is the town's golden boy, you know, and he's been a decent mayor for years. No scandal in his family, ever." While Ted Brody was saying this, he was picturing the time, just recently, when he had seen Olson angry. He supposed he could have described his state that night as extreme rage.

"It's got to be one of them, Ted. It's the only way this could have happened," Tyke said, realizing it was the first time he'd ever used his boss's first name. Maybe it was time to level with him about everything.

But he didn't. Not yet.

"Katherine will be staying at the house," Brody said then. "Do you want to stay here at the station while she's in town?"

"There's a whole other half of the house for her to use. I think we should just keep things the way they are right now. It may be good to have a badge at the place," he added, recognizing a look of skepticism cross Brody's face. "You never know how this town will react when the details are released and charges are finally made."

"How close are we to making charges?" the captain asked.

"Not close enough," Tyke grumbled. "Let's see what this latest development produces. It may result in reactions that get us closer to the truth."

"I hope so," Brody said. "Meantime, I'll check with Katherine when she gets here to see how she feels about having a roommate. If it's okay with her…"

Tyke gave one nod to Brody as he left the office. He'd get back to the house and make sure everything was tidy. He didn't want Katherine, with all that she had to deal with, to walk into any mess that he had made.

* * *

HER ONLY WAY OUT WAS DEATH! the *Bangor Daily News* screamed in bold headlines the next morning. Other papers as far away as Boston and Hartford carried the story with similar front-page headlines. BURIED ALIVE, was the headliner in the *Globe*. LEFT TO DIE, blared across the *Courant's* front page. And the Boston *Herald's* headline mirrored the worry of everyone in town: A MONSTER AMONG THEM! It went on to detail the horrific circumstances that someone had subjected Meghan Murphy to until death released her.

* * *

Gloria read the Bangor article over and over, each time zeroing in on the one detail that haunted her more each time she read it. The DOT photographer had reported that he had had to solicit help in removing the wooden two-by-four from its bracket. And there had been a picture of two men raising the bar. Every time she read that part, and looked at that picture, a mental image of Harry's arms raising and lowering during his dream flashed into her head.

After about the fourth time she'd read the piece, she ran to the bathroom, where she became violently ill.

* * *

Ricky had overheard all the talk about the discovery of Meghan Murphy's skeletal remains from his cell in the basement of Narrownook's police barracks. He'd been rearrested just hours after Harry had successfully gotten him out. Since then, that creep Robinson had confiscated most of his belongings, and for the last five days had been canvassing the homes of every fuckin' customer he ever did any work for. He knew they were looking for more "doggie doors," as the cops liked to call his clever workmanship, but they wouldn't find many. That was because most of his homeowners were happy to entrust him with a key to their premises. He never had to crawl in and out of too many other houses like a freakin' rat except for the Warrens', the Griffiths', and the Dyers', all on Pleasant Street. They'd been too high and mighty to let a lowly caretaker have something as personal as a fuckin' key.

There was one good thing about being in this jail, though. He was able to keep up on all the latest gossip in town. All he had to do was listen to their chatter. This morning he was even allowed to read the paper after the cops on duty had seen it. It pissed him off, though, because they had already done the crossword puzzle—his favorite part.

He'd read through the articles thinking it might give him an idea of how he could maneuver his way out of jail by putting more pressure on Harry so he'd speak up for him. But after reading the reports several times, he could hardly think of anything except what Olson had allowed to happen to that poor girl.

The paper had run several pictures of Meghan. She was looking happy, smiling hopefully in each one, and really beautiful in the graduation photo they had printed. The more he thought about what had happened to her, the more he felt sick to his stomach when he thought about the man who had done this—the man now responsible for his lucrative future. What did his own association with a monster like this say about him? he wondered. Part of him actually began to wish he'd never gotten mixed up with Harry Olson, and he didn't know which scared him more, his dependence on Olson or the sudden appearance of his own guilty conscience. He certainly had a lot to think about and wished he had Sue to talk to. She could rationalize with the best of them.

So he began shouting to get the attention of the guy on watch just outside the annex where his cell and another empty one were located.

"I need to see Sue Hayes," he told the cop when the blue suit finally showed up a good five minutes after he'd started yelling. He passed him a scrap of paper on which he'd scribbled a phone number. "Call that number and tell her to get here ASAP," he instructed.

"Is this your attorney?" the officer asked.

When Ricky said it wasn't, the cop crumpled up the paper and chucked it into the nearest wastebasket. "Does this look like a lonely heart's club?" the cop growled. "We aren't in the business of managing our tenants' social affairs," he sneered as he did a mocking curtsy before going back to his post in the hall.

Dejected, Irving retreated to the cot in the corner of his cell to do some thinking on his own.

* * *

Russ kept reading and rereading every article he could get his hands on. He had even made a special trip to Ben's BookNook to grab the *Herald* and *Globe* for their accounts. It was beyond belief that anything as evil as this could have happened in Narrownook, in this small, peaceful little Maine town. How could there have been anyone horrible enough to do what these papers were reporting had been done to such a sweet girl?

Finally, in late afternoon, he'd read enough, and his business, which had been unusually slow today, had come to a complete stop, so he punched some numbers into his desk phone and waited. When he heard Olson say hello, he kept his voice on an even keel, though he would have liked to have yelled full blast. "Meet me on the walkway behind your office in ten minutes," he said, and slammed down the receiver.

* * *

Lanie spent Friday morning like everyone else in Narrownook. She had first tuned in to the early news broadcasts out of Bangor and then poured over the *Bangor Daily* articles. After Mahitabelle had seen the paper, they commiserated with each other about Meghan and wondered who could have been responsible for such a monstrous act.

It was painful, of course, for Lanie to contemplate what had happened to her classmate, but what made it even more haunting for her to remember was Meghan's last few normal hours in hopeful celebration at the top of her world on the peak of Cadillac Mountain.

So steeped had Lanie been in the news all day, she had not done her customary morning exercise routine. Late in the afternoon, she decided that some movement would help her work her way out of a depressing funk that thoughts of what had happened to Meghan had created. So, in late afternoon, she set off for a walk along the Penobscot River.

August humidity had been threatening to bury Narrownook in fog all day, and now Lanie saw a low ceiling of thick white cloud cover over the water when she arrived at the shore. During her hour-long walk, that fog bank lowered, closing in around her and becoming more and more opaque. She had been keeping her head down against the ever-increasing dewy moisture in the air as she walked and continued to think troubled thoughts about Meghan that she just couldn't seem to shed. She wondered if she should call Gloria and Sarah and Crystal once she got home. It would be a relief to talk with them about some of the emotions she was dealing with.

That made her think about the upcoming reunion, which was scheduled to take place in just a couple of weeks. How inappropriate it would be to gather and celebrate that devastating graduation of 1994 now! How could they ever celebrate that day again? It was the last day of Meghan Murphy's freedom, and afterwards, in the days that followed, while they were reveling in *their* freedom from school, Meghan was...

That was when she finally looked up out of her thoughts, and was amazed at how little she was able to see now. The thick fog had blanketed much of the low area next to the river. She could see her feet, but above them, everything looked distorted or had no shape at all.

She knew there were benches along her path, so she began peering in earnest to her right until she thought she could make out a series of objects on what would be the grassy area lining the walkway. She figured the objects had to be benches, so feeling around with her hands, she located a firm, wooden surface and knew she had found a seat. She decided to rest a minute and get her bearings before she went any further.

No sooner had she sat than she heard voices. Some of the words were being distorted by the low cloud cover that enveloped them, and what reached her ears was a wispy kind of dialogue at first, sweeping in and out, faint one moment, louder the next. She thought the male voices sounded angry. She could detect, even in the fainter segments an edginess in their tones.

She recognized the louder voice eventually. Russ was angry, and his voice was more successful in cutting through the cloud cover because he was beginning to yell.

Lanie stayed quiet and tried to concentrate on what they were saying.

"I can't..." the quieter voice began, but the rest was garbled.

"I should never had listened to you, let alone believed you!" Russ hollered.

Lanie tried to determine where she was on the walkway. Beyond her, at her left, neon lights from the Main Street gas stations at the eastern end of the brick path were managing to penetrate the heavy fog, but she had trouble fathoming how far away they were from where she sat.

"You...and made me...Meghan was okay when..."

Lanie's head snapped and turned in the direction of Russ's voice when she heard him mention Meghan's name. Russ was talking to someone about Meghan Murphy. Of course he was. Everyone in Narrownook was talking about Meghan today. But why was Russ so angry with the person he was speaking to? What had he made him do?

"You son of a bitch! You did this!" Russell yelled.

"Prove it!" The quiet voice was no longer quiet.

"You got her over to the island and your secret rendezvous spot!"

"What would you know about my *secret* rendezvous spot?"

"You forget I went to high school with you, Olson. How many times did we hear you bragging in the locker room about your hideaway under the bridge and your sexual victories! My God! You bastard! If only I had told them what I saw! There would have been time for someone to put two and two together and save her!"

It was Olson; Russ was talking to Harry!

Suddenly there were no voices. In their place, Lanie heard heart-wrenching sobs. A man was crying. She knew it was Russ.

They thought they were alone, and she wanted to keep them thinking that, so she quietly stood and turned to her right, inching along until she found the brick walk again. Once connected to it, she hurried faster, going over the words she had heard in her head to keep them fresh in her mind as she moved toward Oak Street. The glow from the art center's lighthouse became her westerly beacon.

The fog thinned out a bit as she climbed partway up Oak's slight elevation toward Ames Avenue and the public works building housing the fire, rescue, and police departments. She asked for Officer Robinson when she arrived, and was told by the uniformed attendant who buzzed her in that he wasn't on duty.

"What is it you wish to see him about?" he wanted to know.

When Lanie said it was regarding the Meghan Murphy case, he picked up a phone and repeated what Lanie had told him.

A ruddy-faced, middle-aged fellow immediately appeared from an adjacent hallway. "I'm Captain Brody," he told her, extending his hand. "How can I help you?"

"I really wanted to see Officer Robinson," Lanie said after she had introduced herself. "He's the one who has been interviewing us about the Meghan Murphy disappearance. I don't know what to make of the conversation I just overheard, but I think it might be important, and Officer Robinson might be able to make sense of it."

"You overheard someone talking about the Murphy case?" Brody asked.

"Two people."

"Do you know who they were?"

"We were in thick fog down on the walkway. They didn't know I was there, but I heard names. I recognized the voice of Stan Russell, and Russ addressed the other person as Olson."

Lanie saw Ted Brody's face go feather-white. He looked at the officer behind the desk and held out his opened hand. "Give me my car keys," he instructed. He turned back to Lanie. "I'll take you to Officer Robinson, who is at home today. I'll want to sit in on the conversation, too."

Lanie nodded and followed the captain to one of the cruisers parked behind the building. They sped off, over Ames and up Pleasant Street, past the Warren house and into the next block, where Brody pulled into the Murphy driveway.

Lanie hadn't been at the Murphys' since she'd attended a party there on Meghan's eighth birthday. That would have been almost thirty-five years ago. The place looked exactly the same as it had then, and Lanie wondered how that could be when everything else had changed.

Lanie heard a pleasant chime announce their arrival after the captain rang the bell.

The blond woman who opened the door looked very tired, and Lanie wondered who she was. Could it be that Tyke was married? Why did that surprise her? More importantly, why did it disturb her?

Ted Brody didn't seem surprised to see the woman, and called her by name. "Katherine," he said, as he hugged her, then stepped to one side to introduce Lanie. "This is Lanie Warren," he told the woman named Katherine. "We won't be long. We need to talk to Tyke for a minute. Is he here?"

Katherine nodded and invited them in with a step backward and a sweep of her hand. Lanie decided that along with looking tired, the woman had been crying. She was a pretty woman even without makeup and even looking as weary as she did. That was when the name Katherine clicked in her brain. Katherine Murphy! The last time Lanie had seen her, Katherine had been seven years old. Quick math made her thirty-two now.

It was Lanie's turn to hug her and express a worthless condolence in her ear as she identified herself as a fellow 1994 graduate with Meghan.

Tyke appeared then and led them into a parlor to the right of the foyer.

Brody cut right to the chase, explaining that Lanie had just overheard a conversation between two men she believed to be Stan Russell and Harry Olson while she was on the Penobscot walkway and had come immediately up from there to the station to report what she had heard.

Tyke leaned forward in his chair to hang on each word as Lanie repeated the conversation.

"Let me get this straight," Tyke said when Lanie had finished her brief report. "The tool room in the pylon was a regular place where Harry and Meghan would go to have privacy? You clearly heard that?"

Lanie nodded.

"Russell knew about this place, and Russell accused Olson of what? Of locking Meghan in there?"

Lanie nodded again. "He accused him of taking her to the island and to their 'rendezvous spot.' He clearly said, 'You did this!'"

"And you heard Russell say something about Olson made him do something?"

"I heard him say, 'You made me,' and then the last part was garbled, something about Meghan being okay *when*. That last part was not clear."

"And you heard what you thought was Russell crying, after he said that he should have told the truth?"

Lanie nodded.

"The truth about what? The rendezvous spot?"

"I don't know," Lanie shrugged, feeling totally inadequate, especially when she'd glanced over at Katherine wiping at her tears through the entire conversation.

"How long ago was this?" Tyke asked.

"Lanie got to the station a little after six. It's now ten of seven," Brody answered.

"I need to go down to the walkway and see if, by chance, they're still there," Tyke said, standing up. "Lanie, do you have time to come with me to help figure out where this took place?"

"I'll try," Lanie nodded. "It was totally fogged in."

"It's probably worse now," Brody said, "but you should give it a shot. I've got to get back to the station. You two go ahead. I'll send Jared down as backup."

They waited for Brody to back out of the driveway, then Tyke pulled out and down Pleasant Street all in what seemed like one simultaneous swoop. Lanie knew he had activated the emergency lights of the cruiser when the fog turned into blue swirls in front of them.

"I'll be more accurate in getting my bearings if we start at the art center," Lanie told him when they pulled onto Main Street. "I was able to follow its lighthouse beacon through the fog."

Once out of the car, they moved into thick, wispy veils of fog that became more and more dense as they got closer to the water.

Tyke produced a flashlight with a potent sliver of beam that managed to cut successfully through the otherwise impenetrable curtain directly in front of them.

Lanie stumbled once when they began their journey along the brick path, and Tyke reached out, fumbling for her hand. "Don't take offense," he said as he secured her hand in his, "but I don't want us to get separated. I'd have to hunt for you instead of them. Besides, without you to guide this operation, I'm not doing anything productive."

His palm, warm and rough, swallowed her hand, and she was suddenly a teenage girl, holding hands with that special boy for the first time. They had stopped directly behind the art center when Lanie had stumbled, and she began silently scolding herself for her foolish reaction to Tyke's touch. She forced herself to calculate the distance she had traveled almost an hour ago from the bench where she had been sitting to the spot where they now stood.

"We should walk until we have the neon signs of the Irving and Exxon stations in sight," she said, managing to sound like a rational adult instead of a silly schoolgirl. "We'd be close to my bench at that point. The men were just a little further beyond me to the east."

They began to walk again. Lanie knew the path pretty well because of the daily routine she had established for herself, and she was aware that her trek from the bench to the art center had been a brief one.

They both saw the lights at the same time and stopped again. "A little further, I think," Lanie said, and they kept walking. Tyke began alternating his flashlight beam between the walkway and the lawn area in search of a bench.

"There," Lanie pointed, as the light grazed a heavy object to their left. Following the beam of light, Lanie drew her hand from Tyke's and went over to what indeed was one of the seats. Tyke saw her lean over and briefly sweep the bench with her hand. "I know this is the one I was sitting on because there are initials or something gouged into the left side. I think N.H.S. by the feel."

"You'd make a good detective," Tyke laughed. For a moment he lifted the beam of light off of Lanie and further down to reveal a second bench about a dozen feet away and tucked into a natural curve in the walking path.

"Even without the fog bank, Olson and Russell might not have noticed you if you stayed quiet," Tyke told her when she had joined him to look at the second bench. It was unoccupied, of course, and Tyke gestured just a bit further along the path at filmy rays of lights coming from the municipal building up on Main Street. "Harry met him right behind his office," he said. "Probably prearranged, not accidental."

"What now?" Lanie asked him.

"Now I get you home and come back for a chat with Olson before the office closes. I'll want to see Russell, too, but I'll start with Harry before he leaves for the day."

"You don't have to get me home. I managed to get to the police department on my own, and my house is just a couple of blocks further from there. I'll be fine."

He turned to face her. "I don't like you trying to go it alone in this increasing fog," he argued. As he was speaking, they both heard the footsteps approaching and turned to see a pinpoint of light coming quickly toward them from the east.

Tyke turned and backed up against her, facing the oncoming flashlight.

The move was an apparent defensive one, and for the first time, Lanie felt the danger in what they were dealing with. That was when Russ's accusation hit home to her. The one where he had charged Harry with murdering Meghan. His words replayed in her head. *You son of a bitch! You did this!* and Lanie felt herself begin to shiver.

"Tyke, is that you?" the intruding flashlight asked.

"Jared?"

"Yeah, we got anything here?"

"Not yet. This is Lanie Warren, who heard the conversation."

As he spoke, Lanie knew he had turned to face her again. He felt for her hands, which were suddenly ice-cold. She knew he must sense her sudden unease, and she felt embarrassed for her newly acquired weakness.

"I'm going to send you home with Jared," he told her. His voice had changed, had cemented into a quiet commanding tone. This was no longer a discussion. She would let Jared escort her home.

And that's what Jared did. Lanie followed the young officer's pinpoint of light up onto Main Street where his cruiser waited.

"Let me off in front of the house," she told Jared as they neared the corner where McKay's Restaurant sat in a hazy glow. "I went out for a walk hours ago and didn't take my key. My mother will have to let me in her door on Pleasant Street."

Jared turned the car left and climbed the hill, leaving some of the dense fog behind as they neared the top and approached the house.

Lanie thanked her escort when she got out of the car and hurried up the walk to the front steps. Halfway there, she noticed the car in the driveway that the hedges and mist had managed to briefly conceal. Just as she got to the top step and reached out to ring the bell, she heard her name.

"Lanie," he said, and Lanie turned to see a figure emerge from the parked vehicle and begin the short approach to where she was standing.

"Harry!" she said. She felt as if her voice should be thin and trembling, but her shakiness had suddenly been exchanged for a rush of intense anger. How dare this man show his face anywhere in Narrownook, and why, of all places, would he be here?

But she knew she needed to stay cool, so in a light tone that would qualify for an academy nomination, she said, "What brings you by?" The flippancy in tone and the smile she flashed told Harry she was delighted to see him.

"I needed to see you." His tone was totally opposite of hers, a dejected tone to match the slack posture of the man. "This news has left me stunned and devastated."

Lanie poked the doorbell for the first time.

"As it has all of us," she agreed.

"I'm going to have to go away. Distance myself from this place, from everything that is a reminder of what has happened. It's so difficult to..." His voice cracked, and his head lowered on his already bent shoulders.

"I understand," Lanie said, pushing the bell a second time. "Where will you go?"

"I wondered," he raised his head to look at her with wistful eyes, "where *you* would like to go."

"Whatever do you mean?"

"I want you with me. I want you to come, too."

"I have to be back to school in less than a month, and I have dozens of things to finish up here before I go anywhere," Lanie said, hitting the bell a third time.

"I'd pay all expenses," Harry argued. "Hell, you can retire. You've worked long enough. Time someone took care of you."

Lanie forgot her acting award and stammered, "That's crazy. Why would you want to do that?"

"I need you with me to help me forget this horrific event." He took a step closer to her, and Lanie rang the bell a fourth time, this time giving it three urgent jabs in succession.

"I told you once it should have been you and me," he persevered. "Things would have worked out differently if it had been you and me from the start."

"This is very unexpected," she said, managing to keep her voice free of the panic that was threatening to eat her alive.

"I don't see why you're so surprised," he said, actually looking bewildered. "Haven't I always come to call on you every time you were in town? I'd see your car and here I'd be, keeping you up-to-date on my life and trying to stay close to yours."

"Yes, I suppose that's true," Lanie agreed, beginning to suspect that Harry Olson might be dangerous in more ways than one. She wasn't a psychiatrist, but she knew insanity when it was staring her in the face. She decided she had two chances of getting away from this man. One was to convince him that there was a possibility she'd accompany him in his bizarre scheme, and the second was getting her mother to answer the freaking door!

"When would you be leaving?" she asked, hitting the bell again and keeping her finger on it. She could hear its frantic tolling way out here, through the heavy oak door, across the porch, and through the storm/screen combination in front of her, but with a sinking feeling, she realized her mother must not hear it at all.

"I can't stay any longer," Harry sighed. "It's too painful to see the sympathy in everyone's eyes, hear their condolences over and over again. I need to leave tomorrow."

"Leave for where?"

"I'm not sure. You decide. I'll make all the arrangements."

The inside door opened and Mahitabelle, looking puzzled, came out onto the porch. Seeing Lanie, she rushed to unlock the screen.

Lanie, in turn, rushed to get inside the porch and resecure its lock before she spoke again. She had noticed her mother's disoriented appearance and knew the woman had been sleeping in her recliner all this time, which explained her confused state, so she shrugged as she addressed her visitor through the screen. "My mother, as you can see, hasn't been feeling well lately or I'd invite you in," she told Harry.

"Oh, yes, of course," Harry nodded. "Let me know in the morning what you've decided," he said, coming closer to the steps. "We leave at ten. Just throw a few things into a suitcase." He stepped up onto the first stair. "I'll buy you a whole new wardrobe at our first stop," he managed to say before Lanie gave him a quick wave while she ushered her mother into the house and closed and dead-bolted the oak door.

CHAPTER 30

LANIE HAD GONE TO FIND AMY AS SOON AS HER MOTHER WAS RESETTLED in her recliner. Out of Mahitabelle's hearing, they went over the afternoon's events and went through the house checking locks on windows and doors, as Lanie kept emphasizing the need to keep the house completely secure at all times.

Amy agreed that they shouldn't alarm Grandmother with what had happened. "We need to keep her calm," Lanie told her daughter as her own shivering returned big-time.

Then Lanie called the station. As she suspected, Tyke had not returned, nor Jared, either, and Brody was not available, whatever that meant. So she left a long message for any one of them to call her regarding her new conversation with Harry Olson, who, she said, intended to leave town at ten tomorrow morning.

By ten o'clock that night, when Lanie hadn't heard from anyone at the police station, and her mother and Amy had gone to bed, she finally went over to her quarters. She had left both telephone numbers, hers and the main house's, with the officer she'd talked with at the station earlier. As she prepared for bed, she expected the phone to ring any minute, but it remained silent.

Finally, at eleven, thoroughly exhausted, she fell into bed and into a deep sleep almost at once.

* * *

When the phone rang a little after three a.m., it took several rings to penetrate Lanie's consciousness. Even as she reached for the receiver by her bed and spoke an automatic hello, she wasn't fully awake. However, Tyke's voice, quiet but still clearly in command mode, revived her instantly.

"Lanie, it's Tyke. Throw something on over your nightwear and meet me in your driveway—*now*. Stan Russell is on the Waldo–Hancock Bridge threatening to jump. I need you to talk him down. I'm just coming off the Thegan Bridge. I'll be there in two minutes." And the line went dead.

Lanie sprang out of bed, shoved her feet into a pair of sneakers, ran to the bathroom to relieve herself while she gargled with mouthwash at the same time. She scooped up the garage door opener lying on the kitchen table, and in her flight past the hallway closet, threw on the first thing she could grab—a Columbo-style raincoat that had belonged to her father. From there, she raced down into the garage.

As she poked the red light to release one of the doors, a fleeting thought that the voice on the phone might have belonged to Olson in a scheme to gain entry, vanished immediately as the cruiser, its lights flashing, tore up the driveway.

"Here's what I know," Tyke began even before Lanie had thrown herself into the front seat completely. "A motorist on his way to work the early shift at the Belfast Bakery Café saw the car ahead of him smash through the barricade at the bridge about two thirty. The motorist stopped at the entrance and observed the driver of that car get out, run around his vehicle, which he had stopped halfway across the span, and hurl (that was his word—*hurl*) himself onto the side of the bridge, where he seemed to just hang. The passerby dialed 911 on his cell phone, and we got the call at the station at two thirty-five.

"When Jared and I got to the scene at two thirty-nine, there was Stan Russell, just as the motorist, Ken Burgess, had described, dangling on the side of the bridge. He was doing a lot of twitching and squirming when we got to him. What had happened was, he had hit that railing so hard, he had rammed his foot between two lateral steel rods that rim the sides. Rods on that bridge have been collapsing against each other for years as the bridge aged, and Russell's impact had been in just the right place to pin his foot and save him from going any further. If someone didn't believe in a divinity before tonight, this scene might convince them otherwise. Unless he tears his foot off, he's not going over the rail, and then Burgess just happened along at the right moment."

"Thank God," Lanie murmured.

"Exactly."

The cruiser had crossed the Thegan and was headed over the short strip of land that led to the two bridges. The fog of the evening before had disappeared, once again supporting the old Maine adage, "If you don't like the weather, wait a minute."

"I thought that because you and Russell are..." Tyke paused in search of a word, "...close," he said, finally, "I figured you could calm him down long enough for us to get a piece of equipment over to him to sever the two rods that are pinning him. He let us know he didn't want any of *us* anywhere near him. That's when I called you."

"I think Crystal would have better luck than I," Lanie said.

"Crystal?"

"Crystal Murray. She's been in love with him for a very long time, and they do see each other a lot."

"I didn't know that. How did you know that?"

"Crystal and I have become good friends. She confides in me. I think she should be informed about this—tonight."

Lanie thought she saw Tyke's head nod before she became distracted by flashing blue, red, and amber lights as they drew up to what used to be the entrance to the Waldo–Hancock Bridge.

In contrast, the peaceful necklace of lights over on the new Penobscot Narrows Bridge backdropped the chaotic scene on the old span, and Lanie imagined that her heart began thumping in time to the pulsating strobes of emergency lights that were engulfing them.

"Helicopter has already been dispatched," Jared announced as he rushed over to greet Robinson. He was a novice officer, clearly rattled by his first experience with a jumper.

"Let 'em know we won't need it," Tyke said. "No one's going for a swim downriver tonight."

Lanie felt herself shiver inside her Columbo raincoat as she followed Tyke toward the center of the old bridge and her friend Russie hanging like a rag doll against the side of it.

"Stan!" Tyke shouted as they got nearer. Russell wasn't wriggling now, he just seemed frozen in place, probably tired from his defeat against the grip of hard steel. "I've brought Lanie Warren, who wants very much to talk with you. Okay to move closer?"

They had stopped about ten feet from where Russell was entrapped, his torso hunched over his hands, which were gripping the railing.

"Lanie can," Russell answered weakly.

Tyke gave Lanie a go-ahead nod, and Lanie approached the side of the bridge. She automatically looked down to watch her step, anticipating the need to step up on the sidewalk that had always been there on the Narrownook side of the span when she and her teenage friends, often including Russie, would hike to Fort Knox on a Saturday afternoon for a day of adventure. That was long ago, when all the dark and mysterious original compartments in the fort were still open to the public, and every nook and cranny was accessible to young and eager explorers.

Now she was surprised when she didn't find any sidewalk until she remembered reading in one of the local papers last year that they had removed it in a last-ditch attempt to lighten the weight on the bridge's cables. In the end, it was too small an effort and done too late to save the bridge.

Edging herself up to Russ, she reached out and touched his arm. He was gripping the rail so tightly that his arm felt like one of the steel rods that was imprisoning him.

"Russ," she said quietly, "what are you doing? Why are you here like this?"

"I let her die," he wailed, loud enough for the police and firemen and EMTs lined up a short distance away to hear. "I can't live with myself, knowing what I allowed her to suffer." He began yanking at his trapped foot in another desperate attempt to free himself.

"Stop that!" Lanie scolded. "The police and fire are here and can get you out if you let them come over."

"I don't want them to rescue me. I want to die right here. Slowly is okay. Just like she did. It's karma. *My* karma."

"What do you feel guilty about? Did you lock her in that room below us?"

Russ suddenly strained to peer down over the rail as if this was the first time he had realized he was close to that ill-fated room.

"Of course not," he murmured when he raised himself back up and looked at Lanie. "But I didn't try to save her," he choked out.

His face was colorless and streaked with dirt that had mixed with his tears. They had etched his inner turmoil into grotesque pathways across his countenance.

"But you didn't know she was trapped in that place."

"It's a long story."

"Well, I'm here as long as you are, so tell me what you're talking about."

"I've said enough."

"You really haven't, Russ. I don't understand why you're condemning yourself about what happened to Meghan. If you think you could have saved her *then*, help bring her justice *now*. Tell the authorities what you know, and do what you can *now*. This selfish act you're attempting will not rectify anything but your own misguided conscience. If you feel badly that you didn't do enough twenty-five years ago, please do the right thing *now*, Russie."

Lanie was never sure if it was the content of what she had said or her slip of the tongue when she absentmindedly returned to the use of his childhood nickname, but less than a minute later, he relinquished his grip on the bridge rail, threw up his arms, and announced, "Okay. Tell them to get me out of here."

The fire department crew moved in at once. So did Tyke and Jared to give assistance if necessary, but Russ didn't put up any resistance. He allowed the men to lower him onto a stretcher and place him in a waiting ambulance. Those left behind stood as if in a trance until the drama was over. Most were Russell's friends, and all of them knew of his fair-minded and generous practices that had been the cornerstone of his business from day one. And so they watched, paralyzed, as the vehicle, its lights flashing, its siren mute, drove away to a Bangor hospital where Russell would be physically and mentally evaluated.

Tyke looked at Lanie then to thank her. "You did it," he said. "I knew you would. Russell trusts you. So do I. Let me get you home. You're shivering." And he whipped off his bulky jacket and draped it over her shoulders. "Where in the devil did you get that enormous raincoat? You look like—"

"I know. Columbo. It was my father's. I keep it to wear whenever someone calls me out at three a.m. in my skimpy pajamas."

It pleased her when she was rewarded with a healthy laugh from Tyke.

They hiked back up to the cruiser and rode in silence across the Thegan Bridge, where they stopped at a red light at the entrance to Narrownook's Main Street.

"What are all those people doing over there?" Lanie asked, pointing to her right. The cruiser's dashboard clock said four thirty. The sun was only managing to paint a dim swath of dawn in the eastern sky, yet Lanie could see a small crowd gathered on a Main Street corner.

"I'm surprised you don't know," Tyke told her. "It's your good friend Penelope and her crew picketing the memorial. They think it is immoral and indecent, not to mention disrespectful, to have the leg of a woman on a gravestone."

"Oh, good grief!" Lanie laughed. "She hasn't been around lately. I didn't think she was still in town."

"She's obviously busy," Tyke grumbled. "They start at the crack of dawn and go all day over there when they're not trying to get into Olson's office to file a formal complaint and beg for town support. So far, I guess he's refused to see them."

The light turned green and Tyke guided the cruiser up Hanks Street and over Sawmill Road. At his request, Lanie repeated for him the conversation she had had with Harry the night before. "I tried to pin him down about where he would go, but he kept leaving it up to me. I don't know if that was a dodge or if he truly was willing to let me make his decision. When I told him that I was surprised that he wanted me to go with him, he managed to look stunned that I hadn't figured out, somehow, that we were supposed to be a couple long ago. It makes me question his mental stability."

Tyke swung into Church Street without comment and took a quick left through the Warren gate and up to the three-car garage.

Lanie released her seat belt and began fishing through her pockets for the clicker that would open one of the doors. That's when Tyke turned to remove his coat from her shoulders, and in the light of the floods over the center door of the garages, Lanie saw a bloody gash on the left side of his face for the first time.

"You're hurt," she gasped, raising her hand toward his injury.

"It's just a scratch," he shrugged, blocking her touch. "A loose sliver of steel must have caught me when I leaned in to be ready to stop Russell if he tried to go over the rail once he was freed."

"Come in and wash that before you leave. I've got some disinfectant you can use," Lanie said.

"I'll take care of it," Tyke said, dismissing her concern.

"It should be treated now," Lanie argued. "You come in. It will only take five minutes."

"I've got a first aid kit right here in the cruiser I can use when I get back to the station," Tyke insisted.

"Where?" Lanie asked, reaching her hand toward where the glove compartment should be.

"Here, under the seat," and Tyke raised a lever to reveal a blue steel box.

"Let's see what's in it," Lanie said, springing its latch and displaying a sizeable collection of salves and ointments, gauzes and bandages. She reached in and grabbed a package of medicated wipes.

"Turn toward me," Lanie instructed as she tore open the small envelope with her teeth.

"What do you mean?"

"Turn and face me, and let me clean up that wound. I'll tell you if you need to see a doctor for a tetanus shot."

"I'm up-to-date," Tyke assured her grudgingly, but he unsnapped his seat belt and turned to face her. If she had dared to look him straight in the eye, she would have recognized a mixture of mischief and challenge in Tyke's expression that might have discouraged her further attempts at administering first aid.

But Lanie took Tyke's chin in one hand as she leaned forward to gently swipe at an area of dried blood on his left temple. They were inches apart as she worked, and Lanie willed herself not to think about the infinitesimal distance between them. Above all, she concentrated on looking at what she was doing and not into his eyes, which she knew were trained on her.

She had expected him to flinch when the pad caught an opening in his skin, but he showed no reaction. "You're a brave soldier," she kidded him.

She took her eyes off of Tyke's injury for just a second to assess his reaction to her teasing, and, as a result, met his gaze despite her resolve not to do that—not to gaze, for even a moment, into this man's dark eyes at this close range.

Too late!

They moved toward each other in one magnetic motion, and when their mouths met, the kiss exploded into sighs from Lanie and groans from Tyke. Through her thin raincoat, she felt the pressure of his hands grow stronger as he pressed her against him.

Then the police radio crackled once before a voice asked, "Car One, what is your location?"

It was over abruptly.

Tyke threw himself back against his seat. A few seconds went by before he answered the page. Then, in a husky voice, he gave his location. "Dropping off Ms. Warren," he added, looking at Lanie with what she thought was a look of chagrin. Or was it disappointment? She couldn't tell. Was he already feeling regret about the kiss? Was she?

Lanie fished around once again for the garage door opener in the raincoat's deep pocket. Finding it, she wasted no time in pulling the handle of the passenger door.

"Lanie," Tyke said.

She paused and turned, one foot all ready to step out of the vehicle.

He hesitated as if unsure what it was he wanted to say. Then he reached for her, drawing her against him again, tender this time, cradling her in his arms. She could feel his lips depositing kisses against her brow. "I'll wait until you're in and the door is down before I back out," he said against her hair, her skin. "That meeting with Olson last night worries me. You need to be extra careful until this whole thing is over." He moved her away to make eye contact. "Promise me you'll be careful," he said.

When Lanie nodded, they kissed again, briefly, a final kiss before Lanie left the car. She hit the remote button as soon as she was in the garage, and watched the heavy door descend and thump closed like an audio exclamation mark on high volume.

Then she just stood numbly staring at the closed garage door and listening to the cruiser's motor grow weaker until she couldn't hear it any more at all.

CHAPTER 31

WHEN TYKE GOT BACK TO THE STATION, HE MET A PILE OF MESSAGE SLIPS on his desk. Two of them said Brody wanted to see him. Five of them said Ricky Irving wanted to see him. The Irving requests had been coming in since late yesterday afternoon. Along with the slips was a report that camouflage teams had been ordered by Brody to canvass specific areas of Narrownook in the wake of Lanie Warren's phone call last evening about Olson's intention to leave town on Friday.

It was a little after five a.m. now. Through his office window, the sun was making a promise that a beautiful summer day was ahead. Tyke knew that, for him, the day's forecast would depend on whether or not he could think straight enough to take the best course of action in a case that seemed to suddenly be sprouting more than one tentacle of guilt.

He had to get his head together and concentrate on what the last twenty-four hours had meant. Why had Russell gone to the bridge? How was Olson planning to get out of town? Where was he going? Tyke's gut told him Harry was the guilty party, but why did Russell try to commit suicide? Was it possible that this had been a co-conspiracy all along?

Brody shoved through the office door without a routine knock and dropped into the chair in front of Tyke's desk. "What have you got?" he asked wearily.

"I need to interrogate Russell as soon as the hospital gives the go-ahead," Tyke told him. "Any sign of Olson?"

"Nope, he isn't answering telephone calls or opening his door to the officers we've dispatched. He left the office before five o'clock yesterday. We now know why—to meet with Russell and then visit Lanie Warren. No reports of anyone seeing him after that."

"Have you dispersed the surveillance teams yet?"

"Not yet. Waiting for you."

"Let's get it started then. What are the numbers?"

"We've got a dozen; some from Auburn, Ellsworth, and Westbrook. Fort Kent's team hasn't arrived yet."

"Okay. Get one on Main Street near the municipal office, one on Center near Olson's house, one at Church in back of the Warrens', and when The County gets here, put it around Katherine's area. Let's not take any chances that he might not take it upon himself to return to the original scene."

"Olson?" Brody questioned.

"Probably," Tyke said with a shrug.

"Then why was Russell bent on taking his life?"

"When I talk to him, I hope to get the answer to that question."

"What's all the slips?" Ted Brody asked, gesturing toward the scattered mess on Tyke's desk.

"Five are from Irving asking me to meet with him," Tyke grumbled.

"I've got seven of those," Brody chuckled. "He says he's ready to do a deal. He'll trade his freedom for the solid proof he swears he has of who killed Meghan."

"He's a con. Just wasting our time."

Tyke's phone rang. He picked it up and listened as Brody sat quietly waiting.

When he hung up, Tyke stood and adjusted his shirt. Had he straightened it since he'd held Lanie in his arms? He couldn't remember. He told himself not to go to any thoughts of her until he had solved today's problems and the Meghan Murphy case. The two should be a simultaneous wrap if he did his job right and kept himself free of distractions.

"That was the hospital. I'm on my way to Bangor," Tyke declared as he moved to the door. "Set up the teams. I'll be back with important information if all goes well."

In his mind, he replayed what he had just said and determined that it was he who sounded like the boss. Well, he guessed it was because today, he actually was. After all, it was why he had come to Narrownook in the first place, even though Brody didn't realize it yet.

CHAPTER 32

HARRY OLSON HADN'T SLEPT ALL NIGHT. HE HAD PACKED LIGHT STUFF that had taken all of fifteen or twenty minutes to cram into a small duffel bag. He sure wasn't going to hoist tons of baggage onto a plane as a signal to anyone watching that he never intended to return.

He began calling Lanie around six a.m. Friday morning. Her uppity daughter told him her mother was still sleeping, that there'd been an incident on the Waldo–Hancock Bridge last night that she had been called to help with. When he pushed for further information, Amy refused to go into it. So he called Gloria and learned that Russell had tried to take his life and was now hospitalized.

That was the moment Olson felt the world definitely closing in. Stan Russell had never breathed a word to anyone in all these twenty-five years, but after his angry meeting with the man, Harry knew he was no longer able to count on him to keep his mouth shut.

"Anyone who shields the monster who did this to Meghan Murphy will become a monster himself once the world knows the ugly truth about what you did," Russ had told him.

There was only one thing for him to do, and that was run.

A little after six a.m., he grabbed his cell phone and duffel bag and raced to his attached garage, climbed into his car, and pointed it in the direction of Hanks Street. He knew that was where he'd find Penelope Mageloo at this early hour. She had been trying to see him for a while now. Well, this was her lucky day.

He pulled over and stopped on a side street above the gated cemetery where a bunch of folks carrying signs were walking back and forth. He scooped all the papers from his glove compartment and went in search of Penelope.

He'd thought of this secondary plan after her several attempts to make an appointment to see him. She was hardly his A plan, but he congratulated himself for his ability to change horses in midstream when he recognized the necessity to do so. Penelope Mageloo was a nut job, but he needed a getaway driver, and she could be schmoozed. She would never be a substitute for Lanie, but she'd be a malleable accomplice, a lapdog who would not try to interfere with his plan of escape. Lanie had a brain and a mind of her own. It saddened him that she probably was not the person who would have been a worthy partner for him.

As if to prove his analysis was correct, Penelope spotted him immediately and left her group on the run to greet him. Delight illuminated her gaunt face.

"Where's your car?" Olson demanded before she could say anything.

"There," she said. A long skinny finger with a bright-red razor-sharp nail pointed toward an equally red Cadillac CT5.

"Drop what you're doing. I need a chauffeur, and you have wanted to see me, so if you get me to the airport this morning, we'll talk."

"Sure," Penelope decided with a quick shake of her head. "I'll be back," she yelled to a nearby man carrying a sign with a picture of the town founder's historic monument highlighted in a circle of light. A large black X had been superimposed over the offensive leg.

Olson didn't look back one time at the Mercedes he was abandoning. When Penelope beeped her doors unlocked, Harry opened her car's back door. Penelope glanced at him questioningly, saw that he carried a small duffel, and asked if he had other luggage in his car that needed to go into the trunk.

"This is it," he told her. Then he lied and said someone would be along to pick up his car later, and that's when he surprised her further by sliding himself into her car's rear seat.

Penelope gasped. "Sit up front with me so we can chat," she crooned.

"I need to lie down for a few minutes," Harry told her. "I didn't sleep at all last night. Do you have a blanket I can use?"

"I'll get one out of the trunk," Penelope gushed as she hurried to do the mayor's bidding. "I'm so sorry you're not feeling well," she crooned as she spread a plain brown blanket over the already reclining form of Mayor Olson, who had stretched out on the backseat. He pulled the blanket completely over his head and tucked his knees up to his chest so he was entirely covered.

Penelope looked up at the sun, now completely risen, and scowled at its intrusive glow. "You try to sleep then," she said. "What time is your flight?"

"Not until ten," Harry muttered from under his blanket. "I need to do some business at the bank this morning before I take off. I hoped you could wait in the parking lot there until it opens in what...a couple of hours?"

If the request seemed odd to Penelope, she didn't miss a beat to accommodate Harry's request. She got the name of the bank and its address on Main Street and started up the car. "We'll talk a bit until you fall asleep," she told him as the car began rolling toward the center of town.

Harry made no response.

"What are the chances my people can get a permit to stay at the gravesite until September first?" she purred.

Still no response from the mayor.

When Penelope got to the bank, she pulled in and parked close to the front door in the otherwise deserted lot. Then she turned to observe the lump of brown blanket on the backseat.

"Mayor, are you awake?" Can we talk a bit?"

There was no answer.

Now and then, Penelope thought she heard a low-pitched growl from her passenger, but there was no conversation. Penelope Mageloo sat in an empty parking lot, delighted on one hand to have scored an audience with Narrownook's mayor, but becoming more and more antsy as she waited for him to catch up on his sleep.

CHAPTER 33

Tyke arrived at the Mary of Mercy Hospital at seven a.m. He was escorted to a small conference room by a receptionist and seated at a table almost as large as the room itself. He had time enough to spread out a notebook and scribble some questions before the door opened and Stan Russell, on the arm of a doctor's assistant, entered and took a seat opposite him. Crystal Murray followed and seated herself next to Russ. Tyke had called her, as Lanie had suggested, while the scene on the bridge was playing out, and subsequently had arranged for a car to take her to Russell once his destination was determined.

Dr. Forrester arrived then and took a seat at the head of the table. He was a young man, his face not yet showing the weary creases caused by dealing with the little-understood and often shunned conditions of mental ill health.

"Ordinarily, I'd put the kibosh on a meeting this early in our association, but Mr. Russell is adamant that time is of the essence in this matter, and he made it clear that he had no intention of speaking freely with me until he could unburden himself to law enforcement."

Tyke nodded and sat forward to make eye contact with Russell as he posed the initial and most important question. "Why did you find yourself on the bridge last night, Stan?" he asked gently.

"To answer that, I have to go back to that night twenty-five years ago—or rather, to that next morning," Russell answered. He looked nothing like the defeated man who had hung on the bridge for hours the night before. Except for a couple of scrapes on his cheek and a noticeable limp as he'd entered, he seemed uninjured.

"The morning you dropped Meghan off at her house on Pleasant Street?" Tyke prompted.

"Actually, after I dropped her off. My house at the time was on Surry Lane, off Pleasant Street, a couple of blocks above Meghan's. I watched her walk up her steps to the porch, just as I've always said, then I left for my place. Just before I got to my turn for Surry Lane, I recognized Harry's car on the side of the road. At the time, there were no homes built up in the area, and my first thought was that his old jalopy must have broken down and he'd just left it there. Then, on second thought, I doubled back and cruised slowly down Pleasant. When I got to Meghan's, I slowed enough and spotted Meghan and Harry in conversation at the steps of her porch."

"Did you stop?"

Russell shook his head. "In hindsight I should have, but I just turned around and went home."

Tyke thought through the testimony he'd researched over the years and asked the next logical question. "Did you ever tell anyone you'd seen them together that morning?"

"I told Harry," he said.

"You told Harry you'd come back by and seen him with Meghan?"

"After she was reported missing, I confronted him a couple of times that summer about it. He insisted they'd just talked there on the porch for a while. He told me that she had confessed to him that she'd been seeing someone from Hampden or Holden, one of the Maine towns that begin with H, I forget which one. He said if I told anyone he'd been with her that morning, Narrownook would make his life miserable. He insisted that he'd never be able to amount to anything in this town with that accusation over his head, and he threatened to make my life equally miserable by denying he'd been with her at all that day. It would be my word against his. He assured me it would look like I was the one lying; that I was just shifting the blame to him because everyone knew

I had been the one on a date with her. He said I could kiss my business dreams goodbye for sure.

"So, I stayed silent. I lied by omission to the police. I shouldn't have, but at the time I couldn't fathom that Harry Olson would have actually done harm to anyone, let alone a girl he'd loved through high school. He swore over and over to me that he'd left Meghan on those steps at her home in one piece.

"That's why I was on the bridge last night. When Meghan's remains were found in that equipment room, I knew Olson had done it. If I'd been honest twenty-five years ago, I think the authorities would have learned that room was their favorite place to rendezvous, and they'd have found her in time."

"How did you know that room was their rendezvous place?" Tyke asked.

"Anyone who played sports with Olson knew it. He bragged about it all the time."

"Do you know if anyone ever saw them actually go in there?"

Russell shook his head no. He suddenly seemed very tired.

Dr. Forrester stood up then. "I think my patient needs to rest now," he declared.

Tyke thanked Russell with a handshake and told him that his honesty had made a positive difference in the investigation. It seemed to be what Stan Russell wanted to hear because his face lit up, and his shoulders seemed to lose a bit of weight as he walked taller to the door on the helpful arm of his aide.

Afterwards, alone in the conference room, Tyke made a phone call to Brody back at the station. "I'm done here for now," he told the captain.

When asked for specifics, Tyke acknowledged that Russell had been, in his opinion, very forthcoming. "He confessed to having seen Olson in the Murphy yard when he'd doubled back a few minutes after he'd initially left her on the morning she disappeared. Of course, that doesn't put Olson and Meghan at the bridge that morning, but Russell will testify that the equipment room was a frequent meeting place for the young couple. I'd put an APB out on him, Ted," Tyke advised. "He's definitely our primary person of interest and needs to be questioned extensively."

"This is certainly a first," Brody grumbled, "putting out a notice to apprehend the mayor of Narrownook."

"It has to be done, and soon, before he disappears. He told Ms. Warren he would leave by ten. Let's hope that's not his flight time or he'd already be at the airport. I'll check with Bangor International before I head home to make sure they stay alert for him. He'd probably travel under another name, but I'll check their reservation lists anyway."

With all of that to do, it was after eight when Tyke was finally on the Bangor road headed once again to Narrownook. He'd put the Bangor police on alert for Olson and apprised them of the APB that he hoped Brody had already initiated.

For many, Friday was just beginning, but for Robinson, the day was already half over and moving much too quickly.

CHAPTER 34

THE BANK OPENED ITS DOORS AT EIGHT O'CLOCK. LIKE A GOOD DOOBIE, Penelope poked the blanket and roused the mayor when she saw a lady turn the lock in the front door and flip the "Closed" sign to "Open" on its window.

"Bank's open," she announced to the lump in the rear seat. As happy as Penelope was to assist the mayor, she was becoming more and more disappointed in the time she was wasting just sitting in a parking lot listening to him snore.

"Okay," came a groan from the back, and Harry slowly poked his head up to inspect his surroundings. "This shouldn't take long," he told her as he grabbed his duffel and shrugged himself loose from his rough shroud. "Pull the car around so it's headed right out onto Main Street when I come back," he directed. "Time is of the essence now. I can't afford to miss my flight."

The tellers of the local bank all knew Mayor Olson, of course. The bank had serviced his financial needs all his life. Later, they would remember that on this particular day, he seemed hurried, even skittish as he closed out several accounts, plopping wads of cash into his duffel bag as each was liquidated. If they thought all these transactions were unusual, no one was inclined to question him or put a hold on any of his requests. Lately, he had been drawing out large amounts from his CD's and money market accounts. Today, he also spent about ten minutes in the vault with his two safety deposit boxes.

Once finished, he hurried, head down, duffel squarely over both shoulders, to the waiting car parked, as ordered, across the front entrance, pointed toward Main Street.

Traffic on foot had suddenly picked up along the sidewalks, but Harry was relieved that no one had ventured into the bank, so his movements had gone unnoticed by any passersby.

He didn't waste any time getting himself and his bag back into the rear seat. He sighed slightly with relief as he closed the car door.

But Penelope wasn't sighing when she blurted, "What? You're not going to sit up here and talk with me? You're going back to sleep?"

"I'm still very fatigued," he said, scooting under the blanket after giving Main Street activity one final sweep of surveillance.

"But we need to chat. You said we'd chat!"

"We will. Put the pedal down and get me to Bangor in time for my flight. We'll have time to talk when we get there. You know how delayed those plane schedules can get. Now be careful. No more stopping at pedestrian crossings like you're apt to do. Just go," he muttered as the car began to move.

"I don't do that anymore," Penelope answered defensively. She saw the crosswalk right in the front of the bank to her right, put her signal on to turn into it, looked for traffic that might be coming from her left, and seeing none, stepped on the gas. Immediately, she hit something. There was an audible crunch.

"What was that?" Harry yelped from under his mantle.

"A stupid kid pushing a bicycle across the street. I must have grazed the bike a little."

"Was he in the crosswalk?"

"I guess so. It's okay, the boy's all right," Penelope muttered as she accelerated again.

"Why in hell didn't you stop if you saw someone crossing?" Olson screamed hysterically.

"You told me not to!" Penelope wailed.

Then something else behind them began to wail.

Looking in her rearview mirror, she saw the cruiser, which had been coming from the Bangor direction, flash on its blue lights, and do a U-ey as it descended on her back bumper.

"I've got to pull over," she announced meekly.

"I'm not here," Harry told her shrilly.

"What do you mean, you're not here! Of course you're here. You're the mayor. I can say I was distracted trying to get you to the airport."

"If you ever expect me to help you, do *not* mention that I'm here," he screamed. "This trip is a matter of security; a secret town excursion. Important town affairs hang in the balance. *I am not here!*" he ended in a final yell as he secured the brown blanket more tightly around him.

CHAPTER 35

"LICENSE AND REGISTRATION, PLEASE."

"What!" Penelope scoffed when she saw the familiar face in the blue uniform. She reached over and clicked into her glove compartment to retrieve her documents before she looked back at Tyke. "Let me guess," she said with a smile that looked more like a sneer, "this one-horse town is also a one-cop town, right?"

She thought she heard the backseat growl as she shoved the papers at Robinson, who returned to his cruiser without comment.

The plate came back with an outstanding warrant for an unpaid parking ticket, so he used his cell phone to call the station. "I've got Penelope Mageloo," he told Brody when the desk sergeant connected him to Ted. "She failed to stop at a crosswalk and clipped a bicycle that little Barry Goodin was pushing across Main Street in front of the Diamond Bank. There's also that outstanding parking ticket that she has neglected to pay."

"Bring her in," Brody instructed him.

"One other thing," Tyke said. "She's got someone covered up on the rear seat. There's definitely movement under a blanket by an adult-sized person. Just in case there's a problem, send a unit to back me. What's happened with Olson since we talked?"

"We found his car parked on Gould Street. We've towed it in. The car has been stripped clean. Nothing in the trunk or cubicles."

"Gould Street," Robinson mused aloud, "just above the cemetery. Make that two units. I may find someone we know in Mageloo's backseat."

"Fort Kent surveillance team just arrived. I'll send them down. Are you suggesting Mageloo may have Olson stashed in her car?"

"Penelope Mageloo has been picketing at the cemetery's memorial for weeks. Olson's car was parked near it. They knew each other from earlier this summer, and she's been trying her darnedest to see him at his office. I know I'm connecting two very weird dots, but stranger things have happened. Okay, send the team. I'm making the arrest now."

With that, Tyke exited his vehicle and went the short distance back to the red Cadillac. Halfway there he began cursing himself for forgetting to tell the captain to instruct The County's surveillance teams he was sending to assist him to remove any camouflage paraphernalia that they might have already changed into. He'd heard about how the Maine teams did surveillance—lots of colored sheets and headwear. He didn't relish a spectacle. It reminded him of the one time he'd hunted with some Mainers when he was younger. It was the rowdiest hunt of his life.

They'd used whistles, rattles, and assorted noisemakers to drive the deer out, which was successful in driving *him* out of his mind.

He had to admit, though, they'd gotten a prize buck that morning.

"Ms. Mageloo," Tyke said at Penelope's driver's-side window, "step out of the car, please."

"What in heaven's name for?" Penelope blurted.

Tyke opened the door. "Step out, please," he repeated.

With an offended sigh, Penelope did as he asked.

Out of the corner of his eye, Tyke saw two unmarked vehicles pull up and stop behind his cruiser.

"You have the right to remain silent..." he began.

"Are you arresting me?" Penelope screamed. "All I did was clip a kid's bicycle, for God's sake!"

One of the men from the newly arrived cars rushed over at the sound of an agitated voice. He was still wearing a helmet with blades of grass all over it that bobbed and waved as he ran toward them. Tyke winced and watched a couple of other officers climb out of the cars still in green sheets.

Penelope gawked in disbelief. "What is this? A joke? Halloween?" she shrieked.

Tyke was successful in calming her down and finishing the recital of her rights when he produced handcuffs and gave her the option to go quietly or be subjected to wearing the bracelets. One of the Fort Kent officers escorted her to the cruiser.

Silently, he signaled the green sheets to surround the Cadillac before he opened the back door.

"Step out of the car, please," he said to the blanket. He'd been watching small movements under that brown wrap all the while he had been dealing with Penelope Mageloo at the side of the car. The black duffel bag on the floor next to the blanket was capturing his curiosity, too.

* * *

It hadn't taken Harry long to determine that the jig was up. Now to convince the police that there was a perfectly plausible explanation for the mayor of Narrownook to be wrapped up in a blanket in the backseat of this idiot woman's car! After Tyke's demand, Olson stayed perfectly still for only a mini-second longer before he threw off the woolen shroud, blinked heavily a couple of times, sat up, blinked once more, and rubbed his eyes.

"Mornin', Robinson," he said, with a shrug that he hoped enhanced the look of embarrassment that he tried to manufacture across his face.

"Step out of the car, please," Tyke said again.

"You know how these things are, Tyke," Harry began explaining, as he inched himself over to the opened door. "The lady and I had a lively night together, and by morning, I couldn't keep my eyes open, so I took a short nap while she did some errands." He gave Robinson a good-ol'-boy slap on the shoulder as he exited the car.

Tyke already had the handcuffs out, and once Harry had both feet on the ground, he requested, in a mannerly tone, that Olson turn and put his hands behind his back.

"There's no need for this," Harry said, his voice suddenly a bit crisper. "What seems to be the problem?"

Robinson put a firm hand on his left arm and helped him turn to face the car. "Put your hands behind you," he said again.

"I need my duffel bag," Harry said.

"We'll send it along to the station with you," Tyke told him as he clicked the metal hoops around his wrists.

"You realize, of course, that I am somebody in this town," Olson snarled. "As a newcomer, you have a lot to lose by conducting this obscene display in front of people who know and love me."

"We'll talk more at the station," Robinson assured him. Then he read him his rights and handed him over to the backup team. He took one of the sheeted officers with him and Penelope in the cruiser, and followed the Fort Kent brigade back to police headquarters.

CHAPTER 36

RICKY HAD FELT ABANDONED FOR DAYS. HIS PLEAS FOR A MEETING WITH Captain Brody or Officer Robinson had fallen on deaf ears, and now he sensed a shift in the very atmosphere of this place. Something had happened; something big. No longer was there relaxed chatter coming from outside the holding area; no laughter or good-natured back and forth between officers as they performed their workday duties.

However, he had been aware of an unusual amount of movement in the reception area. Nonstop footsteps hustled back and forth without any pause to pass pleasantries or share a joke. One of the ways he'd entertained himself in this hellhole was listening to the talk. Today, voices that he heard were low and trailed off because of their harried pace.

Something had happened, of that, he was sure.

About ten thirty, Ricky's patience had been completely spent, and he started yelling for somebody, anybody who would give him the time of day. About an hour later, after he had shouted himself hoarse, he finally received a visit from a guy he'd never seen before.

"Who are you?" he asked the man in drab street clothes carrying what looked like a folded green cloth under his arm.

"I'm Officer Reynolds filling in for Bergman at the desk, who is busy with other matters. What did you want to see Brody or Robinson about?"

"I need to see my lawyer. Today. It's an emergency."

"What's your lawyer's name and number?"

After Ricky gave him the information, Reynolds wanted to know what he should tell him that constituted an emergency.

"I'm in possession of vital pieces of evidence regarding the death of Meghan Murphy."

"How often do you normally meet with your attorney?" Reynolds asked him.

"I've only met him once, but I didn't say much. I wasn't comfortable talking to him about things at that time. I'm ready to tell him everything now so I can get out of here."

"I'll see what I can do," Reynolds said before he disappeared.

Ricky waited several more hours. Then, at two thirty, Hogan Lowell, Attorney-at-Law, wandered into the holding area with Officer Bergman.

Ricky had been hearing less and less activity as the day wore on, and with the reappearance of the regular desk sergeant, he figured whatever had been an issue earlier was resolved, and things were getting back to normal.

Lowell was let into his cell and immediately made himself comfortable on the unmade cot, spreading open a loose-leaf notebook on his lap to get ready to jot down some notes.

"What's this new evidence?" Lowell asked him.

"Not new, really. I've had some of it for years, but after the remains of Ms. Murphy were found in the bridge, it's become crucial."

"Tell me what you have and how you came into possession of it."

"Not so fast. First I want to make a deal for my release and a guarantee of total immunity from prosecution for anything I've done."

Lowell looked at Irving with a good deal of skepticism. "You must have some powerful evidence."

"Can you draft up an agreement for law enforcement to sign before I tell all to them?"

"Maybe. Let me hear what you have, and we'll see."

So Ricky told him about the ring and how Harry Olson had been paying him off for his silence. At some point in the story, Lowell couldn't write fast enough and switched to his laptop and began pounding out the details with more vigor. Once Ricky was finished, the attorney sat back and breathlessly stammered, "Anything else?"

"That's it," Ricky shrugged. "Will it buy me freedom?"

"If it bought you the mansion, a quarter of a million, and two Cadillacs—probably. I'll get right on it. The pictures you showed me are helpful. I'll have to see that safety deposit box first, though," he told him, holding up the tiny key that Ricky had had squirreled away in his shoe.

"I'll deny everything without that agreement," Ricky vowed to Lowell's back as the lawyer hollered for Bergman.

"I gotcha," Lowell said on his way out of the cage.

* * *

The Narrownook Public Safety Building had only one conference room, nine-by-ten in size. That's where they had deposited Penelope Mageloo. They had put Harry, still cuffed, in Ted's office. Robinson and Brody took turns questioning the two characters, shuffling back and forth all day at fifteen-minute intervals. Tape recorders were in use at all times, of course. Now and then, they would play back a statement that was a contradiction of what the other had said.

"You say, Harry, that Ms. Mageloo and you spent the night together. She says she only met up with you this morning. Listen to her statement," and Ted would rewind a section of his machine and play Penelope's words.

"Don't you know about women? She's obviously trying to preserve her good name," was Harry's reply.

"Penelope says she didn't have errands this morning, that it was you who had to wait for the bank to open at eight o'clock to do some business before catching a scheduled flight out of Bangor," Brody challenged. And he played back the corresponding statement from Mageloo.

"The woman is a fruit salad," Olson sneered more than once after hearing what Penelope was saying.

"So, let me see," Tyke said, thinking back to Olson's exact words at the time of his arrest, "you spent a lively all-nighter with a fruit salad."

"You know how it is, Tyke, sometimes a guy can't be too particular."

It didn't take long to determine who the liar was. During the back-and-forth questioning for several hours, other officers were interviewing the Diamond Bank employees, and even Tyke escaped to do some of his own sleuthing during the morning.

After a cursory survey of witnesses, a warrant to go through Olson's property was obtained, and further investigation made it clear that Harry had been intending to do exactly what he had told Lanie Warren he'd do. He was leaving Narrownook for good.

About four o'clock, Brody and Robinson left their respective suspects to confer with each other privately in Tyke's office.

"Let's get Penelope into Ellsworth to settle the outstanding ticket. They'll hold her on the accident, and we'll make sure they understand we need her for further questioning in the Murphy matter. That way, they'll release her back to us when we need her."

"Sounds right," Robinson agreed, "and we'll hold Harry for a while here. He isn't going to crack easily, if ever, and that worries me. He totally denies that the equipment room was a private meeting place for him and Meghan. Even telling him we have former classmates willing to testify to that fact didn't seem to rattle him, and he's adamant that Russell is lying when he says he saw him with Meghan that morning. When you lay all this out, we have very little to hold him on for more than a couple of days. It's a he said–he said, and won't get us anywhere without witnesses to confirm what Russell told us. As of right now, we can forget about charging Olson with murder.

"I'll see if I can dig up some witnesses who actually saw Olson and Meghan going into that room sometime during their high school days," Tyke sighed. "That would be a big help."

"And I'll work on finding someone who can testify as to Harry's activities on that morning after graduation in 1994. Unbelievably, there's nothing in the records to indicate that an inquiry about his whereabouts was ever conducted back then," Brody grumbled.

Shortly after that, there was a quick but robust knock on Tyke's closed office door. Hogan Lowell crooked a finger at him when Tyke opened it. "We need to talk," Lowell told him.

"Not today, Hogan. We're in the middle of what we hope is a break in the Meghan Murphy case."

"I doubt that. I think I'm the one with a severe fracture in the case if what I just heard and saw has any merit," Hogan Lowell said. Peeking through the crack in the door, he spotted Captain Brody. "Both you and Ted give me ten minutes in private to share a little of what Ricky Irving just confessed to me."

"Oh, Ricky," Tyke sneered, brushing any thought of Irving away with a sweep of his hand.

"He's got pictures to back up some of the story. I've seen them."

"Pictures of what?" Brody asked, getting up from his chair and joining the men in the doorway.

"This is the best place to talk, then," Tyke said, stepping back and allowing Lowell entry.

Once the door was closed and everyone seated, Brody repeated his question. "What pictures?"

"Before I show you those, Ricky is in possession of a 1994 men's Narrownook High School class ring," Hogan announced.

"There are still quite a few of those around," Tyke remarked.

"Inscribed?" Hogan challenged with raised brows.

"Tell us about the inscription," Brody urged.

"Well, that's the thing," Lowell wavered. "I'm under directions from my client not to share details until we have a signed agreement that if this evidence turns out to convict Olson—and I assure you what I've learned so far has, in my judgment, the power to send him away for life—then in return, my client will go free without prosecution for any of his past offenses."

"A ring, inscribed or not, could have been found anywhere by anyone, including by the person or persons who may have done harm to Meghan," Tyke reasoned.

"True," Hogan said, but this next part is the killer, pardon the pun."

"What else?" Brody asked.

"This picture of a huge foundation just poured in an area at the corner of Pleasant and Surry Lane, which Irving claims to own thanks to Olson's gift of it to him just recently."

"I noticed that just this morning," Tyke said. "During my break, I went up and checked out Russell's story of where he used to live on Surry to compare it to where the Murphy house is. The footing you're talking about is humongous! Whoever is building a house there has a lot more money than Irving."

"This is something that can be checked out quickly," Brody said, picking up the phone on Tyke's desk and dialing the town office. "You must understand," Brody said over the telephone's mouthpiece as he waited to be connected, "Irving is a sleaze with a history full of deceit."

Once Brody was talking with someone on the other end of the line, there was a slew of "Uh-huhs" and silent nods up and down as he clutched the receiver tighter and tighter against his ear and held his face expressionless. When he hung up, he shook his head slowly back and forth for a few seconds before he announced, in Academy Award fashion, "And the winner is…Richard A. Irving! He indeed owns the lot and the mansion that is in the process of being built." All of a sudden, he was resenting the distinct possibility that he'd have to turn the Irving creep back out into the streets of Narrownook.

"According to Gloria, the complete acreage was signed over to Irving about a month ago, and construction started soon after. I did hear recently in passing that Irving had come into money from a deceased rich relative," Brody added.

"And who did they say he got the land from?" Hogan asked, leaning forward in his chair expectantly.

"You are right, Lowell. None other than our friend presently sitting in handcuffs in my office," Ted grumbled, raising his eyebrows in Tyke's direction. "For one dollar, I might add."

"Okay. Let's see and hear all you can tell us," Tyke sighed with another shrug.

He and Brody were thinking the same thing at that moment. If Ricky Irving had been rewarded for his silence by Olson, that was the part of the puzzle that could unite all the pieces they had gathered so far.

"I bet I know what the A stands for," Brody said suddenly.

"The A?" Lowell and Robinson chorused.

"Richard A. Irving," Brody clarified. "I bet I know what the A stands for."

Even Ricky's lawyer had to join the two police officers in hearty laughter.

* * *

When he was alone again, Tyke sat staring out his office window. It was going on five o'clock, and the sun hadn't even begun setting. Could they be lucky enough to wrap this case up today?

Suddenly he was filled with two contradictory emotions: An overwhelming sense of relief flooded over him because the case could finally be solved after twenty-five painful years. But surging through the relief was a sense of loss in knowing that within a matter of days, his time in Narrownook would be finished also, and with it something important that had barely begun would be ending, too.

CHAPTER 37

A MEMORIAL SERVICE FOR MEGHAN MURPHY WAS CONDUCTED AT THE
Methodist Church on Ames Avenue on Saturday, August 10th. It
was followed, just across the street, by a Mass of Christian Burial
at the Ames Avenue Catholic Church. Afterward, attendees at
those functions moved down the same street for a luncheon at the
recently renovated reception hall of the Congregational Church.
All three churches wanted to remember the young girl whose
whole adult life had been so cruelly stolen from her.

Earlier that same day, Harry Olson was arrested and charged
with her murder.

The town that had adored their mayor for so long was staggered
by the news of Harry's arrest. They took his actions personally. It
was, to them, a betrayal of their lifelong trust in him.

* * *

In the back of her mind, Gloria had known the truth about the
mayor for a long time, and over the years, had found it easier to
bury it by second-guessing herself each time it rose to the surface of
her consciousness. Now, she went through the motions of being a
secretary to Joe Davis, the temporary replacement for Olson, while
she berated herself whenever she had idle time in which to reflect.
At those times, she automatically went back to the years in which
she had dismissed her better instincts to escape to the comfort of
denial and felt immediate disgust with herself for being so weak.

Gloria and Stan Russell carried a lot of guilt, but at least Russ,
who was still receiving treatment in a Bangor hospital, could feel

he had been able to help bring justice to his classmate by continuing to be thoroughly helpful to law enforcement now. Already, there was talk that his present cooperation, along with his obvious remorse, would minimize his ultimate punishment for deceiving authorities in 1994 and during the years since.

Once the story of Harry's arrest was publicized, no one in Narrownook rushed to defend him—for several reasons. There was immediate talk about how Harry Olson had helped cover his tracks. In retrospect, people began remembering how Harry had hyped the story about Meghan running off with a lover, which had served to diminish a sense of urgency about conducting a more thorough hunt for the girl.

Many also began to remember one or more times when they had witnessed a sudden, unexpected explosion of Harry's hot temper. "I knew" or "I should have known" started hundreds of conversations, followed by recitations of past volatile episodes with the man.

Skip Dyer and Charlie Briggs had witnessed such a moment too recently to have it even begin to blur in their memory. The two men, in fact, paid a visit to Harry in his new home behind bars in the Ellsworth jail the morning he was charged with the crime. Unlike Gloria and Russ, Skip and Charlie didn't feel guilty about their lifetime friendship with the murderer. Instead, they just felt like damn fools—extra-angry damn fools!

Harry was forced to listen to their ravings for several minutes until a guard put a stop to the duo's rants by escorting them out of the building.

But Harry had gotten their message. They were determined to help authorities by gathering at least a dozen character witnesses who would testify at Olson's trial about the many times they had been on the wrong side of his temper tantrums.

* * *

After law enforcement had signed the papers that waived any and all culpability for past wrongs, Ricky had produced the ring, the tie clip, and his recent bank records showing that he had, indeed, been able to amass a sudden and large quantity of money and land, all trailing back to Harold Olson.

At first, Sue had not been happy with Ricky's decision to confess all, but after sleeping on it for a few nights, she came to the realization that there was no positive outcome for them if they continued to protect the man who had done such a horrific act without even a single pang of conscience. Besides, they already had two new SUVs and a quarter of a million. The property on the corner of Pleasant and Surry was in their names, too. The foundation had been poured for a mansion there that they probably would never build now that Harry would not be around to finance the construction, but the way the town was growing, it was a sure bet it soon could be sold for a fortune. So could the dozen adjoining lots that were also theirs, thanks to Olson.

Ricky still had one major ongoing worry, though, and that was how to manage Sue, the spendthrift, to keep her from going through the assets as soon as they were liquidated.

* * *

Tyke hadn't seen Lanie Warren in over a week. In truth, he was slightly dreading their next meeting because it would probably be the last time they'd be together. Every time he thought about that, he ached in the pit of his stomach. So he had kept himself busy to avoid lamenting over what could never be.

It certainly had not been difficult for him to find a lot to do. Since the night Russell had found himself on the Waldo–Hancock Bridge, there had been lawyers to deal with, depositions to witness and record, and an iron-clad case against Harry Olson to put together before they could officially indict him for murder.

Finally, on what had been a very long Friday, August 9th, the case was solidified. It was time for Tyke to tell Captain Brody the truth. It was another goodbye that he had been dreading, but he knew he had to do it before all the Murphys arrived in town for the weekend tributes to Meghan. If he kept quiet any longer, Ted would figure it out on his own during those ceremonies because one of the Murphy clan would surely spill the beans. Tyke recognized the unfairness of his letting it happen that way.

At ten thirty that Friday night, Ted went into the lavatory and dumped his and Tyke's stale coffees down the sink and came back to his office, where Robinson was getting ready to head home.

Ted Brody sat and pulled a bottle out of the lower drawer of his desk and poured two generous shots of brandy into the two empty cups. With a wide smile, the captain stood and passed one to Tyke. "A toast and a sincere thanks to you for breaking this cold case wide open and then solving it!" he announced, raising his drink in a salute to Robinson before taking a large swallow for himself.

Very deliberately, Tyke put his cup down on the top of Ted's steel desk without drinking to the toast and sat back down in the chair he'd just vacated.

"Captain," he said, "it's past time for the truth." Tyke leaned forward in his chair and cupped his hands as he rested his elbows on his knees. "I'm afraid I haven't been honest with you. In fact, at times, I've blatantly lied to your face by omission. I owe you the courtesy of hearing an explanation from me before tomorrow, when you'd have found things out for yourself."

Ted Brody looked at his favorite cop with a stunned expression and lowered himself slowly into his desk chair.

"I'll be leaving you soon," Tyke blurted. "My work, my reason for coming here is over. I'll stay a reasonable length of time to help with any transition problems, of course. The one bright note in all of this is that Jared has learned well during the time we've worked together, so I'm not concerned that I'm leaving you completely high and dry." Tyke paused to let what he'd just said sink in and to let Ted respond. When Brody just sat staring at him blankly, he went on.

"The truth is," he said, sitting back and clearing his throat, "I'm a Boston detective on temporary leave. My coming here, my looking for a job, was a ruse to get me situated in your department in order to solve what happened to my cousin..." he paused to take a long breath before he dropped the bomb, "...Meghan Murphy."

Brody reached for his brandy and took a copious swig. It took him several seconds to swallow the liquor and find his voice. Finally, he murmured into his cup something like, "I should have known you were too good to be true for my small town." Then he took another healthy quaff.

"Katherine and I have been working on this for many years, ever since she moved to Massachusetts to be near her mother's family," Tyke said. "Katherine's mother was my mother's sister." Tyke paused again to give the captain a chance to respond. When Ted still said nothing, he kept talking.

"I've been one of Boston's detectives for going on fifteen years," he continued. "I signed on as a Boston cop at age twenty-four and rose in the ranks to lead detective by age thirty. The Boston department has known about and been sympathetic to what my family has been enduring for these twenty-five years."

Tyke shrugged with a sigh and sat forward again. "Always in the back of my mind, I was going to solve Meghan's case. It was something I felt I had to do for my family. I had to use my talent to bring some closure to them. In order to do that, though, I had to be in Narrownook, and I had to be in an official capacity."

Brody remained silent. Tyke watched him tip his cup up and drain its contents.

"So, with Boston's permission, and with their full knowledge of the reason for my sabbatical, I took a leave from my detective job. Then, with Boston's recommendations, I got myself hired here." Tyke paused again. The pause lasted for almost a minute as the two men squinted at each other.

"That's quite a story," Ted finally mumbled, picking up his cup and starting to take another swallow. When he discovered the cup was empty, he reached for Tyke's.

"I have a great deal of respect for you, Ted," Tyke said, standing up to leave. "You run a top-notch department here. It's been a privilege knowing and working with you. I hope, in time, you'll forgive my deception. Answer me this: If I'd told you this story when I interviewed with you, would you have hired me?"

Brody tipped Robinson's cup way back and swallowed the contents in three large gulps. Then he made a move to stand, thought better of it, wiped his mouth with the back of his hand, and sprawled back in his chair. "I dunno," he growled.

The two men eyed each other for a few more seconds before Tyke turned toward the door.

"I'll see you tomorrow at the Narrows, then," Tyke said and left the office.

Once outside Brody's closed door, he felt the momentary relief of a good confession before tremendous regret flooded through him; regret that he had had to put a competent professional like Ted Brody through this wringer. He hoped that the captain could forgive him eventually. He wondered how long it would take for him to forgive himself.

CHAPTER 38

IT WAS A BUSY WEEKEND.

The day after the churches' events, the state finally opened the tallest public bridge observatory in the world and the only observatory bridge in the Western Hemisphere.

The Penobscot Narrows Observatory at the top of the Penobscot Narrows Bridge was christened "Meghan's Vista," and the Meghan Murphy Memorial Garden of flowers was unveiled along the bank of the river beneath the giant obelisk.

The name Meghan's Vista was meant to help form a mental image of the girl's spirit rising gloriously and looking down, with pride, upon her earthly garden and her hometown of Narrownook.

The 1994 reunion committee had decided they'd use their reunion get-together to honor Meghan with the rest of the people celebrating the opening of the observatory and her garden. They helped prepare statements that were presented by her high school senior class officials and friends. They also voted to begin every future reunion in her dedicated place here at the Narrows.

In the meantime, long lines had been forming all morning with people who wished to ride the single elevator forty-two stories up to the observation deck. Only a handful of folks could be accommodated on the elevator at one time, but no other restrictions were in place. There were no time limits placed on how long visitors could tarry once they reached the top of the 420-foot tower.

Along the entrance, massive slabs of engraved granite from Waldo Mountain (the same granite that had helped build another famous obelisk, the Washington Monument, on which the Penobscot Narrows Observatory was modeled) gave information about this engineering marvel. Among the notable facts mentioned was its stature among other American landmark structures. At 420 feet, it stood taller than the Statue of Liberty, which measures 305 feet.

Once up on the observation deck, there was a lot to see because there was a 360-degree range of view. Those at the top could rely on plaques to inform them of every town, mountain, and body of water they were observing as they made their way completely around the massive walls of windows.

* * *

Lanie, Mahitabelle, and Amy had attended all the events that weekend, and had stood with the large crowds on the eleventh of August to cheer the public opening and dedication of the bridge's observatory.

Once the formal ceremonies were completed, however, Amy took Mahitabelle home. The elderly woman confessed to being tired and not anxious to ride up forty-two stories in an elevator. Besides, she said, she had an important meeting scheduled for later.

Amy and Lanie guessed that Mahitabelle's "meeting" was probably Penelope dropping by to say a quick goodbye before heading home. Word had reached the Warrens that now that the investigation was completed, Penelope would be permitted to return to her home in New York with the understanding that she would be called as a key witness when Olson's case went to trial.

Penelope Mageloo had stubbornly refused to have an attorney during her incarceration, saying there was nothing she'd done wrong, and she would not waste her money on some crooked lawyer. Nevertheless, she had been released after a brief stay in the Ellsworth jail, where she had been held for a week on the outstanding traffic ticket and a charge of violating a pedestrian's safe passage in a crosswalk. Even though she was free, however, she had not been allowed to leave the Downeast Maine area until the case against Olson was airtight and he had been placed behind bars indefinitely.

* * *

After she took Mahitabelle home, Amy would not be returning to the observatory. With a fear of heights, she had declined the opportunity to go to the top of the Penobscot Narrows Bridge. Ever!

Lanie, on the other hand, wanted the experience, so after the two had left, she waited in line with the rest of the public to climb to "where the osprey fly," a quote from a recent advertisement about the new tourist attraction.

As Lanie waited, she had a chance to scan the area carefully. She had seen Captain Brody and Jared with other officers moving around the grounds earlier, but she hadn't seen Tyke today. She wondered if, somehow, he'd drawn time off even with this major event occurring.

Yesterday, she'd seen him at the church services sitting with Katherine Murphy and her large family. He'd been in uniform, obviously there in an official capacity.

Though she had tried not to focus on him, she found it difficult to keep her gaze away for any length of time. During all of the activities that day, their eyes met sometimes, and in those moments, Lanie would feel the familiar heat surging through her before she looked away.

It had been over a week since that night on the bridge. Lanie knew it had been a time full of unparalleled obligations for Tyke and the rest of the police force. She understood why she hadn't heard from him, but as time went on, she began to wonder about the meaning of their brief but impassioned embrace. Had it simply been the result of their both coming from an adrenaline-driven crisis? She knew that was not the case for her, but was Tyke trying to send her that message by his absence now?

In a way, she was already regretting any future meeting with him because she knew it would be their last. She'd be going back to school in a couple of weeks, and if they met, she would have to say goodbye. She hated even thinking about it.

She had feelings for Tyke Robinson. Since her divorce several years before, she had not, for even a minute, entertained the idea of ever letting herself feel this way about a man again. She'd forgotten how painful being in love could be, and in this case, she imagined she felt more wretched because any relationship between her and Tyke had been doomed from the start.

An hour went by before Lanie reached the front of the line and gained access to the elevator. A cheery lady in casual dress with a pin on her collar that said *Beverly*, instructed their small group about the ascent. She cautioned that if anyone was nervous about heights, they should stare down at their shoes when the elevator door opened and keep focusing on their feet to give themselves time to gradually become acclimated to the new elevation.

It was good advice. To ensure an unobstructed 360-degree view, the elevator did not go to the top level. It was brought to the forty-first floor, and the area where the elevator stopped to release passengers was small. When the elevator opened, only about eight feet separated the visitors from the sudden appearance of the osprey's sky. The sightseers then had to walk toward the windows, turn right to go up a set of stairs beside those windows, and walk up steps that faced a new set of windows climbing directly into that sky. Another set of stairs to the right finally brought them up to the forty-second floor of the tower. (A lift was available for the disabled.)

For anyone with the mildest sensitivity to heights, those first few seconds out of the elevator could, as the first-floor greeter had warned, rattle even the toughest men. "When I covered the top foyer, I saw many adult males turn right around and go back into the elevator to return to terra firma," Beverly had said with a smile.

So Lanie had listened well and was doing what the greeter had suggested. When the elevator ride ended and the door opened, she was looking at her shoes.

"Lanie!" his voice exclaimed.

She forgot about acclimating and looked up from her footwear. Tyke was standing with his back to the high windows that overlooked a forty-one-story drop full of nothing but sky.

An intense terror of falling suddenly shot through her, and it froze her in place. Her face must have recorded the fear because Tyke rushed over to her and gently took her by the arm.

"Look back down at your shoes," he said both to Lanie and an older man who also had become immobile when he stepped out of the elevator.

"I'm just going off duty on a break," he told them, "so I'll lead you up one at a time to the forty-second level while you keep your eyes on your toes."

Lanie stayed on the inside of him as they climbed. That way, he managed to block the view from the windows on Lanie's left, as she concentrated on keeping her eyes firmly planted on her sneakers and her right arm and shoulder deliberately hugging the firm concrete walls.

After Tyke had gotten Lanie to the forty-second level, he went back down to escort the middle-aged gentleman.

By the time Tyke returned, Lanie had raised her head to look around. Placing her feet squarely on the carpeting helped her develop a sense of grounding, and the fact that she was now a bit back from the tall panes of glass and behind railings that held the plaques of information had eased her discomfort, too. When Tyke returned to join her, she apologized for being such a nuisance.

"Don't give it a thought," he said kindly. "Something over half of our visitors react the same way the first time here."

"Did you?" Lanie asked, pinning him with an accusatory look that said she doubted it.

Tyke grinned. "No, but three out of our four greeters had to repeat the ride and entrance up here several times before they were comfortable enough to do their job." In an effort to get her mind off of her initial reaction, he changed the subject and pointed toward the view they were presently facing. "Cadillac Mountain," he noted.

Lanie looked straight out as far as she could see. "Where?" she asked. She could see several mountains in the distance.

"The two largest mounds next to each other straight ahead," he directed.

"There's a tower or something tall and skinny in the center of those ridges, right?" she nodded.

"Yes," Tyke answered, putting his arm around Lanie's waist and turning her toward another direction, "and there's Whitecap Mountain over there next to Saddleback."

He was helpful in pointing out many landmarks as they enjoyed the spectacular array of landscape. But Lanie gazed the longest on Narrownook, far below, a tiny village of neat, white buildings nestling on the Penobscot. Despite what the little town had been through, it looked peaceful. So many horrific events had taken place there. The untimely and grizzly death of a young girl at the hands of a man who had been adept at portraying himself as a highly respected mayor, the demolition of Narrownook's paper industry, and now its beloved signature bridge about to be razed, had not seemed to change the town's serene appearance. The ability of a community to defy brutality and destruction was a testament to its grace and strength of will. Lanie knew the people of Narrownook had long possessed those important qualities along with the Yankee ingenuity that always got them over seemingly insurmountable obstacles.

"That clear-edged body of water," she asked, "what is that? It looks sculptured."

"Diamond Lake," Tyke answered. "You can tell from here that it's manmade."

Lanie sighed. "I love Narrownook," she said. "I'll hate to have to leave it."

"That's right," Tyke suddenly remembered. "You're only here for the summer. Where do you live? I never asked you."

"Medford," Lanie told him.

Tyke's head snapped around and his eyes left the scenery they'd been admiring to stare at Lanie. "Medford?"

"Medford, Mass," she said.

Immediately, Tyke's face took on a different expression. Lanie thought he looked awestruck. "I had no idea!" he uttered in a voice that was barely a whisper. Then, in a totally opposite tone much too robust for the tightly enclosed room they were in, he howled, "That's wonderful!" just before he swept her into his arms and kissed her fiercely.

The middle-aged gentleman grinned over at them, and a young couple and several others on the deck began applauding.

"You must really love Medford, Massachusetts," Lanie gasped when the two of them came up for air.

"You have no idea!" Tyke beamed, and he kissed her again while he mentally scrambled around in his brain about how to break the same news to her that he had delivered to Ted less than twenty-four hours ago. The difference this time, though, was that he was delighted to do it.

"Did she say yes?" someone in the sightseer group shouted.

"Not yet," Tyke laughed.

And Lanie turned crimson.

CHAPTER 39

TYKE WENT BACK TO WORK, AND LANIE WALKED HOME.

Just like in the old days, she hiked from the bridge and across Orphan Island as she had done so many times when she was growing up. Then she took the long way along Main Street, turning up Pleasant between McKay's and The Jed, and arriving finally at the house on the top of the hill. The Maine blue sky that she had just been in followed her all the way home.

She had needed the walk, needed exercise to bring herself down to earth after the forty-one-story elevator ride and the even loftier emotional journey. It was good to feel the ground solidly beneath her while her spirits stayed at an all-time high.

She and Tyke would not have to say goodbye. In fact, they had swapped their Massachusetts addresses and phone numbers and had found great delight in learning that they had several favorite Boston area restaurants in common. They couldn't wait to enjoy every one of them together.

Lanie had finally been able to ask him about his name, something that had intrigued her since the day she had first heard it.

"Where does the name Tyke come from?" she'd wanted to know. She had guessed that it must be short for something.

"I get that question a lot," Tyke had laughed. "My father gave me that name almost the moment I was born. I was his thirteenth child. The family doctor looked at him as the midwife was wrapping me up in a blanket to present to my mother, and asked, 'So, what's the name going to be for *this* tyke?'

"The story goes that Dad shrugged and said that was as good a name as any, and the doctor recorded *Tyke Robinson* on the birth certificate."

Lanie had found herself chuckling about that all the way home.

Without the car again, she had no clicker to let herself into the Church Street garages, so she had to go to the front door. As soon as she had turned into the walk, she stopped in her tracks. "This is never good," she muttered when she saw a car parked in the driveway. She'd expected that Penelope would have been gone by now. Then she looked again. She had time to register the fact that it wasn't Penelope's Cadillac just before she recognized the BMW.

Her inner voice had just begun screaming hysterically at her when the front door suddenly opened, and Amy appeared, grinning from ear to ear.

"It's okay, Mom," she greeted her. "Grandmother has known all the time. Come meet my brother, John Dyer. He turned out to be the 'meeting' that Grandmother was referring to."

"How in the world did your grandmother, my mother, figure out she had a grandson and then arrange a meeting?" Lanie demanded. They were still standing on the front porch. Lanie had blocked her daughter from entering until she got some answers.

"To quote Grandmother," Amy laughed, pausing while she got herself geared up to imitate her grandmother's voice, "'I wasn't born yesterday, and I keep my ear to the ground and figure things out just fine on my own when people try to pull wool blankets over my eyes.'"

"Sounds like your grandmother," Lanie had to admit, still blocking Amy's attempt to enter the house. "What's he like?" she nodded toward the half-opened door.

"Go see for yourself," Amy answered, giving her mother a tug.

"I'm suddenly very nervous," Lanie admitted, resisting Amy's pull.

"Don't be, he's very down-to-earth and very bright. In fact, he's the CEO of the new yacht club that is coming to Narrownook. He's about to open an office on Main Street and get things lined up for construction now that he's got all the permits he needs.

The fact that his company happened to move here, plus we both contacted AAAA around the same time, was how he found us. I haven't been able to wrestle out of Grandmother how the two of them hooked up yet, though. I'd be willing to bet money that Grandmother has known about him all along."

"Sometimes she can be a scary lady, can't she," Lanie nodded.

Then she took a deep breath and silently decided that the way this day was going, it could possibly be on its way to even greater heights.

So she followed her daughter into the house, where a very tall, very handsome young man immediately rose to his feet.

Mahitabelle remained sitting quietly in her recliner, wearing that familiar and infuriatingly smug expression.

The Varied Genres
from Jane Harvey Meade:

The Mystery...

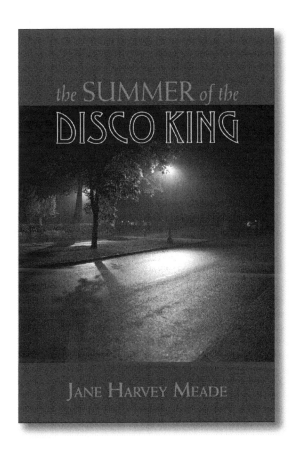

Think Your Home Is Safe? Think Again!

*Winner of Honorable Mention
at the 2011 New England Book Festival*

available in paperback and eBook from
local bookstores and Amazon and at
www.maineauthorspublishing.com

The Spiritual Memoir...

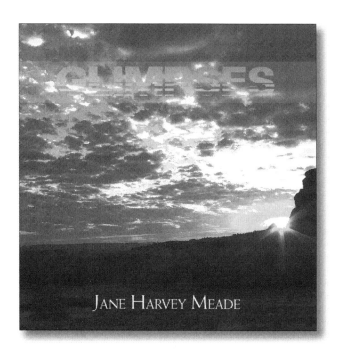

True Stories of Unexplained Events in Everyday Lives

Coincidence? Imagination? Chance?
Fluke? Accident? Fate? Luck?

Maybe not!

*Winner of Honorable Mention
at the 2011 New England Book Festival*

The Dramatic Fiction...

How Does a Woman Escape Abuse?

A TEACHER STRUGGLES TO FLEE AN ABUSIVE RELATIONSHIP WHILE NAVIGATing her role at a new school.

...the heart of this novel involves Kate's evolution from battered housewife to empowered single woman. It's an emotionally resonant story, and Kate's fear and anxiety are palpable...

...Meade offers a window into the deep struggles of an abuse victim...

A page-turning story of a woman's struggle to overcome abuse and make a new path forward.

—*Kirkus Reviews*

available in paperback and eBook from
local bookstores and Amazon and at
www.maineauthorspublishing.com

The Poetry Collection...

PIPER'S SONG, MY LIFE IN POETRY IS A COLLECTION OF POEMS WRITTEN over the course of the author's lifetime. Highlighted by more than 25 years of spousal abuse, readers of *Piper's Song* will see the brighter moments as clearly as they will see the darker times.

available in paperback and eBook from
local bookstores and Amazon and at
www.maineauthorspublishing.com

ANOTHER MAINE MYSTERY!
ANOTHER PAGE TURNER!

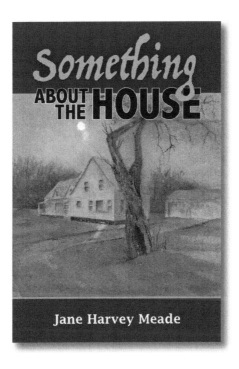

CONFLICTS ERUPT INTO VIOLENCE WHEN A SMALL MAINE TOWN ATTEMPTS to form a new school district with neighboring communities. Abby and Dan Morgan, newly hired teacher and principal, must work to resolve growing hostilities as they struggle to get settled into their new home.

When the house they just purchased becomes a target of many odd and disruptive occurrences, they are forced to wonder if the town is taking its vengeance out on them, as newcomers, or if it is something else. Maybe "Something About the House" itself!

available in paperback and eBook from
local bookstores and Amazon and at
www.maineauthorspublishing.com

TRUE ACCOUNTS OF UNEXPLAINABLE EVENTS IN THE LIVES OF ORDINARY PEOPLE (a sequel to *Glimpses*)

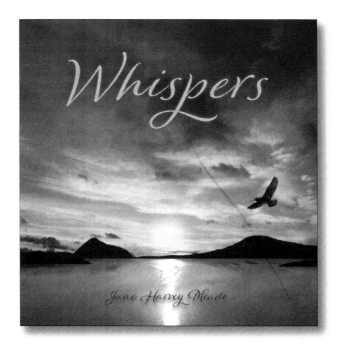

WHISPERS IS A REMINDER THAT MIRACLES HAPPEN. SOMETIMES THE miracles are small, and you don't even notice. Other times, they make you stop to wonder before you chalk them up to coincidence or imagination.

The people who have volunteered to tell their stories in this book know better than to make excuses for what they have experienced. They carry the moments forever in their hearts.

available in paperback and eBook from
local bookstores and Amazon and at
www.maineauthorspublishing.com